continued . . .

"Great storytelling . . . makes a strong case that to enjoy and live life, 'to thine own self be true' . . . Teen readers will jam with the heroine."
                                                                —*Midwest Book Review*

"The perfect mix of real life, romance, and magic."
                —Wendy Mass, author of *Jeremy Fink and the Meaning of Life*

"For readers who like just a bit of fantasy with their reality . . . Even if you have no hair issues, you are sure to find this book well worth your reading time. I highly recommend it."
                                                        —*Flamingnet*, Top Choice Award

"This is a funny, smart book that readers are sure to love!"
                                        —TeensReadToo.com, Gold Star Award

Praise for the novels of
Maryrose Wood

"Irresistible . . . hers is a voice that is way plugged in."
                                                —*The Cleveland Plain Dealer*

"Uproariously funny . . . strong, pitch-perfect narration will easily win readers."
                                                                —*Booklist*

"Will provide hours of laughter and empathetic nods from readers."
                                                —*School Library Journal*

"Pure entertainment."
                                                        —*Kirkus Reviews*

what i wore to save the world

Maryrose Wood

BERKLEY JAM, NEW YORK

THE BERKLEY PUBLISHING GROUP
Published by the Penguin Group
Penguin Group (USA) Inc.
375 Hudson Street, New York, New York 10014, USA
Penguin Group (Canada), 90 Eglinton Avenue East, Suite 700, Toronto, Ontario M4P 2Y3, Canada
(a division of Pearson Penguin Canada Inc.)
Penguin Books Ltd., 80 Strand, London WC2R 0RL, England
Penguin Group Ireland, 25 St. Stephen's Green, Dublin 2, Ireland (a division of Penguin Books Ltd.)
Penguin Group (Australia), 250 Camberwell Road, Camberwell, Victoria 3124, Australia
(a division of Pearson Australia Group Pty. Ltd.)
Penguin Books India Pvt. Ltd., 11 Community Centre, Panchsheel Park, New Delhi—110 017, India
Penguin Group (NZ), 67 Apollo Drive, Rosedale, North Shore 0632, New Zealand
(a division of Pearson New Zealand Ltd.)
Penguin Books (South Africa) (Pty.) Ltd., 24 Sturdee Avenue, Rosebank, Johannesburg 2196,
South Africa

Penguin Books Ltd., Registered Offices: 80 Strand, London WC2R 0RL, England

This book is an original publication of The Berkley Publishing Group.

WHAT I WORE TO SAVE THE WORLD

Copyright © 2009 by Maryrose Wood.
Cover illustration by Sarah Howell.
Cover design by Monica Benalcazar.
Interior text design by Kristin del Rosario.

PRINTING HISTORY
Berkley JAM trade paperback edition / December 2009

Berkley JAM trade paperback ISBN: 978-0-425-22967-5

An application to register this book for cataloging has been submitted to the Library of Congress.

PRINTED IN THE UNITED STATES OF AMERICA

10   9   8   7   6   5   4   3   2   1

For Peaches, Ralph and Lil, who prove that "unlikely" does not mean anything remotely like "impossible."

acknowledgments

Thanks to my agent, Elizabeth Kaplan, editor Jessica Wade, publicist Caitlin Brown and all the lovely people at Berkley JAM. Special thanks to illustrator Sarah Howell and designer Monica Benalcazar for yet another magically eye-catching cover.

Many thanks to the readers of this series! You are a hilarious bunch of incurable romantics, and your e-mails always brighten my day.

And remember, you don't have to be a half-goddess to save the world. I hope each of you will find some way, large or small, to make your own communities a better place to live. Clean up a park, tutor a kid, visit a nursing home or volunteer for a cause you believe in. Maybe you could even run for office! You've got my vote.

Maryrose Wood
July 21, 2009

one

"And so, in the immortal words of Polonius—"

"In the words of Shakespeare, he means," Sarah hissed in my ear. "Polonius was fictional! God, that ex-boyfriend of yours is such a *dweeb*—"

Raph stepped back from the mike and adjusted the tassel that hung over the edge of his mortarboard an eighth of an inch to the right. Apparently it had slipped from the perfect photo op–ready angle.

"'To thine own self be true,'" he intoned, nodding like he'd just thought of it.

Some goofball guys in the seats up front whooped with fake enthusiasm, but I couldn't see who they were. Sarah and I were seated in the back with the rest of the juniors, way out past where the white tents cast some badly needed shade over the graduating seniors and their guests.

The metal folding chairs were heating up in the sun. My cotton sundress was sticking to my legs, my legs were sticking to each other and my ass was sticking to the seat. If the school administration had actually buttered the chairs before the ceremony they could have served sunny-side-up juniors for lunch. "Hot East Norwich Teens Actually Fry to Death," the headlines would read.

At least that would have put me out of my misery. Instead, I had to watch cool-as-a-cucumber Raphael, my onetime boyfriend, now senior class president and valedictorian, as he wrapped up the Speech of His Awesome Lifetime So Far.

This was his perfect moment, the one he'd fantasized about since he was voted Most Likely to Color Inside the Lines in kindergarten. Raph on the podium. Raph at the microphone. Raph telling his classmates how to live the rest of their lives, while his proud parents snapped one flash photo after another.

"My fellow graduates of East Norwich High School!" He was practically yelling now, as he built up to his big finish. "You are ready, you are willing, you are *totally* able! Be true to yourselves and you cannot fail!"

The black-robed seniors jumped to their feet, cheering. Following Raph's lead, 522 square black hats flew into the sky. Raph grinned and pumped his fists in the air like a rock star.

His girlfriend du jour, a bubbly, pretty junior named Alyssa, was sitting two rows in front of Sarah and me. She was the only junior to leap up from her seat and clap along with the seniors.

Leave it to a cheerleader to show excess enthusiasm, I thought. I wondered how long Raph would wait after graduation before ditching her. When it came to girls, Raph liked to wipe the slate clean at the end of the school year. Like emptying out your locker. This I knew from personal experience.

The senior class of East Norwich High School had been set free. The boys yelled and pounded one another's backs; the girls hugged and cried. There was some comical ducking and evasive maneuvers as the mortarboards crash-landed back on earth.

What goes up, must come down . . . But the rules of gravity didn't seem to apply to Raph.

"*So* obnoxious. It's like he's the freakin' king," Sarah muttered as she washed her hands. "Why do they make the juniors sit through the ceremony, anyway? I have more valuable things to be doing on a beautiful day like today."

Now that we were inside the air-conditioned chill of the school, I was too busy trying to peel my sweaty dress away from my body to answer right away. My face felt like it had spent the morning in a toaster oven, right under the broiler.

"Can you believe all those people are waiting outside for the Porta Potti?" Sarah shook the excess water off her hands. "Guh-ross."

Of course, none of those poor shlubs were on a first-name basis with the school janitor. He was a major b-ball fan who was only too happy to let Sarah, star center of the school's undefeated girls' team, and me, her unathletic but needing-to-pee friend, into the building to use the facilities.

"Yikes. Your face is really red." The soap dispenser by my sink was empty, so Sarah gave me a squirt from hers. "Ever hear of sunblock?"

"I forgot."

"Skin cancer, Morgan. Wrinkles. *Freckles.* You have to be more careful."

Sarah, always sensible, had been wearing a wide-brimmed straw hat all morning. On her it looked ironic-retro-glamorous, like she was the star of one of those made-for-cable movies based on a Jane Austen novel. On me, a hat like that would look like a stack of pancakes had fallen on my head.

"If I'd known they were going to leave us stranded in the desert to die . . ." I bent over the sink and gently splashed cool water on my scorched cheeks.

"I know, right?" Sarah laughed. "Why does the school administration hate the juniors so much? Maybe they're still punishing us for what happened at prom."

I lifted my head and saw Sarah watching me in the mirror, waiting for some kind of reaction. It'd been three months since the junior prom. All Sarah knew about my adventures that night was that, ten minutes after I'd arrived, I was sprawled on my butt in the lobby fountain of the East Norwich Country Club, dripping wet in my ironically pink prom dress and looking like I'd just woken up from a truly excellent dream.

I'd never told her what really happened, but what was I supposed to say? Should I tell her that, while she and her boyfriend, Dylan, and all the rest of our class were *ooh*ing and *aah*ing over the streamers and balloons, I'd swum through a portal to the faery realm?

Where—*surprise!*—I'd arrived at my own seventeenth birthday party, thrown by Titania, Queen of the Faeries, with music provided by Kiss and mosh-pit diving provided by a happy leprechaun? I'd even scored a truly magical birthday kiss from my one, my only, my true love, Colin, the freckle-faced hunk o'Irish hottie who pwned my heart, even though he lived an ocean away.

Surely *that* was the kind of newsworthy development that needed to be reported to my BFF, ASAP, right?

Nope. I'd never mentioned any of this to Sarah, or to anyone else, either. She and the rest of my classmates had interpreted my pink taffeta–clad water ballet as a cool and rebellious act of anti-prom performance art. So much so that nearly all of the other prom-goers had repeated the stunt at some point during the evening. Truly, it was the soggiest junior prom ever.

The school administration had not been pleased. Neither was the management of the East Norwich Country Club. The owners were frantic that those "awful teenagers" might have damaged their precious fountain. Little did they know: It takes more than some pranking kids to mess up a portal to the faery realm.

But when the principal, Mrs. Calhoun, tried to suspend any student who'd been seen going home wet, a bunch of parents (some of whom were lawyers) sent threatening letters about "the school's liability in endangering our children by placing them in an environment known to contain hazardous bodies of water." After that the incident was mysteriously dropped, which just goes to show that the ability of the Faery Folk to conceal all evidence of their existence pales next to the ability of East Norwich parents to protect their kids from the consequences of their own stupid behavior.

I patted my wet face gently with a paper towel before answering Sarah's questioning look. "They just want to give us something to look forward to. Graduation: proof that our suffering will someday end."

Then I crumpled the paper towel, tossed it at the trash can and missed. Sarah chuckled as I retrieved my bad toss. Sarah had once settled a bet between Dylan and some wiseass by burying twenty free throws in a row. The ball never touched the rim, and the wiseass had to wear Sarah's "Chicks Rule!" T-shirt to school every day for a month.

"A year from today it'll be us throwing our goofy black hats in the air. Oh my God, I can't wait! College is going to be so awesome compared to this." Sarah fluffed her hair and put the pancake hat neatly back in place. Then she looked at me with her legendary I-have-a-great-idea-that's-against-the-rules expression. "Hey! Let's go look at the college wall."

"Sarah, we're not even supposed to be in the building—"

But she was already loping out of the bathroom door into the cool, empty hallway.

It beat going back out into the sun, so I followed.

* * *

the college wall was right outside the school's main office. It was where the guidance counselors posted copies of the seniors' acceptance letters as they came in.

Personally, I hated the college wall. To me it was just another way for the seniors to put themselves in rank order, and I'd had enough of that kind of posturing when I was with Raph. But most of the juniors were drawn to it like pod people being summoned back to the mothership. It was as if there was some magical clue about our own futures hidden in all that official-looking correspondence.

Sarah let out a whistle. "Sweet! Two more people got into Brown."

I didn't bother to ask who they were. East Norwich was the kind of school where practically everyone who graduated went to college. But there was the posse of superstar seniors (led by Raph, of course) who were genetically programmed to attend Ivy League schools and for whom nothing less would do.

I figured the two future Brown undergrads must be from Raph's crowd. Naturally, Raph had gotten into his first choice: MIT, early admission. Like there was ever any doubt.

Sarah was transfixed by the wall. Watching her read each letter, slack-jawed with concentration, reminded me of how my little sister, Tammy, would go all glassy-eyed in front of the TV, watching the same Disney movie over and over and over . . .

"Hey, look. Curtis Moore got into Northwestern."

"Good for him." I kept glancing down the dim hallway to see if the security guard was coming to throw us out.

"Cute! Eileen Rossiter and Mark Schmidt are both going to Stanford." Eileen and Mark had been a couple since middle school.

"Adorable," I said. "I predict they'll break up by Christmas."

Sarah punched me in the arm. "Don't be such a cynic."

"What about you and Dylan?" I countered, not very nicely. "Will you be filling out 'his and her' college applications? Or will higher education be the end for true love?"

Sarah scowled. "It's not funny, Morgan. Dylan has his heart set on BCM."

The look on her face made me instantly sorry that I'd joked about it. Sarah was a star athlete with good grades, and it was just a matter of time before the basketball scholarship offers came rolling in. She would have her pick of a dozen schools. However, the Boston Conservatory of Music was not likely to be one of them.

"Sorry, bad joke. You two will work it out." I knew all too well how hard it was to be apart from the guy you loved. "You and Dylan are meant for each other."

"I know." She spoke softly, still staring at the wall. "I mean, it feels like we are. But how can you really know something like that?" She turned to look at me. "Anyway, what about you?"

"What—what do you mean?" I didn't want to discuss my long-distance whatever-it-was with Colin, mostly because I knew Sarah thought I was nuts for holding out for a guy who was already in college and lived so far away. Especially when our status as a couple was a lot vaguer than I wanted it to be.

If I closed my eyes I could still hear his lilting Irish voice in my head: *Ye're still in high school, Mor. Have some fun . . .*

"I mean college, dum-dum!" Sarah rolled her eyes. "You haven't toured any campuses. You haven't decided on a major. Your SAT scores were, frankly, kind of weak—"

"They were pathetic," I corrected. "Extremely pathetic."

"Indeed they were." Sarah was very good at scolding me. "And yet, I do not see a test-prep book tucked under your arm, Morgan Rawlinson! Are you even going to bother taking the test again?"

"Somebody's going to have to make the lattes of the future," I joked.

"It's too late to kid around." All of a sudden Sarah had her game face on, and it was scary. "Junior year's over. It's time to figure out what you want to do after high school."

The click of high heels echoed down the hall moments before the all-too-familiar voice rang out:

"What are you girls doing in here?"

It was Mrs. Calhoun, high school principal and object of mockery and revulsion to all self-respecting East Norwich teens.

"We came inside to use the bathroom." Sarah smiled brightly.

"This is the college wall. Not the bathroom." It wasn't a question, but Mrs. Calhoun stood there like she was waiting for an answer.

Sarah kept her smile frozen in place and stood up very straight. She was a full head taller than Mrs. Calhoun, and she worked it by stepping a little too close and talking straight down at the unnaturally blond head of our school's fearless leader. "Mrs. Calhoun," she said somberly, "the truth is, Morgan is having a *really* hard time figuring out what color her parachute is."

"My what?" I blurted.

She ignored me and kept spewing BS. "So we came to the college wall for, you know, inspiration! Wow! *So* many great schools! You must be *massively* proud—"

"Inspiration? I hope you found some," Mrs. Calhoun said, cutting her off. "Now, back outside, please."

"We *totally* found some! We're done now. Thanks *so* much!" Sarah kept babbling as she dragged me away by the arm.

"What was that crap about a parachute?" I asked, as soon as we were out of earshot and had recovered from our giggle fit.

"Duh, it's this famous book about planning your life, everybody knows that."

"Well, duh, obviously 'everybody' *didn't* know that—"

Together we pushed open the main doors of the school.

"Admit it, Morgan. You spent your whole junior year obsessing about Colin." Always prepared, Sarah pulled the brim of her hat down low against the sun, but the light and heat hit me like a slap. "Too bad you can't major in *him*."

two

by the time we walked back to the field they were already taking down the tents. Sarah ran off to find Dylan, who'd been stuck playing the cymbal part in "Pomp and Circumstance" all morning in the concert band. I stood in the sun and watched as the workers tried to fold each tent into a nice, neat, obedient square, while a gust of welcome breeze made the white fabric billow and fight back.

Okay, fine: What color *was* my parachute?

Was it the sparkling cornflower blue of Colin's eyes? Or the soft red-gold of his strawberry-blond hair?

Was it the cream of his fair skin, or the tawny peach of his freckles?

Maybe it was the lush velvet green of Ireland, as seen from the window of an Aer Lingus jet.

Maybe I should go find out. All I had to do was buy a ticket.

Yeah, right. As if my parents would pay for me to go to Ireland just to see Colin. My parents had met Colin, and they liked him, but the notion of me being that involved with someone, at my age, was not their idea of wisdom. When Colin's grandmother had died shortly after he got back from his trip to the States, I'd even hinted around about flying over to Ireland for the funeral, but they wouldn't bite.

He's in college. He lives in another country . . . I could recite their arguments from memory. *He has his own life. It's time for you to plan yours, Morgan!*

When Sarah made that crack about majoring in Colin, I knew she was teasing me the way best friends do, but it hurt anyway. Probably because she was right.

"I know you love him, but it's such a long shot, Morgan," she'd said quickly when I ducked my head to hide how my eyes had suddenly filled with tears. "Why risk your heart on something that's so unlikely to work out?"

But isn't that what you're supposed to do with a parachute, a voice inside me whispered in reply. *Close your eyes, take a breath and jump?*

My mom, the queen of anti-clutter, was facing down approximately six thousand different pieces of paper, arranged with obsessive neatness in dozens of stacks that completely covered the surface of the table my family used to eat off of.

College brochures. Course catalogs. Applications. Financial aid forms. I watched her march around the table, tapping each pile into perfect alignment with her hands while maintaining a strangely neutral look on her face in order to hide her hysteria about my impending failure to launch.

Finally she spoke. "If you would take the time to actually *read* some of the brochures, Morgan, perhaps it would jump-start your thinking about college."

"I'm not *stalled*, Mom. I don't have a dead battery." I'd been in super-snarky mode ever since I got home from the graduation ceremony. Blame it on the sunburn. "I don't need to be 'jump-started,' okay?"

"So forget 'jump-start.' What I meant was—"

"It sounds like you're going to clamp cables to my earlobes or something."

"I said forget it!" She stopped marching. "I'm just saying, if you could bring yourself to *participate* in the college selection process, it might raise your interest level. You don't even seem to be thinking about it."

"Not thinking about it? It's all anybody talks about!" Whoops, involuntary eye roll. "I'm sick of thinking about it, that's the problem."

Mom sighed her heaviest, most exasperated mom-sigh and leaned back against the edge of the kitchen island. "If that's the case, then perhaps you should let me in on what you've been thinking. Then I can be sick of it too. Because right now, what I'm sick of is *not* knowing what you're thinking about college!"

Okay, that logic officially made my head hurt. But she wasn't finished.

"A lot of arrangements have to be made in preparation for your higher education, Morgan. A lot of planning and juggling of finances and all kinds of considerations that have to be, you know—"

"Considered?" I deadpanned. It was a dangerous moment to yank Mom's chain, but I couldn't resist.

"Right," she said, narrowing her eyes. "My point is, it's not just about you."

"Mom, I hate to tell you this."

She started to say something else, then stopped. "What?"

"Me choosing a college? Me choosing a career? Me choosing what I want to do with my life?"

"Yes?"

"It *is* just about me."

I liked the sound of that as soon as I'd said it, so I said it again. "It's about *me*. It really is."

Mom backed off after that little piece of insubordination, but she made me repeat the whole drill when my dad got home from work. With him I took a different approach.

"It's just that I don't know what I want to do, career wise," I said, little-lost-girl style. That was usually the best strategy with him. "So I don't know what I want to study. And so I don't really have any, you know, whatayacallems—"

"Criteria," my mom threw in, before I could think of the word.

"'Cry teary *ahhh!*' That is the saddest word ever!" My sister, Tammy, was lying on her belly on the rug, scribbling into a composition notebook. She was so worried that she'd forget how to spell over the summer that she'd decided to make her own book of spelling words to keep her sharp as a tack until September. For a kid who'd just finished second grade, she was showing a lot more concern for her academic future than I was showing for mine. "How do you spell that sad, sad word?"

"With a C," my mom answered. "Now hush, Tammy, we're talking."

"So like, there's no way to pick," I went on, to my dad. "It just seems so random."

My dad nodded and said nothing. It was hard to tell if he was listening.

"There's no shame in getting a liberal arts degree," Mom offered.

"Oh my God, there so is," I countered. "Liberal arts means you have no clue."

"How about a gap year, then?" Mom was not going to give up. "If you can find something constructive to do, of course."

"Please! Gap year means you *really* have no clue."

Dad got up from the sofa and walked the full length of

our oversized, no privacy, open-plan house. He marched across the living area to the dining area to the kitchen area and then to the refrigerator. He got himself a Diet Coke and popped it open. He even thought to pick up a coaster. Then he walked all the way back and sat back down on the sofa.

"Well, at least we all agree on something," Dad announced.

"What?" my mom and I said at the same time.

"You, Morgan," he said, raising the can to his lips, "have no clue."

the two of them had one of their late-night kitchen conversations that night, the kind I could hear from my room without being able to make out any of the actual words. Like two anxious bees, buzzing and buzzing until well after midnight.

The buzzing must have been about me, because by ten o'clock the next morning my mom had booked an emergency appointment with Mr. Cornelius Phineas, private college counselor.

He was *very* expensive, my mom explained proudly after she'd hung up, and came highly recommended by her snootiest friends. As soon as she heard his name Tammy immediately added "Phineas" to her book of summer spelling words.

"'Phineas.' What does it mean?" she asked as she carefully wrote it in the PH section, on a page that already contained "phone" and "phyllo dough"— two of my mom's phavorite accessories, heh heh.

"It's an ancient word meaning 'bad-smelling person who kidnaps obnoxious smarty-pants girls and gives them nothing but dictionaries to eat, forever,'" I explained with a sneer.

"Mommmmmmmmm! Morgan's acting like a meanie!"

Mission accomplished.

Of course, what it really meant was one more person prying into my business and telling me what to do with my life, but I didn't say that to Tammy.

Mr. Phineas was one of those older men who hadn't gotten the memo about how balding guys should embrace the aging rock star look and keep their hair buzzed really short.

His look was more like aging mad scientist. The top of his head was a shiny dome of pink scalp. Halfway down, a fringe of long gray frizz erupted, sticking out at weird angles and drifting over his collar. And there were serious ear hair issues. Guh-ross, as Sarah would say.

"What's Morgan?" was his first question.

Huh? I thought. Then I wondered if it was one of those *Inside the Actors Studio* questions, like, "If Morgan were a tree, what tree would Morgan be? If Morgan were a type of pasta, what type of pasta would Morgan be?"

"I don't get it," I confessed. "Do you mean, like, what color is my parachute or something?"

"Who said anything about a parachute?" Now he looked as puzzled as I was. "A moment ago you said, 'It's Morgan.' *What's* Morgan?"

"My *name's* Morgan," I said, slouching in my chair. "You called me Morganne."

And he had. My mom had tried to weasel her way into the appointment, but Mr. Phineas had blocked her at the office door. "It would be best for Morganne and I to speak privately," he'd said firmly while closing the door in her face. *Whoosh.* Two points for Mr. Ear Hair.

Of course, in the faery world everybody called me Morganne. It was the mythical goddess-version of my name. But normal humans did it all the time too, just by mistake.

"It should be Morganne, but it's not," I explained. "Personally I always thought Morgan was a boy's name. You can take it up with my mom when she comes back."

"Morgan, of course! I do apologize." He shuffled the papers around on his desk. "At my age it's far too easy to get things mixed up. I've met so very many people in my lifetime, you see. And I seem to be meeting new ones all the time!"

Then he leaned back in his swivel chair and folded his fingers into the *here is the church, here is the steeple* formation. "Now, before we begin, is there anything you'd like to tell me about these rather—let's call them 'unfortunate'— documents?" My high school transcript was spread out in front of him, on the dark wood surface of his large antique desk.

"I'm an underachiever," I explained helpfully.

"Wonderful! I'm thrilled to hear it." Mr. Phineas smiled warmly. "I would hate to think these lackluster report cards are an accurate reflection of your abilities. Well! Now that we know *who* you are, and *what* you are capable of, the only question that really matters is: What is it that interests *you*?"

"If I knew *that*—"

But he kept talking, in a voice that was both calm and strangely hypnotic. "What puzzle would you most love to solve? What subject do you return to again and again—not because you have to for school, or because some parent or teacher or friend thinks you should, but because you simply can't stay away from it?"

"Mythology." The word slipped out of my mouth without me even planning to say it.

He leaned forward, suddenly interested. "Really? I so rarely hear that from today's students. Which branch of mythology do you prefer? The tales of White Buffalo Woman, from Native American lore? The German *Nibelungenlied*? The Icelandic saga of Snorri Sturluson? There are some positively hair-raising tales from ancient China—"

"I guess I'm mostly interested in Irish myths. You know, faeries and stuff." I thought of all the adventures I'd had last summer, in Ireland, where I'd first met Colin. And more recently, when I had to do some wee-folk matchmaking to help get Colin unenchanted in time for the junior prom. "And leprechauns, of course. And all those ancient goddesses and warrior-dude types."

Morganne, the half-goddess daughter of a faery mother and a mortal father . . . According to legend, it was the

Queen of Mean, nasty Queen Titania herself, who was the source of my magical mojo. Luckily for me, the faery-human booty call that created my half-goddess DNA had taken place many millennia ago, where I didn't have to think about it. I mean, gag. I didn't even like seeing my parents kiss, and they were both human.

Mr. Phineas lifted his feet and did a slow 360 in his swivel chair, interlacing his fingers and muttering as he twirled. "Fascinating . . . Irish myths . . . faeries and leprechauns and ancient 'warrior-dudes' . . ."

When he faced front again he stopped and pounded the desk in enthusiasm. "Brainstorm! Have you considered Oxford University? In England?"

As soon as he said "in England," I perked up. England wasn't Ireland, but it was a whole lot closer than Connecticut.

"Not really." I tried to remember anything I knew about Oxford, and came up blank. "Is it hard to get into?"

"Quite competitive, in fact! But for someone of your unique qualifications, it should be possible. And it would be ever so much closer to your boyfriend."

Wait—had my mother coached this guy in advance? I scooted to the edge of my chair and looked him in the eye. "Why did you just say that? About my boyfriend?"

"You have a boyfriend?" he murmured innocently, staring at his fingers. "How nice. Is he applying for colleges too?"

Okay, my weirdo radar was starting to bleep. In the past I'd sometimes had this same feeling when an encounter with the faery realm was about to happen. But other times it just meant that I was talking to a weirdo. I was pretty sure this was one of those times.

"You just said," I replied slowly, "that Oxford was a lot closer to my boyfriend."

Mr. Phineas unfolded his hands and looked at me quizzically.

"If I'm not mistaken, Morgan, you and I have just met. And our conversation has consisted solely of a discussion of your professional and educational aspirations." He leaned forward until his chair squeaked for mercy. "So how would I know if you have a boyfriend?"

We sat there, stymied. Or at least I was. He just looked at me calmly, with his big watery brown eyes. I had the sense that he was trying not to laugh. It was annoying, frankly.

After a moment, he sat back and resumed our meeting as if nothing freaky had just happened.

"All right then! I have your transcripts here, and I am quite familiar with the admissions requirements at Oxford. I have some personal contacts there, in fact. Let me review the situation, and I will send you my specific recommendations as to how to proceed."

He reached inside one of the file drawers of his desk and pulled out a large white envelope with an emblem printed on it—a circle containing a picture of a heavy book, surrounded by three crowns. The words UNIVERSITY OF OXFORD ran around the edge of the circle in capital letters.

"Here's some background information, which you might find of interest." He slid the envelope across the desk to me.

"Do you think you would be capable of writing a particularly strong application essay? It would have to explain your special interest in Irish mythology in some detail."

"Oh my God, yes!" I exclaimed without thinking.

"Excellent." He rose from his desk and escorted me to the door. For the first time I could see that he was wearing strange, goofy-looking pants, which ended at the knee.

"They're called breeches," he said, reading my mind. "Much more practical in this hot weather than trousers."

"I bet," I said, while thinking, *Eww, freak*.

"The essay will be key. Because, with these grades . . ." He held the door open for me and smiled. "Frankly, Morgan, if you want to get into Oxford, your essay is going to have to *kick ass*."

three

"Oxford? Oxford *University?*"

My parents were staring at me with the most open-mouthed, *what-the-fek* expressions imaginable. Which was gross, because we were in the middle of eating dinner and their mouths were both full of half-chewed vegetable lasagna.

Since the dining table had been turned into college application central, my family now ate dinner on trays in the living room. TV trays, my mom called them. If she'd let us watch TV during dinner this might have made sense.

"Are you sure that's what he said?" My mother put down her fork and reached over to feel my forehead. What else but a sudden case of malaria could explain this bizarre delusion about my own academic prospects?

"I feel fine." I batted her hand away. Tammy took advantage of the sudden distraction to steal a buttered roll from my tray.

"I knew this counselor guy must be a rip-off." Dad held the TV remote like he was itching to turn it on, but that would be the start of a whole other argument.

"Isn't there another college called Oxford?" Mom carefully put down her tray. "Oxford Community College, perhaps? There must be! I'm almost positive there's a town called Oxford in Connecticut somewhere." She got up and speed-walked back to the kitchen, bypassing the piles of "safety school" literature and diving straight into the "loser school" brochures. These were stacked precariously on the countertop and weighed down with a large rock, which Tammy had hand-painted in kindergarten and was insanely proud of.

Dad was still griping through his food and longingly fingering the remote. "Two hundred dollars an hour . . . a cardiologist doesn't make that much . . ."

"He was *highly* recommended. Esther Finley told me he was a genius." Mom shuffled through the papers. "Here's one: 'Oxford Technical Academy.' Hmmm." She skimmed the brochure. "This can't be right. This is for people who want to be X-ray technicians. Morgan, you didn't tell Mr. Phineas you wanted to be an X-ray technician, did you?"

I struggled to power down my sarcasm reflex and speak normally, but it was a struggle I lost. "Mom. Dad. I told Mr. Phineas I was interested in mythology, and he said I should apply to Oxford University. The real one. In England."

"Did he actually *look* at your grades?"

"Yes! He said I just needed to write a really good essay."

Both of my parents were avoiding eye contact with me all of a sudden.

"What? What's the problem?" I asked.

"It's just—really, honey—I mean, *Oxford* . . ." Mom was never speechless, but at the moment she seemed close.

"Bill Clinton went to Oxford," I argued. "So did some of the Monty Python guys. So did the guy who wrote *Lord of the Rings.* How cool is that?" I'd gleaned these tidbits from looking at the pictures in the brochure Mr. Phineas had given me. You can fake your way through a lot of homework by skimming captions, I'd always found. Though maybe my over-reliance on that particular study technique helped explain the sorry state of my grades.

I tried to remember what else it said in the captions. "I mean, show some enthusiasm, people! We're talking about Oxford. Home of Rhodes Scholars. The place is, like, practically a thousand years old or something."

Now, my mom was a woman who could spot the label on a Prada bag or a Pucci blouse from a mile away. You'd think she'd be doing a major happy dance that her firstborn child was aiming for a university of global reputation. You'd think she would already be planning how to deploy the Oxford bragging rights to maximum effect among her peers.

You'd think. But no. She stared at my dad with her hands on her hips and her lips pressed flat into a long straight line—the universal marital signal for *say something, you doofus, I'm all alone out here.*

"You don't want me to go so far away?" I asked, lost. "Is that it?"

At last, a reaction from Dad. He burst out laughing.

"England isn't that far, compared to some places," he said, once he regained control of himself. "Anyway, your mother and I are the ones who sent you to Ireland last summer, remember?"

"So what is it, then?" I was running out of patience. "You're worried it'll be too expensive? You're afraid I'll come back with a funny accent? What?"

Dad shook his head. Mom just *hmmm*ed and *mmmm*ed.

"They don't think you're smart enough to get in," Tammy said cheerfully. "Can I have more bread?"

But then even Tammy shut up, so we could all inhale the pungent stink bomb of truth the kid had lobbed into the living area.

Major. Awkward. Silence.

Mom was the first to crack. "Morgan. Honey. The thing is, your grades have not been stellar."

"Grades aren't everything," I protested weakly. "There's the application essay, like Mr. Phineas said. And, you know. Extracurricular activities and stuff."

"Name one," Dad shot back.

Whoosh. Two points for Dad.

"If only she'd run for some kind of office," my mom said to him, like I wasn't even there. "Treasurer. Secretary, even."

"Why not class president?" I snapped, pushing away my lasagna. "Or don't you think I could do that, either?"

"It's not that we think you couldn't," Dad said, as he wiped the tomato sauce off his mouth and defiantly clicked on the TV. "It's that you didn't."

fek. i hated it when my parents were right.

Morgan Rawlinson, senior class president. That would have sounded so much better on my Oxford application than *Morgan Whatshername, third junior from the left.* "One of the more nondescript students in her class." How's that for a yearbook caption? But it was true. Hardly anyone at East Norwich High School even knew who I was before I hacked off all my hair in a fit of heartbreak when Raph ditched me. Then I went from being "Raph's girlfriend" to "crazy buzz-cut girl."

Even then, a lot of kids assumed I was going through chemo. Come graduation, I fully expected a significant percentage of my classmates to sign my yearbook, *Congrats on finally beating leukemia!*

But it's not like I didn't *do* any extracurricular activities. It's just that none of it was stuff I could put on my college application without sounding like a nutcase. I started to make a list:

- Can talk to horses and swim with mermaids.

- Has a very special relationship with her dad's garden gnome collection.

- Magically finds prom dates for lonely leprechauns.

Clearly, writing that kick-ass application essay was going to be a tad more complicated than I'd let on to Mr. Phineas. On the other hand, I could still be an X-ray technician.

But that wasn't going to get me on the same side of the Atlantic as Colin, would it?

No, it would not. I wasn't ready to give up on Oxford, not without at least giving it a try. But I did need advice. Getting into college was a competition, and I had to learn to think like a winner.

What I needed was a coach.

Whoosh.

"Can you even get a job doing that?" Sarah panted, as she passed the ball at light speed between her legs, under and around until her hands were a blur. "The mythology thing, I mean?"

Getting on Sarah's calendar for a BFF coaching session meant that I had to meet her at the basketball courts at eight in the morning. Normal people slid into summer vacation mode the minute school let out. Sarah slid into summer training mode. After warming up for an hour at the YMCA, she'd be spending the rest of the day in a training camp for "hot prospects" at UConn.

That was one difference between Sarah and me. Not only did she know what she wanted, she was willing to work her ass off to get it.

"I guess so." I hadn't thought about a job, to be honest. "Teaching or something."

"Oh my God!" She snorted with laughter. "Sorry. I'm imagining you teaching college."

First my parents, now Sarah. Among the people who knew me best there seemed to be a consensus that whatever I tried to do with my life, I would suck at it.

"Mythology interests me." I tried to sound firm. "I want to study something interesting. I'll figure out the job thing later."

Sarah put down the ball, loped to the side of the court and grabbed a big, pee-yellow Gatorade out of her duffel bag. Watching her guzzle it so early in the morning made me feel like I might as well skip breakfast.

"Morgan, if that's what you want to do, fine. It's just like, so out of the blue." She wiped her mouth on the hem of her shirt and picked up the ball again. "Some weird guy in knickers—"

"Breeches," I corrected.

"Whatever, tells you to study 'mythology at Oxford' and suddenly you're all over it, like it's your life's dream or something. I mean, I've never even heard you mention it."

"I know. But trust me, it's not just because this guy said so. The subject has been on my mind for a while. Ever since I went to Ireland, really." It felt good to share a tiny piece of the truth, even though I had to leave most of it out. "Anyway, I know my grades are bad and all, but this counselor says he knows people at Oxford. It sounds like he can pull some strings."

"Ever since you went to Ireland, huh?" Sarah spun the ball idly on the tip of her index finger. "And Oxford is in England."

It was obvious where she was going with that geographic news flash, but "stubborn as a mule" was both my best and worst quality. I glared at her with an I-dare-you-to-say-it expression that would melt an ordinary person into slush.

"Yeah, so?" I challenged, in the world's least witty comeback.

Sarah tucked the ball under her long arm. "In my personal opinion, this mythology-at-Oxford obsession is just a ruse to get you to England so you can be closer to Colin."

"England is not Ireland, ding-dong," I countered.

"England is way closer to Ireland than Connecticut, doodlehead."

"Close is irrelevant. It's still a different country." Our voices echoed strangely in the empty gymnasium. "Why are you always so snarky about Colin?"

"Colin, Colin, Colin." She dribbled the ball to emphasize each word. "You know what? The whole two weeks he was in Connecticut, I never even met him. And I'm your best friend. So that kind of makes me think there might be something dubious about the you-and-him thing, in the first place. And in the second place—"

"That wasn't his fault," I blurted. Though how could I explain that Colin had been under an enchantment the entire time he'd been here?

"In the *second* place," she went on, "I really don't care if he's the reason you're suddenly interested in planning your future. Because if the Colin factor is what makes you finally pick a school and get your act together to apply, then that's all that matters. It's your life."

"I *know* it's my life!" I sounded like Tammy at her whiniest, but I couldn't stop. "Why does everyone keep saying that?"

Sarah ignored my question. "Listen. You asked for my advice, and I'm going to give it to you. Bad grades, bad SAT scores, no sports or extracurriculars. Two words for you, Morgan: Community. Service."

I made a face. "Really? You think that would help?"

"Help? It's your only hope." She wheeled and nailed another layup before turning back to me. "And it has to be something major. It would be awesome if you could cure cancer or achieve world peace or something. That's pretty much all that can save you now."

Whoosh.

four

fine. i admit it. the Colin factor was, you know, a factor.

A major factor.

Colin, of the overwhelming Irish adorableness, the strawberry-blond hair, the cornflower blue eyes. Colin, with the soccer-star bod and just the right amount of freckles, like a big connect-the-dot puzzle you wanted to trace with your fingertips, over and over again.

But Colin was way more than the sum of his cute parts. He was funny in a way that no one else was. He got me in a way no one else ever had. When he kissed me, which he'd really only ever done twice (once in Ireland on a moonlit beach, and once on the night of the infamous junior prom, at my magic faery birthday ball with Gene Simmons looking on—trust me, you had to be there), it was beyond magic.

It was like a million leprechaun rainbows covered with little MySpace glitter hearts, and silver unicorns with flowers sprouting out of their horns dancing underneath, and a zillion helium birthday balloons floating up into a perfectly blue sky, all crammed in a blender and frappéed into a delicious milk shake of happiness. With two straws.

Sarah had no way of knowing all this, of course, because she'd never met him. But what could I say? Colin made me feel one hundred percent goddess, one hundred percent of the time. Wasn't that worth crossing an ocean for?

Or, to be more specific—wasn't that worth spending the summer volunteer-tutoring a bunch of hyperactive third-graders for? It wasn't going to cure cancer or bring world peace, but it was all I could find on such short notice.

Two words, Morgan: Community. Service.

Oh, fek.

"Morgan. It is the *summer*. I do *not* have to *learn* over the *summer*." Tammy looked at me with eyes as round and cold as two Ping-Pong balls that had spent a year in the freezer. "It's against the law, I'm almost sure."

She stretched back on the chaise longue and let out a little *ahhhhh* of contentment. The regular babysitter was sick and I was on duty, which normally would have been a fairly tragic development. But today I had my own agenda, and I was acting my magical-big-sister chummiest.

I'd grabbed some chips and lemonade from the kitchen and pulled the chaise longues to the shady side of the backyard, since I was still peeling from the commencement on Saturday. We were hanging out in style: I was wearing my favorite bikini top, the one with the polka dots, and a pair of cutoffs. I'd even streaked some lemon juice in my hair to see if I could get a few highlights going. Tammy had dressed for the occasion too, and was accessorized with scuba flippers, movie-star sunglasses and a hot-pink feather boa from her extensive Disney-inspired costume collection.

"Tammy, come on," I pleaded. "You're my guinea pig. Let me try to teach you something. It doesn't matter what. I just want to practice before I have to face all those kids at camp next week."

"Pay me." She held out a hand.

My first instinct was to squirt her with a hose, but I resisted. "Tammy, get this through your head: I'm volunteering for the Y day camp. It's community service. That means I'm not getting paid." I smiled my most reasonable smile. "Now, I shouldn't have to pay you to practice doing work that I'm not going to get paid for, right? That wouldn't make sense."

"'The East Norwich Y's "SmartYCamp" helps kids maintain academic skills over the summer, while having fun, fun, fun!'" she chanted. "I've read the posters too. Do you know what Daddy says they charge for that camp?"

"A lot, but that has nothing to do with—"

"You bet a lot! It has the S word in it, that's how much. Daddy says it's an s-load of money." She stuck her hand in my face. "If you want to maintain *my* academic skills, you have to pay, pay, pay!"

"Fine," I said, digging in the pocket of my shorts for change. "How much?"

"Enough for a box of Tic Tacs. The orange ones. You shouldn't give me potato chips for breakfast, you know," she added, shoving a handful into her mouth. "Pay me extra and I won't tell Mom."

"All Tic Tacs cost the same—never mind." I plopped a couple of quarters into her salty fist and waited while she tucked the change in her special Pocahontas purse, which already contained an empty ChapStick, some crayons, a plastic toy cell phone and her broken zipper collection.

"It's a pleasure doing business with you." She crossed her arms. "Teach away."

"Um." I realized that I hadn't remembered to bring a pencil or paper outside with me. "Okay. What do you want to do first? Math, or spelling, or—"

"I want to learn about photosynthesis." She unfolded her arms and swung her legs over the side of the chaise longue. "It's about how plants turn green and make air for us to breathe. And it's a P-H word! I already put it in my spelling book. P-H-O-T-"

"Cool," I interrupted. The summer was too short to listen to Tammy spell every stupid word that crossed her mind. "Photosynthesis. There's this stuff in plants that's green, see, called chlorophyll—"

"I just told *you* what it was," she said impatiently. "The plants turn green and make air. What's next?"

Already I was feeling cranky. "Let's do the times table," I suggested.

"Bo-ring!" she sang out, but obliged. "Zero times one is zero. Zero times two is zero . . ."

Then Tammy and I recited the times table together. It went pretty well until we got to the eights. I kept getting eight times seven mixed up with six times nine, but she knew it all like the back of her grubby little hand.

"*Fifty-six,*" she corrected, "fifty-six, fifty-six! Say it, Morgan!"

"Fifty-six," I mumbled. Then, to save face, I tried to show her the cool thing about how the answers in the nine times table always added up to nine.

"See? That's like, magical, right?" I said, faking enthusiasm.

"So what? Everybody knows that. I can do *two*-digit multiplication." She waggled her scuba flippers with pride. "I'll show you. Say two numbers."

"Uh, seven and five."

"I said *two*-digit numbers! Never mind, I'll do it myself. Seventy-eight times twenty-four . . ."

Then she grabbed my fashion magazine, took a crayon out of her Pocahontas purse and started to draw little lines and triangles and arrows all over the page. At the end of this exercise she came up with some random number.

"That's not two-digit multiplication, Tam." I took the magazine back, glad that there was finally something I could teach her. "Two-digit multiplication is when you put the numbers on top of each other like this, see?" I started to write it out in crayon, all over Paris Hilton's hideous spray-on tan. "And you times the ones and carry the tens and . . . hmmm . . ."

She'd gotten the right answer.

"This is the *new* kind of multiplication," she said smugly.

"But multiplication is just—multiplication." I threw the magazine down. "How can there be a new kind?"

"They invent a new kind every year." Tammy leaned forward, and her sunglasses slipped down to the tip of her nose. "It's because they don't have enough math. I think they're running out."

"What?"

"Shhh!" She put a finger to my lips. "It's a secret. I think math is going stinked."

I mulled that over for a minute. "You mean extinct, Tam."

"I mean they don't have *enough*." She pushed the glasses back up. "And that's why they keep changing multiplication. Because once you know how to do it, they have to invent a new way. Otherwise they would run out of math to teach you. And if they ran out of things to teach us at school," she concluded with a shrug, "*then* what?"

Then what, indeed. I had no answer for that.

"Miss Wallace is a way better teacher than you," Tammy offered.

"I'm sure she is." This tutoring idea was starting to feel like a huge mistake. World peace would be easier.

"I hope you don't get Marcus. He goes to that SmartY-Camp." Tammy leaned back on the chaise longue and shook her head, which made the pink feathers fly everywhere. "Marcus will eat you up and spit you out."

Providing job security for her beloved Miss Wallace might have been enough to keep Tammy cheerfully relearning the same crap year after year, but my patience was already shot. My failed attempt to teach her anything had given me a massive headache, plus, some of the lemon juice had gotten in my eye and it stung like hell.

Here's a new kind of multiplication, I thought, as I bent over the garden hose and splashed cold water in my eye: Take a dozen smart-ass kids forced by their overachieving parents to "maintain academic skills" over the summer, then multiply them by one C-average seventeen-year-old who's desperately padding her college application at the last minute, equals what?

Even I could do *that* math. It equaled disaster. It equaled a totally not-fun summer. It equaled me being eaten up and spit out by Marcus, Tammy's arch-nemesis at Idle Hour Elementary School: a snub-nosed bully who had single-handedly brought many a substitute teacher to tears, according to Tammy.

What it did not equal was me getting in to Oxford. Who was I kidding?

Tammy was so entertained by stomping around the yard in her scuba flippers while I chased her with the hose that she decided she wanted to go swimming, but I didn't have the nerve to take her to the pool club. I knew as soon as we got there the manager would offer me some shifts flipping burgers in the Snack Shack, because the job was so greasy and unpleasant they were always looking for people.

And I knew I should say yes, because I was going to crash and burn as a volunteer tutor and I had no paying gig lined up for the summer, but saying yes to being Burger Girl seemed like sealing my fate in the most pathetic way possible. Of course Burger Girl didn't get in to Oxford. Burger Girl would be lucky to even end up as an X-ray technician.

And she sure didn't end up with the cute Irish boyfriend.

Forget the pool club, then. Instead I filled the bathtub, the big one in my parents' bathroom, and poured half a bottle of Mr. Bubble into the swirling water. Tammy was psyched. She kept the flippers on and put on her Little Mermaid pink plastic snorkel mask. She'd be good for at least forty-five minutes in there, until the water got cold.

My fate is so *not ready to be sealed,* I thought, as I dragged the kid-sized pink beanbag chair from Tammy's room into the hallway, close enough to the bathroom for me to hear her splashing around. I wanted it all: Oxford and the cute Irish boyfriend (okay, one of those things I actually wanted more than the other). And I knew there must be some kind of half-goddess destiny in store for me. But was I supposed to wait for it to show up and ring the doorbell? Or was I supposed to go looking for it?

And how do you go looking for something when you don't know what it is?

"Behold, I am Tammy! Mermaid Queen of the Bubble Sea! *Blub blub blub blub blub* . . ."

I sank into the beanbag chair, took out the Oxford packet that Mr. Phineas had given me and started to read it—not just the captions this time, but the whole thing.

Founded nine centuries ago . . . the first University in the English-speaking world . . . graduates include twenty-five British Prime Ministers, forty-seven Nobel Prize winners, six kings, twelve saints . . .

And, oh my God, Hugh Grant. How cute was he in *Bridget Jones's Diary?*

Clearly, Oxford rocked. Just as clearly, I was way out of my league. Two-digit multiplication had proven beyond a doubt that Morgan Rawlinson was not even close to being smarter than a third grader.

On the other hand, in all those centuries of churning out heads of state and Archbishops of Canterbury and Olympic gold medalists, nowhere in the brochure did I see any mention of a half-goddess graduate. Wasn't it about time they added one?

Major splashing sounds were emanating from the bathroom. It sounded like entirely too much fun was being had.

"Hey, take it easy in there!" I jumped up and pushed open the door. "Am I going to have to clean this whole bathroom or what—"

Tub full of bubbles. Floor full of bubbles. Bubbles stuck all over the tile walls.

No Tammy.

"Tammy!" I plunged my whole upper body into the

water and batted away the suds. It was a big tub, too big, like everything else about this stupid house. *Why did I pour in so much Mr. Bubble,* I thought frantically as I pushed the foam away, *it's all suds, I can't see anything . . .*

There, beneath the bubbles, with her snorkel apparatus still on but fully submerged, was Tammy. Her eyes were closed, and she lay flat against the bottom of the tub. She looked like she was sleeping, or—

I yanked her up as if she weighed nothing, water streaming everywhere. As soon as she was out of the tub she opened her eyes. No sputtering, no choking. She just looked surprised.

"Oh my God, Tammy, are you okay? Can you talk?" To think of the millions of times I'd wished this kid would just shut up for a minute, but at that moment all I wanted was audible proof that she was alive and breathing.

"I got a new P-H word," she said. Then she started shivering. "Can you g-g-get me my sp-sp-spelling book?"

five

i wrapped tammy in the biggest bath towel i could find, brought her downstairs and sat her on the sofa, safely away from any bodies of water, active gas lines or open flames. Then I went to her room and got her favorite Disney Princesses comforter—"and m-m-my sp-sp-spelling book!" she yelled after me through chattering teeth—and wrapped her up again, even though she was already squirming and trying to get loose.

The more I asked her if she was all right the more she looked at me like I was insane.

"Do I look drownded to you?" she snapped, flipping her spelling book open to the right page. She pushed it into my hands. "You write it for me, my fingers are all wrinkly from the water."

"It's 'drowned,' not 'drownded'—okay, shoot."

"P-H-I." She stopped and thought. "N."

I was getting a twitchy feeling down my spine. "What word is this?"

"Just write it. N," she repeated.

"The same N? Or another N?"

"How many did I say?"

I glanced at the book. "Two."

"Two is enough. The rest is easy. B-A-R."

"No offense, Tam, but I don't think that's a real word . . ." Then I saw what I'd written:

PHINNBAR

Finnbar? My faery half brother? The magical brat whose well-intended efforts to help me out usually caused more problems than they solved? And who really sucked at spelling?

"Tammy," I said, grabbing her a little too hard. "What does this word mean?"

"*Ow ow ow*," she squealed. "It's not a word, it's a name, *let go let go let go.*"

The phone rang. I ignored it, but Tammy lunged at the handset on the end table.

"A name? Whose name?"

"The boy who was blowing bubbles in the bathtub while I was drownding—look, it's him on the phone!" she squealed, reading the caller ID. "P-H-I-N-"

How could Finnbar be calling my house, I thought in a

panic, *as if he were some neighborhood kid looking for a play date and not an immortal faery prince*? I grabbed the phone away from Tammy and looked for myself.

"Phek! I mean, Mr. Phineas—hello!"

"Took you long enough to answer, Morgan." Mr. Phineas chuckled. "I was about to give up on you."

"Sorry, I was just—in the middle of something." Now Tammy was mouthing *I'm hungry* and rubbing her stomach.

"In the middle of something, eh?" Mr. Phineas sounded positively jolly. "I'm not surprised. After all, a person is generally located somewhere between the past and the future, which could fairly be described as the middle, don't you agree? Of course, there are exceptions."

Only half-listening, I followed Tammy as she shuffled into the kitchen, still mummy-wrapped in her towel. The way this day was going she'd probably shut herself in the refrigerator next. Mr. Phineas kept babbling.

"I have some wonderful news for you, Morgan! My contacts have informed me that the University of Oxford is hosting an orientation session for their 'special admissions' candidates. And you fall right in the *middle*"—he chuckled again—"of that category."

"Sounds great," I said wearily. "When is it?"

"This Friday, ten A.M. Punctuality absolutely required."

"Hang on a sec." I scribbled it down on the message pad on the kitchen counter. "And, where is it?"

"On campus, of course."

"On campus, cool, okay—" Now Tammy was staring at

me with big round manga-girl eyes, making begging gestures and pointing to her mouth in a truly obnoxious way. I turned my back to her and covered my free ear with my hand.

"Sorry, Mr. Phineas, I was distracted. Which campus did you say?"

"The University of Oxford, located in the city of Oxford, approximately sixty miles northwest of London, England." He sounded very matter of fact, like he was giving me directions to the local pizza place.

"You mean—I have to be in England in *three days*?" I had to lean against the counter for support. "But there's no way—"

"Perhaps I'm not being clear." Mr. Phineas's attitude went from chuckles to chilly in a heartbeat. "This is a *special* orientation session. For *special* applicants. It is by invitation only, and a campus tour is a *mandatory* component. Your plane ticket is already purchased and paid for, courtesy of the Oxford admissions office. You have a valid passport, I presume?"

Though I knew he couldn't see me, all at once it felt weird that I was talking to him in my polka-dot bikini top and bare feet. "Sure. I mean, I went to Europe last summer, so I guess the passport is still good." I shoved a banana into Tammy's mouth to make her get out of my face. "But, Mr. Phineas? Seriously—the plane ticket is free? Is this really on the up and up?"

"The 'up and up.' What a curious expression," he said,

not bothering to answer my question. "Travel instructions will arrive via e-mail this evening at eight o'clock sharp. Please follow all instructions to the letter! Understood?"

"I understand, but I kind of have to talk it over with my parents first—"

"Morganne," he said, so sternly I didn't bother to correct him, "where you go to college and what you do with your life—it's not about your parents, or anybody else, for that matter. It's about *you*. Now don't forget to check your e-mail, please! Eight o'clock. Do exactly as it says; that's very important. Goodbye."

I hung up, as dizzy as if I'd just spent an hour riding the Cyclone at Coney Island.

"Yuk!" Tammy spit out the banana into my hand. "You could have *peeled* it first!"

"Oxford is paying for you to fly over for a campus tour? They must think you're incredibly special!"

Morgan, how we've underestimated you! Clearly your academic potential is limitless! Why didn't we see it before?

At least, this was the kind of ego-boosting crap I was imagining my parents would say, when they both got home from work and I tried to explain what Mr. Phineas had told me over the phone.

"He says I have to go to Oxford. I mean, *go*. In person. Like, this week. The Specials Admissions something-or-other wants me to be there Friday morning. I'm supposed to get all the details later—"

They stared at me like I was speaking a foreign language. Then, piercing through the air like a hundred smoke alarms going off at once:

"Morgan is the worst babysitter *ever*!"

Tammy had been happily watching *SpongeBob* in her room until she realized Mom and Dad were home. Now she ran downstairs screaming. "She gave me potato chips for breakfast and she almost let me get drownded in the bathtub and she doesn't even know how to peel a banana!"

I knew Tammy was really only upset about the banana, but after they heard "drownded in the bathtub," I pretty much lost my parents' attention. Mom started screeching at Dad to hold Tammy upside down by her ankles in case there was any water left in her lungs, and Tammy started crying because she hated being upside down, and Dad started yelling because Mom and Tammy were both hysterical.

From the noise Tammy made it was obvious her lungs were fine. She'd still be happily underwater playing mermaid games with her bubble-blowing faery friend if I hadn't yanked her out of the tub, but I didn't think there was much point in trying to convince my parents of that.

I'll tell them about the trip to England later, I thought dejectedly, as I slunk back to my room to wait until eight o'clock rolled around.

At seven fifty-nine I was sitting in my room in front of my computer, staring at the screen and feeling like a fool.

Don't get your hopes up, I told myself. The more I thought about it, the more unlikely the whole offer seemed. Mr. Freaky Short Pants was probably just yanking my chain. Nevertheless, I'd already piled a dozen potential campus tour outfits in a big messy heap on my bed. I'd also swiped some travel-sized bottles of shampoo and conditioner that my mom had nabbed from various hotels during family vacations.

I'd found my passport stashed in the bottom of my underwear drawer, where so many valuable but rarely needed items eventually find a home. Most important, I'd fantasized at least twenty different ways of trying to convince Colin to meet me in London.

Now I was just sitting there at my desk, watching the screen and the clock.

Sure enough, at eight o'clock exactly, right when my mind started to wander, the new mail alarm on my computer went off. The alarm was a snippet of a heavy metal riff from Kiss, which was kind of an in-joke between me and Gene Simmons, you might say.

I reached for the mouse, but my hand froze when I saw who the e-mail was from.

Mor,

What I've got to tell you is complete lunacy so I'll just spit it out.

Am in Wales on holiday with Grandpap (long story)— but something unbelievable happened and I'd give anything if you could cross the Atlantic, quick. Is

there a chance? Wales is just few hours' bus ride
from London, details below. Tell your da, I'll pay for
your travel myself, no worries.

Hate to say emergency but that's what it is in my
humble opinion. Unless I've gone mad, of course! A
tragic but real possibility.

Sorry to dump this on you, darlin', there's no one else
I can turn to—anyway, you've been summoned by
name (& not only by me) so if you possibly can, you'd
best come quick.

Colin

My heart was pounding like a basketball being dribbled
in double-time. Colin had attached a page with some cheap
flights and the bus schedule from London to the place in
Wales where he and his grandfather were staying. It was
called "Castell Cyfareddol." I was not even going to guess
how to pronounce that.

    *. . . Travel instructions will arrive via e-mail at eight
o'clock sharp. Please follow all instructions to the letter . . .*

    Was this some kind of insane coincidence? Or was Colin's distress signal the e-mail Mr. Phineas was telling me to
wait for?

    And if so, what did Mr. Phineas have to do with whatever was going on with Colin?

    And what the phek, sorry, fek, was Finnbar doing in my

parent's bathtub? The weirdness was reaching critical mass. Something must be up.

My mom knocked on the door before opening it a crack. "Can I come in?"

"Uh." I glanced back at the computer to make sure I hadn't left Colin's e-mail open on the screen. "Sure."

"Mr. Phineas just rang the bell, didn't you hear it?"

I looked at her stupidly. "What bell?"

"The doorbell, silly. He dropped this off." She handed me another envelope with the official Oxford emblem on it, sealed and addressed to me.

I stared at it, speechless. It was like when cartoon characters get so flustered that smoke starts spewing out their ears and their eyes bug out on springs. My mom just smiled.

"Your plane tickets are in there. He said you'd be getting your itinerary in an e-mail. Did you?"

"Um, yeah." I stared at the envelope, not wanting to open it in front of my mother in case Tinker Bell flew out of it, trailing a stream of magic sparkle-dust.

"He explained about the tour to your father and me. You leave tomorrow."

"Wow." It was the kind of all-purpose word that seemed to cover the complexity of the situation nicely, so I said it again. "Wow."

"Wow indeed." Mom sat down on the edge of my bed. I knew that move. It meant she "wanted to talk." This was definitely not a good time.

"How's Tammy?" I asked, as a diversion. "Did you drain all the Mr. Bubble out of her lungs?"

"She's fine." Mom sounded weirdly calm, considering the big drama that had just transpired. "She was probably playing with Barbies until Dad and I walked in, right?"

"Watching *SpongeBob*, but yeah."

"We overreacted," she said simply. "But you didn't. After your father put her down Tammy told us the whole story: that you were right outside the bathroom door the whole time she was taking a bath? And you came in and pulled her out of the tub the minute you heard something suspicious?"

"Yeah, the bathroom is probably a mess, sorry about that—"

My mom threw her arms around me and squeezed so hard I lost my breath. "Morgan! Do you realize that you saved your sister's life?"

"Mom—ouch—I think you still might be overreacting." I wriggled free, gently, because I could tell she was on the brink of getting weepy, and I didn't have time to deal with that. "Maybe you're having one of those hormonal surges that afflict women your age and cause temporary fits of insanity."

"Most serious childhood accidents occur in the home," she said, wiping her eyes. "But not this time, thanks to you. And now this!" She tapped the envelope with her finger. "Oxford University is pursuing *you*! Morgan, I don't know what to say. I feel like there must be a whole side of you that we've missed, somehow."

Oh my God, you have no idea, I thought. "Does that mean I can go to England, then?"

"Sweetheart, you *have* to go! I know it's short notice, but it's not like it's the first time you've traveled to Europe alone." She looked at the pile of clothes on my bed like she wished she were the one with the plane ticket. "Do you need any help packing?"

"I'm fine." I really wanted her to leave so I could print out Colin's travel directions. "I can manage. Thanks."

She started to leave, but stopped in the doorway.

"This is going to be a real adventure for you, Morgan." She put her hand over her heart, drama-queen style. "I just have a feeling. This trip is going to be a *truly* unforgettable experience."

six

i waited until i heard my mom's footsteps going down the stairs, counted to ten, and then turned back to the computer. My reply to Colin was short and sweet. "I'll be there Friday morning," I wrote. "Whatever it is, you're not crazy. Love, Morgan."

I stared at the screen for a moment before pressing SEND. Of course I was dying to know what was going on— for one thing, what the fek was he doing on vacation with his grandfather? He was supposed to be working the bike tour this summer—but there'd be plenty of time to ask questions in person. Right now, the less I knew, the less I'd have to lie to my parents about. I just needed to get my half-goddess butt to Wales without anybody realizing that I was taking a detour. Call it the really, really scenic route to Oxford.

Feeling totally spylike, I printed out Colin's e-mail and

travel instructions, then deleted the file. I changed my pass-word too, just in case some nosy kid named Tammy felt like playing with my computer while I was gone.

And I wrote an e-mail to Sarah saying I'd be out of town for a while to look at college campuses. "Cheerio!" is how I signed off at the end, instead of goodbye. I was pretty sure she'd figure it out. I made it a "send later" e-mail and timed it to get to her when I would be high in the sky, halfway over the Atlantic. Detailed explanations would have to wait until I got back to Connecticut.

Of course, I had no idea when that would be.

the next morning, with some small part of me still suspecting I might have dreamed the whole thing, I found myself standing in the lobby of the local Marriott, waiting to board the airport van to JFK.

The Oxford brochure poked strategically from the out-side pocket of my wheeled suitcase, where everyone could admire it. My secret itinerary from Colin was folded up and hidden inside the private zipper pouch of my backpack, where I usually stashed my SGS (SGS was Sarah-and-Morgan-speak for Secret Girl Stuff, meaning tampons and panti-liners and supplies of that nature, though math tests that had failing grades scrawled on them in red ink some-times got crumpled up and shoved in there too).

I promised my mom that I'd be careful and not get kid-napped by perverts, my dad that I'd take plenty of pictures and not get arrested by a "constable" and Tammy that I'd buy her crappy souvenirs from every overpriced gift shop in the United Kingdom.

And then, with multiple hugs all around and my mom doing a final frisk to triple-check that my passport and plane tickets were safely stashed on my person, I climbed in the van and took my seat. Taking the van was my idea—I figured there was no need for either of my parents to miss a whole day's work just to drive me all the way to the airport when the Marriott was only two miles away from our house. I already had enough guilt that I wasn't telling them the whole truth about where I was going.

"I want to handle this trip myself," I argued, when Mom made a boo-boo face about my van plan. "That's what a true Oxonian would do." I'd been waiting for a chance to use that word ever since I'd read it in the Oxford brochure. Privately, I imagined the Oxonians as a small, nerdy race of aliens from the planet Oxon. Their incompetent rulers would be called the Oxymorons. Anyway, just saying it did the trick. Dad puffed out his chest, Mom got a tear of pride in her eye, and they let me go.

"My goodness," Mom whispered in my ear, during her final-final-final-positively-this-is-the-last-one goodbye hug. "You've grown up so much since last summer, I can't get over it."

She doesn't know the half of it, I thought. Last summer I'd been a cranky-to-the-point-of-emo-girl whose world revolved around a twisted axis named Raphael. Now I was a legendary half-goddess who'd been summoned to a far-off land, "by name," Colin had written—but by whom? And to do what?

Like a dork, I waved through the van window until I couldn't see my family anymore. Then I took a deep breath and settled into my seat. I'd brought my MP3 player for the ride but I didn't feel like turning it on. There was too much to think about: Finnbar blowing bubbles in my parents' bathtub, Colin's e-mail, even the phreaky Mr. Phineas—all signs pointed to some kind of magical disaster brewing.

I could handle it, right? I'd done it before. *The half-goddess Morganne, at your service. Magical Disasters R Us.*

But something was bothering me, and the van was half-way to the airport before I figured out what it was:

Whatever faery mischief was percolating this time, it sounded like my utterly non-magical, one hundred percent-skeptical-human Colin had already come face-to-face with it.

Not in a dream, or while under an enchantment that would make him forget everything he'd seen by morning—but for real.

That had never happened before.

the whole seven-hour flight to london, in between naps, gross airplane meals and multiple screenings of *Be Kind Rewind*, I kept thinking about Colin, and magic, and—wait for it—photosynthesis.

I mean, come on: The fact that a blade of grass, or a tree, or a weed growing in the sidewalk could have the ability to turn carbon dioxide into oxygen and keep an entire planet alive had to be the greatest feat of magic ever.

Photosynthesis was something Colin had absolutely no

trouble believing in, but faeries? Leprechauns? Not a chance. He thought all that "faery claptrap" was leftover junk from the "old Ireland," the backward, superstitious country of his grandparents' day.

Colin believed in the future. He believed in an Ireland whose high-tech factories manufactured laptop computers, and where heavy metal bands rocked the night away in two-hundred-year-old pubs. What would he say if he found out his very own Morgan, the bad-ass American girl whom he'd taken for a band chick when he first met me, was really a magical half-goddess from Ye Quaint Olde Days of Irish lore?

Would he think I was insane? Or worse, ridiculous? Some stupid fairy-tale character, like a cheap plastic toy you'd get by sending in the top of a Lucky Charms cereal box plus $3.95 shipping and handling?

Or would he be too mad at me to care, once he found out that I'd basically been lying to him since the first day we met?

Correction: It was more like the third day. But still.

Fek, I thought, as I stared out the window at the swirl of gray clouds below. *If my goddess half gets busted in front of Colin, I'm going to have a* lot *of explaining to do.*

After my flight landed at heathrow i followed the crowds and the signs and figured out how to get through customs and retrieve my suitcase from the luggage carousel. I was briefly stumped trying to find the terminal where Colin had instructed me to catch the bus to Wales, but once

I realized the buses were called "coaches" I figured it out. The idea of traveling by coach made me feel like I might be going to Wales in a pumpkin pulled by enchanted mice, which would hardly surprise me at this point.

When it was my turn at the ticket window I read the information directly off the itinerary from Colin, to make sure I got it right. "One round-trip to Castell Cyfareddol, please."

The clerk looked at me like I had a horn growing out of my forehead.

"Pardon me, miss—but *where* did you say you were going?"

"I must be pronouncing it wrong." I pressed the sheet of paper against the glass so he could see. "This place. It's in Wales."

He looked at the paper, then back at me, an expression of total horror on his face. "KASSul Kuh-FAIR-uh-doll? Why on earth would you want to go there?" Then he removed a pencil from behind his ear and tapped it on the glass to make sure he had my attention, even though I was already looking at him.

"Castell Cyfareddol is a *profoundly* silly place," he said ominously. "The type of destination that attracts budget-minded couples on second honeymoons. Rock stars on ironically low-brow vacations. Disgraced members of the royal family hiding from the paparazzi." He leaned down and spoke in a fearful hiss through the hole in the bottom of the ticket window. "Personally I can't imagine going there. Speaking for myself, I would rather go nearly *anyplace* but there."

What a head case, I thought. *This guy could definitely use a dose of my mom's Xanax.*

Thanks to my dad, my wallet was pimped out with my very own AmEx card for traveling. I pushed the card through the window. "Awesome." I smiled, trying to be friendly. "It sounds like a total piss. How much did you say the ticket was?"

He scowled back at me from under his wire-rimmed glasses. "Forty non-refundable pounds. And for a mere one pound extra you can buy insurance against accidents that are highly likely to befall your person, including loss of life, loss of limb, loss of personal property and personal liability in case of unforeseen but practically inevitable catastrophe—"

All I knew was I didn't come all this way just to miss my coach. "Just give me the ticket," I growled, switching to my scariest deadpan death glare.

"Forty pounds, then. It's hardly worth it. 'Castell Cy-fareddol,' ugh!" You could practically hear the quote marks of distaste in his voice as he punched the information into the ticket machine. "You know what it means, don't you? 'Magic Castle.' Please! They might as well rename it 'Disneyland.'"

The ticket finished printing. He pushed it through the window with the tip of his pencil, as if he didn't want to touch it.

"That would be a lot easier to pronounce—hey." I looked at the ticket. "This is one-way. I asked for round-trip."

He threw his hands up in the air, as if I'd proved his point. "See? That's another reason not to go! It's a preposterous place. Completely preposterous! Yet once people get there they never want to leave. Journey time is three hours. Overpriced snacks and refreshments will be available on board. Express Coach wishes you a pleasant trip. Next!"

I looked over my shoulder. There was no one behind me.

"Next!" he called again, even louder.

"Never mind, I'll buy the return ticket in Wales." I hoisted my backpack into place. "Thanks anyway."

"Believe me, you shouldn't be thanking me at all." His voice rang after me as I walked away. "Arrivederci, Miss Mouseketeer! Have a good time at Disneyland!"

the clock had magically zipped ahead five hours because I'd crossed the Atlantic, so it was early morning when I got on the bus to Wales, even though my body was insisting it was still the middle of the night. I kept having the urge to check the time on my cell phone, but the arrangements for my trip had happened so fast I'd never figured out how to get my phone set up to work in England. In the end I'd left it home.

The good part was I'd be spared hourly calls from my parents asking whether Oxford was everything it was cracked up to be. *Sure, Oxford is great! I'm chillin' with the archbishops! I'm Facebook friends with Frodo and Samwise! And the prime minister invited me for tea, but I had to blow him off because I'm having drinks with Hugh Grant later . . .*

Yeah, right. The nagging question of how I was going to explain to my parents why I never actually made it to my campus tour at Oxford was buzzing around my head in a most annoying way. I filed the whole problem in my mental "I'll deal with it later" pile. That pile was getting kind of large, but at the moment I had other stuff to worry about.

For one thing, without a phone I had no way of getting in touch with Colin to tell him I was a mere pumpkin ride away. I'd have to check in at the front desk of Castell Cyfareddol—fek it, I was just going to call it Magic Castle, it was easier—and have them call Colin's room once I got there.

Disgraced members of the royal family hiding from the paparazzi . . . I hoped the ticket clerk was right about that much, at least. It would be kind of cool to run into some royalty.

As long as it wasn't Queen Titania.

from the outside, Castell Cyfareddol's main hotel looked far too much like the Cinderella Castle at Disney World for my taste, but when I walked through the revolving doors and saw who was at the far end of the lobby arguing with the desk clerk, I knew I was definitely not in Orlando. My own personal version of heaven, maybe.

"It's a fairly simple question, innit? What I'm asking is, d'ye happen to know if there are any horses living wild on the grounds? A herd of Welsh ponies, maybe?"

"Sir, if you want to take riding lessons as part of your

holiday it can easily be arranged. Starlight Stables is in the next village and offers a discount to the guests at Castell Cyfared-dol. I can call them right now to make an appointment—"

"I'm not interested in takin' any bloody lessons . . ."

The decor of the lobby was a cross between the Taj Mahal in India and the Bellagio casino in Vegas, two places I'd never visited but had seen pictured in my mom's alphabetized collection of *Travel + Leisure* magazines. However, in this half-goddess's opinion the rear view of Colin O'Grady was one of the true wonders of the world, so much so that I would have been happy to stand there admiring it until lunchtime, at least.

But during the argument about the ponies the exasperated desk clerk had spotted me waiting with my luggage, and she pounced on the opportunity to change the subject. She called to me loudly, over Colin's shoulder, "Can I help you, miss?"

Colin glanced behind him. Then he did a double take. He turned to face me. His mouth fell open but nothing came out.

I was so happy to see him I was almost afraid to breathe, in case it was all a dream. There was so much I wanted to tell him—how much I'd missed him, how glad I was to have any reason, even a crazy one, to come join him in Wales, how heart-stoppingly yummy he looked from head to toe—but the expression of pure shock on his face shut me up.

"Mm—Mm—Mm—*Morgan?*" he finally choked out.

I raced over and threw my arms around him. "See, I made it! Your directions were perfect. Oh my God, Colin, what's going on? When I got your e-mail I was kind of freaked out—there's so much I want to ask you—"

"What e-mail?" He pulled me off of him and stared at me like he was seeing a ghost. "No offense, darlin'—but what the fek are ye doin' here?"

seven

Okay. this was not the greeting i'd expected. We stared at each other like two people having a WTF? contest.

"You sent me an e-mail," I said, bewildered. "You asked me to come. You said it was an emergency."

He was shaking his head *noooooo*, side to side—

"I swear, Colin! I can show you, I printed it out—it says something weird happened and I was 'summoned by name.' You even sent me all the directions on how to get here, the address and the coach schedule and everything . . ."

I'd never actually seen Colin in a fight, but I knew from what he'd told me that he wasn't above exchanging friendly fisticuffs in a pub when the occasion called for it. Now I knew what he must look like in those moments. He looked very focused, and very pissed off.

"Now who the bloody hell would do somethin' like

that?" he muttered, looking away. "And why?" He exhaled sharply and turned back to me. "At least it proves yer not hallucinatin', because ye'd never find yer way here otherwise. As destinations go, this place is unlikely as they come." Then his eyes filled with concern. "Are ye all right?"

"I'm fine." The thrilling nearness of Colin was quickly being preempted by the sickening realization that he hadn't actually asked me to come. Was I losing my mind? I shook off the feeling. "Confused, but fine. Are *you* all right?"

"Sure, sure. Grandpap is too. Well, bollocks! I can't believe ye're standin' in front of me. The plot bloody thickens, doesn't it?" He lowered his voice. "Listen, Mor—this mysterious e-mail of yours was right about one thing: Somethin' *did* happen; I guess ye could call it weird. But I hadn't yet made up me mind what to do about it, and I surely didn't ask ye to come to Wales." Finally his face softened, and there was a hint of a smile. "I'm not sorry ye're here, though."

I tried to reply, but the attempt forced me to inhale, and as soon as I did that my poor oxygen-starved brain demanded that I yawn, and then yawn again. My intention to form words got completely overruled.

"Ah, ye poor jet-lagged thing!" He took my backpack from me. "Last time I saw ye I was the one who couldn't stay awake. But ye've got a good excuse. Ye've been travelin' all night, haven't ye?"

"I'm fine, really," I protested, fighting another yawn. Being handed a whole new mystery to unravel must have pushed me over the edge, because the accumulated fatigue of my trans-Atlantic all-nighter suddenly crashed down on me. "But wait"—*yawwwwwn*—"what was this 'weird thing' that happened?"

He glanced around the lobby. "There's an awful lot to tell ye, Mor, but this isn't the place to tell it. Let's get ye settled and rested first. Grandpap and I are staying in one of the guest cottages on the beach side o' the boardwalk. There's plenty of room, if you don't mind sharing the place with us."

A cottage by the beach? With Colin? Take away the bizarre circumstances and the grandfather-as-chaperone part and it was like a dream come true. "Of course I don't mind." I mustered a smile. "If your grandpap doesn't, of course."

"Are ye kiddin'? He'll be over the moon to meet ye." Colin heaved my suitcase onto one of his strong shoulders and slung my backpack over the other. "We're in 'Villa C by the Sea,' otherwise known as the Seahorse. All the guest cottages here have names: the Toadstool, the Merry Milkmaid, the Head o' Lettuce. Daft, I know, but this whole place is daft, as ye're about to discover. Are ye up for a walk? They have golf carts for the elderly and infirm, but I hardly think we're in that category just yet. Unless ye're too sleepy?"

"I'd much rather walk. It feels like I've been sitting on buses and planes forever." Colin's use of the word "seahorse" gave me a strange feeling inside. I put a hand on his arm. "Colin—why were you asking the desk clerk about horses? Does that have anything to do with what happened?"

"Like I said, there's a lot to tell." He looked at me like he wanted to say more—but not yet. "Let's get ye settled in first."

i followed Colin through the lobby doors and out into the sun. The late-morning light was bright and lovely but also totally disorienting, since my body was still convinced it was before dawn in Connecticut. The air had that fresh, salty ocean smell.

Colin led me across the wide paved plaza in front of the hotel. "They call this the 'piazza,'" he explained, "and where the Italian flavor comes from you needn't bother askin', because there's no rhyme nor reason to anything about this place. But it's a beautiful view, fer sure."

He was right. From the far end of the piazza you could look out over the water. It looked like somebody had sprinkled the surface with glitter, as the sunlight sparkled and danced across the swells. The water was the same vivid blue as Colin's eyes.

"That, darlin', is the Irish Sea," Colin said proudly. "Of course I'm partial, but in this Irishman's opinion ye'll find no wetter ocean anywhere on the globe."

Colin, Colin, Colin. It was so great to hear his voice again, and to see him looking so fit and rested. This was the old Colin—the one I'd met and fallen for in Ireland last summer, not the exhausted, enchanted wreck who'd spent two unhappy weeks with me in Connecticut only a few months earlier.

And now here we were, together again, side by side in a foreign land. Foreign to me, anyway. Though, as I followed Colin across the piazza toward the boardwalk, it became increasingly obvious that Castell Cyfareddol would have felt like another planet to pretty much anyone who wasn't raised inside a theme park.

For starters, the huge reflecting pool in the center of the piazza offered up a mirror image of the hotel's Cinderella Castle exterior that was so convincing, it had actually caused me a moment of confusion when I'd gotten off the bus. At the time I figured it was because I was so groggy with jet lag, but a second look confirmed it: There was definitely something bizarre about how easy it was to mistake the reflection for the real thing.

We reached the end of the piazza and continued along the main boardwalk, which led to the guest cottages and gardens. The boardwalk was flanked on both sides with tall palm trees, Hollywood Boulevard style. Between the palms were large evergreen shrubs pruned into the shapes of rabbits, squirrels, chipmunks, and other miscellaneous animals of the cute woodland variety, except much bigger than life-sized. They were all about the same height as Colin.

The sculpted shrubs made me think of *Edward Scissorhands*, a film Sarah and I admired hugely due to the sexy-hawtness of Mr. Johnny Depp, who was second only to Orlando Bloom on Sarah's list of celebrity crushes.

Then the boardwalk took a turn, and all at once we were treated to another open view of the water. Leering stone gargoyles perched on a waist-high balustrade, with their winged backs facing the sea.

Colin saw me gaping at the surroundings. "Quite a spread, innit? The whole shebang was dreamed up by this mad architect a hundred years ago. McAlister was his name. The bloke was never satisfied; he kept adding to it and moving things around until he died. Now his grandson's in charge, still fussin' and adding on to the place."

"Nothing matches," I said, rubbing my eyes. On one side of the boardwalk were the gargoyles and shrubby dunes leading steeply down to the sea. On the other side the terrain was mountainous, with pastel-colored guest cottages scattered all over the hills. A distant, snow-capped peak served as the backdrop. Sea, mountains, palm trees, evergreens—what climate were we in?

And I didn't know much about architecture (other than the fact that oversized Connecticut open-plan houses were annoying to live in), but even I could see how a salmon-pink stucco chalet with a Spanish-tiled roof tucked behind a pale yellow, cottage-sized version of a columned Greek temple was definitely out of whack.

The distant, soothing crash of the waves had turned into a strange roaring sound that seemed to be getting louder as we walked. Colin raised his voice to be heard. "Careful of the waterfall, now."

"Careful of the wha—?" I started to ask, but then we took another turn. Ten yards in front of us the boardwalk dead-ended into a waterfall. It was at least fifteen feet high and the width of the boardwalk across, and there seemed to be no way to get past it.

I stared open-mouthed at the wall of turquoise water crashing down into a spray of white foam at our feet. Were we supposed to jump in?

"Watch this," Colin said. Adjacent to the nearest gargoyle was a Victorian-style streetlamp with an incongruously modern button on it labeled "Push to cross," just like on the traffic lights at home. Colin pushed. After a minute, the waterfall trickled to a stop and quickly drained. The boardwalk continued right through the middle of where the water had just been.

"Nice bit of theatricality, that." Colin gestured at me to follow him through. "When Grandpap and I arrived, the gal at the desk handed me the keys and told me: 'Ye're in Seahorse Cottage, down the boardwalk, through the waterfall, fifty meters straight ahead and make a left at the dragon.' I thought she was kidding."

The dragon? I thought, trying not to overreact. The waterfall had resumed its normal operations behind us. Ahead on our left, an enormous dragon carved of weathered stone guarded the entrance to a sandy path that led from the boardwalk down toward the beach. The boardwalk continued on, twisting and turning along the shore and then into the hills until it seemed to disappear into a not-so-distant forest.

Colin stopped to turn down the path, but I stared ahead,

fascinated. "What's up there?" I asked. "At the end of the boardwalk?"

"The forest," he said, after the briefest pause. "And some other things I'll tell ye about in a bit. Come, the cottage is this way."

Seahorse Cottage was halfway down the path between the boardwalk and the beach. It was so tiny I thought Colin would have to duck his head getting through the front door.

It looked sort of like a gingerbread house from a fairy tale, but instead of gumdrops and lollipops, the Seahorse was adorned with the kind of ocean-themed tchotchkes you'd expect to find in a tacky seafood restaurant. Giant crabs clung to the roof. Smiling starfish lined the window-sills. The shutters were latticed like coral, and the curtains had a loose, seaweedy weave. There was even a classic jock-ey-with-a-lantern statue lighting the path to the front door, but this jockey was mounted on a seahorse.

"Let me go in first, in case Grandpap's taking a nap in his Skivvies." Colin rapped softly on the door, then pushed it open. "Grandpap? Put yer trousers on," he called. "We have company, of the female persuasion."

I followed him through the door, feeling shy and strange. The cottage seemed much bigger on the inside than it looked from the front. From an unseen back room there came an answer.

"'Trousers on,' he says! D'ye think I've become a nudist in me dotage, lad?" Grandpap strode into the living room, yawning and still buckling his belt.

"Look at ye, ye codger! Ye were nappin' like a baby, weren't ye? Ye couldn't even stay upright till lunchtime." Colin beamed and gave his grandfather a bear hug, which the old man returned with vigor.

"Don't listen to a word he says, young lady," Grandpap said as Colin released him. "He'll have ye convinced I'm one of the forgetful elderly, instead of the distinguished gentleman in his prime ye see before ye. I'm only eighty-two, after all." He peered at me. "And who are ye, dear?"

"Paps, this is Morgan. My friend in the States that I've told ye so much about," Colin said. "I didn't know she was comin', but I'm glad she's here."

"You must be Colin's grandpap." I couldn't help grinning. As grandfathers go he was just about the cutest thing I'd ever seen—not quite as tall as Colin, or as buff, but very fit-looking for his age, with a head of thick silvery hair. And he had the same twinkly blue eyes as Colin. In Grandpap's case his eyes were half-hidden behind a pair of dorky black-rimmed glasses, but they were still full of that familiar brand of mischief I loved so well.

"Colin's grandpap is what I am, and I'm a better man for it too. Well, this is a surprise! So ye're the famous Morgan." He held out his arms to me. "Colin talks about ye so much I feel like I know ye."

I wasn't usually a fan of hugging old men whom I'd just

met, but on this occasion it seemed perfectly appropriate. Grandpap smelled like licorice and pipe tobacco, a pleasant combination.

There was a knock on the door.

"More company? It's like Heuston Station in here today." Grandpap let me go and padded to the front door. "I bet it's old Devyn, come to beat me at another hand of Forty-fives."

"I hope ye're not playin' cards for money," Colin scolded. "Ye're not a man of boundless wealth, ye know."

Grandpap chuckled as he reached for the seashell-shaped knob. "Shut yer gob, lad, if I want to squander me pension I will—good mornin', Devyn! We'll have to have our card game later. Colin's lady friend from the States has arrived, and she'll be needin' lunch and some decent conversation."

"No need to babysit, Pap," Colin said, giving me a roll of the eyes.

"Says you!" Grandpap scoffed. "If I let you children out of me sight, ye'll be gettin' into all kinds of scrapes and shenanigans."

"And what's the harm in that, William?" The visitor's voice was a deep baritone, with a cultured British accent. "You were young once too, you know. Or have you forgotten?"

Grandpap took a step back from the door, and I was finally able to get an eyeful of his friend.

Distinguished, silver-haired, in a funny old-fashioned hat. To my horror he was wearing breeches, just like Mr.

Phineas. Was this some kind of retro fashion trend only senior citizens knew about?

It wasn't just the knee pants, though. Boy, did this guy look familiar. I tried not to stare.

"Allow me to present me good pal, the ruthless card-sharp, Devyn McAlister," Grandap said proudly.

"The third," Mr. McAlister added quickly. "And you are Morganne, of course! How thrilling that you're here. I've been wondering when you would arrive."

eight

Every trace of fog in my sleep-deprived brain evaporated in an instant.

"My name's Morgan," I said slowly. "And nobody knew I was coming, so why were you expecting me?"

I saw him do a slow take around the cottage—Colin's puzzled expression, my suspicious one, Grandpap's oblivious good cheer.

"Upon second thought, I am mistaken, of course. My sincere apologies," Mr. McAlister said with a strange smile. "But I couldn't be more delighted to meet you, Miss— Did I catch your name?"

"This is Miss Morgan Rawlinson, sir," Colin said.

The old man tipped his hat. "Devyn McAlister the Third. What a distinct pleasure to make your acquaintance."

I looked at him carefully. "You seem very familiar. Are you sure we haven't met before?"

"Is this your first visit to Castell Cyfareddol?"

"Yes."

"Then you must have me mistaken for someone else." Mr. McAlister grandly waved a hand around. "This is my home. I haven't left the grounds of Castell Cyfareddol in many years, in fact. But perhaps it's my name that seems familiar."

"Mr. McAlister is the grandson of the famous Devyn McAlister, the fellow who designed and built this place," Colin explained. "If ye ever want a guided tour of the premises, he's yer man. He knows every nook and cranny."

"You are too kind." Mr. McAlister nodded his thanks to Colin. "I oversee the foundation my grandfather created to maintain his life's work. It was his express wish that Castell Cyfareddol never be 'finished,' so, in addition to supervising the preservation of the existing structures, I oversee the design and the construction of all new additions."

"Ye should see the quarter-scale version of the Parthenon he's planning," Grandpap offered. "Better than the real thing, if ye ask me."

"As if ye've ever been to Greece." Colin patted his grandfather on the back. "I took ye to a Greek restaurant once and ye moaned and groaned because they didn't have corned beef and potatoes."

Grandpap waved off Colin's teasing. "Dev, ye should tell Morgan about the book ye're writing," he urged. "About yer architectural theories. I've heard ye talk about it while we're at cards, and though I confess I only understand every tenth word ye say, it still feels bloody educational."

Mr. McAlister lifted a silvery eyebrow in amusement. "I would enjoy that immensely. But I'm afraid your guest may have other things to do with her holiday than listen to an old man prattle on about mansard roofs and fluted pilasters. What do you say, Morganne?"

Again with the Morganne. He smiled at me, a sly, *yes-I'm-yanking-your-chain* smile. Or maybe it was a secret, *I've-got-something-to-tell-you-privately* smile.

"That would be excellent," I said quickly. "I would love to hear about the fluted thingies, and anything else you'd care to tell me."

"And it's Morgan, Mr. McAlister," Colin corrected. "Not Morganne."

"I am sorry; perhaps I will just refer to you as Miss Rawlinson, to avoid confusion! But I do appreciate your keen interest in my favorite subject. Come visit me any time to discuss. My cottage is called Tip of the Iceberg. It's just down the path toward the beach."

"Great," I said. "I'll look forward to it."

"Devyn's quite an intellectual," Grandpap added. "Why he squanders his time hanging around with us ordinary blokes I'll never understand. The man studied at Oxford! Didn't ye, Dev?"

"I did indeed, William. Dear old Oxford! A school, by the way," said Mr. McAlister, tipping his hat in my direction, "that I would highly recommend."

*   *   *

Oxford, cute. the guy had something to tell me all right. Getting some private face time with Mr. McAlister definitely belonged on my to-do list—somewhere between food and sleep.

After Mr. McAlister left, Colin fixed lunch in the cottage's tiny kitchen—grilled cheese and delicious sliced apples from the Castell Cyfareddol orchards—accompanied by endless cups of tea and a nonstop monologue from Grandpap. This was despite Colin's protests that the old man "stop bendin' the poor lass's ear with yer creaky old tales."

I didn't mind the old stories, but maybe that's because I hadn't already heard them hundreds of times, the way Colin had. Grandpap told me the whole saga of how he and his wife, Nancy, had grown up together in a rural town in Ireland, fallen in love as teens, married young and honeymooned right here at Castell Cyfareddol.

"Now it's almost three months already, since me ol' girl's passed on," Grandpap said sadly. "I miss me Nan every second of the day, but what a grand life we had! When Colin was a wee boy-o, we used to keep him summers on our farm. Ye should've seen him back then! All day playin' and runnin' around the woods like a wild thing."

"I'm sure it was wonderful," I said warmly. I *was* sure. I'd once gotten a glimpse of this very same farm in the days when Colin was a "wee boy-o," thanks to a little faery time-travel with Finnbar. The farm was gone now, though—sold to a real estate developer years before.

"Sweet memories are a priceless treasure, lass. Better than money in the bank." Grandpap gave me a wink. "If ye've set a good store of those up along the way, ye'll have done the very best job of livin' a person can do. That's my philosophy."

Colin pushed his chair back from the table. "Well said, Socrates, but speakin' fer meself that's all the wisdom I can absorb in one sittin'. I'll show Morgan to her room now. Leave the dishes, Paps, I'll get 'em when I come back."

"Five minutes, Colin!" Grandpap wagged a finger playfully. "Yer allowed five minutes and then I'm comin' in after ye."

Colin rolled his eyes. "Paps, I'm twenty years old."

"Sure ye are, but she isn't."

"I'm seventeen!" I piped up. "That's old enough to—" They were both staring at me. "Drive," I finished lamely.

Colin snorted and got up. "Use the egg timer, then. I don't want to be shortchanged." Then he picked up my suitcase from the foot of the stairs and carried it up the tiny staircase to the cottage's attic bedroom.

"Trust me, lass, I know what I'm doin'," Grandpap stage-whispered to me as I rose from the table to follow. "A few obstacles here and there never did true love any harm. In fact, it's the best thing fer it."

the upstairs bedroom was tiny, with a ceiling that peaked in the middle and sloped gently down on each side. This wasn't much of a problem for me, but Colin could only stand straight up as long as he was in the absolute center of the room. And in the center of the room was the bed—a fact we both realized at the same moment.

I started to giggle.

"I'd say it's either the bed, or a trip to the chiropractor," Colin observed. He held out a hand, and together we toppled onto the covers.

It must have made a mighty thump down below, because Grandpap felt it necessary to bellow, "Four minutes!" from the bottom of the stairs.

We wasted another thirty seconds laughing at that. Then Colin touched my face, and suddenly it was all I could do not to cry. I'd missed him so much, and now that we were together I didn't know whether to make out—only three minutes left!—or pepper him with questions: What was the "weird" thing had happened here at Castell Cyfareddol that caused him so much concern? Where did he think that e-mail could have come from? Most important, had he been seeing anybody else while he was at school in Dublin, and did he still love me like he did before, and what was going to happen with this relationship anyway?

But I didn't ask. Not yet. This perfect moment of us lying snuggled in each other's arms was too sweet to interrupt with anything but a kiss.

Somewhere downstairs a cuckoo clock went off. *Cuckoo— cuckoo—cuckoo—*

"We're running out of time," I whispered, only half-kidding. My fingers crept under the bottom of his rugby shirt. His skin was impossibly, deliciously warm.

He kissed me again, the kind of careful kiss that said, *Let's not get too crazy right now.*

"I know yer probably wonderin' what I was talkin' about earlier," he said softly. "And I want to take a look at this mysterious e-mail that pretends to be from me. But the Q&A portion of our program can wait until after yer nap is complete."

I lifted myself up on one elbow. "Colin, I'm fine. There's so much I really want to know—"

"Eh, no arguments!" he said, placing a finger on my lips. "It's fer yer own good, darlin'. Ye've been up all night. What if I told ye something that made it hard for ye to sleep?"

"What does *that* mean?"

"Time's up!" Grandpap yelled from downstairs.

"On my way, Admiral!" Colin yelled back. Then he kissed me on the forehead and slipped out the door.

the attic room was too small to be crammed full of fish tchotchkes like the rest of the house, but there was a small painting hanging above the dresser. It caught my eye when I rolled over in the bed. Something about it made me get up and take a closer look.

The painting was of a mermaid, but not your typical Disney mermaid with a flipper instead of legs and a pink clamshell bra. This was more what I would call an accurate depiction—two strong legs, webbed toes, seaweed hair, a little red cap on her head. It was a merrow, the kind of Irish mermaid I'd actually met once. I recognized her face, in fact—

"Fek!" I yelled without thinking.

"What?" Colin stuck his head in so fast it was as if he'd been sitting outside guarding the door.

I turned, instinctively blocking the painting from his view. "I just realized, I-I-I forgot my—toothbrush." I flashed a weak smile.

"No worries, luv, I'll find ye a spare." Colin looked at me quizzically. "Why so jumpy? Are ye all right?"

"I'm fine. Just tired."

"Morgan's nap, take two." He smiled and pulled the door almost shut, but not all the way. "Sweet dreams."

Sweet dreams? Not likely, with Queen Titania's cold, snarky face staring down at me from the wall.

She made an ugly mermaid, I had to admit. Before I got back in the bed I dumped out my suitcase and found a gray sweatshirt hoodie to throw over the picture frame. It helped, a little. And it gave me real satisfaction to drape such an unflattering garment over the vain and fashion-conscious queen.

Morgan's nap, take two. The bed had two pillows on it. I put my head on one, and hugged the other one close to my chest. It smelled faintly of Colin's aftershave. Yum.

If I'm lucky I'll have no dreams at all, I thought, as I sank into an exhausted sleep. If Titania was anywhere close by, any dreams I'd have would probably be extremely unpleasant.

* * *

i came to hours later, completely disoriented. Was I in my room in Connecticut? Or dozing on an Irish beach?

Or was I waking up in a tidy Oxford dorm room, just in time to get ready for my campus tour?

Oxford. My parents. Mr. Phineas—

That's all it took to snap me wide awake.

I sat up. The merrow painting was still covered by my hoodie, and the door to the bedroom was fully shut. Colin must have closed it after I'd fallen asleep. It was sweet that he'd been checking on me. But why had he been so worried?

My room had its own "lavatory," a tiny room with a toilet and sink, but no tub. I grabbed my toiletry bag from my suitcase and went in, brushed my teeth and washed my face. I ran my damp fingers through my hair, but it was still a post-nap mess.

"Mor?" Colin cracked open the bedroom door. "Are ye awake?"

"In the bathroom, I mean the lav," I called.

"I brought ye a toothbrush. I heard the water running, so I figured ye might need it."

Right, the toothbrush. As he handed it through the bathroom door I sucked in my breath so he couldn't smell that it was already minty.

"Perfect timing, thanks." I left the bathroom door open and made a big to-do about brushing my teeth, even though I'd just done it. When I came out, I saw Colin staring at the hoodie-covered painting.

"Not a big fan of art, then, are ye?"

"It has spooky eyeballs," I said sheepishly. "It made me feel like I was being watched."

I held my breath as he peeked underneath the hoodie.

"Whoa! I see yer point; that's bloody hideous." He let the hoodie drop. "But those spooky eyeballs are nothin' compared to Grandpap's ears. The man's a medical miracle; four score and two with perfect hearing on both sides of his thick Irish head. And not one ounce o' shame about listenin' to other people's conversations, either."

"Are ye talkin' about me, lad?" Grandpap yelled from downstairs. "Speak up! The kettle's on, I can barely hear ye over the whistlin' of me tea water!"

"No trouble, Paps!" Colin shouted back. "I was just tellin' Morgan how ye're much too much of a busybody to go deaf; think of all the scuttlebutt ye'd miss."

Then Colin lowered his voice to a whisper. "Up for a walk? I thought we could take a stroll to the beach. This way we can talk in private. Bring that e-mail with ye too, I want to have a look at it."

I just nodded. Between Titania's eyes and Grandpap's ears, I was afraid to say a word.

nine

the path from the cottage to the sea led us gently downhill the whole way, but I hadn't realized how far down we'd gone until we were on the beach and I looked back. We stood on a crescent of sand at sea level. The water glittered in front of us, while far above and behind a steep curved bluff perched the wacky skyline of Castell Cyfareddol, like a theme park tottering on the edge of a cliff.

I saw the fairy-tale castle turrets of the hotel, the pastel-colored cottages, the Greek temples, the Swiss chalets, the domed igloos, the tropical gardens and the desert palms. Near the horizon the approaching sunset streaked the sky with colors out of Tammy's favorite cartoons: Powerpuff Girl pink, SpongeBob yellow and Barney the dinosaur purple.

Was this place real, or make-believe? It was hard to say. *Maybe I should tell him,* I thought impulsively. *Maybe this is my chance to come clean about the whole me-being-a-half-goddess thing. Here it might actually seem normal.*

"Sit or walk?" Colin asked.

"Let's sit for a while."

We found a quiet spot, as close to the water as we could get without the sand being too wet to sit on. Colin turned to me. Before he spoke he looked in my eyes, hard and searching—what was he trying to find? He took a deep breath and exhaled slowly, like he was trying to work up the nerve to do something scary.

"Before you start," I said, squeezing his hand, "let me ask you a very important question: What the fek are you doing in Wales?"

That broke the tension and made him laugh, which was what I'd hoped for. "Well, that's a lot easier to explain than what comes next, so I might as well start there. It was all Grandpap's doing, the troublemaker."

Then his mood changed. He looked out at the water and spoke quietly, just loud enough for me to hear him over the surf. "I wish ye could've met Granny, Mor. She'd have thought the world of you."

"I wish I'd met her too," I said, remembering how close I'd come, once. But that was in the faery realm. Yet another adventure I'd never told Colin about. "Grandpap must miss her so much."

Colin sighed. "Poor old bloke. After she passed he didn't know which end was up. Mopin' around, talking to himself, not eatin'. Can't blame him, really. The two of them'd been together since—well, since they were our ages, I suppose."

The sudden, stark image of Colin and me as wrinkled old people, with only one of us left alive to mourn the other at the end of a whole happy lifetime together, flashed through my mind so vividly I had to blink away tears.

He went on. "Then, just last week, clear out of the blue, he announces that there's nothin' he'd rather do than come back to Cyfareddol fer their anniversary. Well, I wasn't wild about the notion. For one thing, the bike tour was supposed to start this week—and I need all the work I can get to earn me tuition fer next year at DCU."

DCU was Dublin City University, where Colin was putting himself through school. He was studying computer science, of course. Something nice and rational.

"I'm ashamed to say I tried to talk the old boy out of it." Colin smiled ruefully. "I warned him how it was short notice and this place gets booked up months in advance, but he wouldn't take no fer an answer. And the idea of comin' here seemed to perk up his spirits no end. Against me better judgment I rang up the hotel. I figgered they'd say they were full up and that'd be the end of it, but it turned out the Seahorse was available—the very cottage Grandpap and Granny had stayed in on their honeymoon. Last-minute cancellation or some such thing. Lucky, eh?"

"Very," I agreed, though I wasn't yet sure that it was.

"Well, now I had to take him, didn't I? So I sucked it up and told Patty at the tour company I'd be startin' a week or two late. You can imagine the colorful language that ensued! But she's got a good heart, does Pat, and she understood. Grandpap and I packed our bags, and here we are."

I drizzled sand on his bare feet, and smiled at the way his toes flexed and curled in answer. "That makes sense," I said. "Now let me hear the part that doesn't."

"Eager for the good stuff, eh?" He gave a wry smile. "From the minute we arrived, Grandpap was happy as a lark. Sometimes I heard him havin' conversations when I knew he was alone in his room. But I didn't think much of it; he's gettin' on in years, after all. Even so, I was reluctant to leave him alone fer any length o' time. But then he befriended that Devyn McAlister fellow. Their card playin' seemed to boost the old boy's mood even more.

"Anyway, a couple of days ago, while Paps and Devyn were safely occupied playing Forty-fives, I finally decided to take a walk by meself. It was a relief, to be honest. I love Paps like anything, but I was gettin' bored playing eldercare nurse, and the pub scene at the hotel is a bit tame for my taste. Ye should hear the bands they book! Barry bleedin' Manilow impersonators! Abba lite, to put it kindly. I'd take the three Irish tenors over that lot any day; they've got more edge."

"Colin—"

"Right. Anyway, I thought it would be good fun to go explorin', so I headed down the boardwalk to the far end. To where the forest begins. You noticed it yerself when we arrived."

I nodded.

"It's a funny walk. Looks like the forest is miles away, but the distance is an illusion, really. Ye just keep walkin', the boardwalk comes to an end, and the forest begins, just like that. There's maybe a dozen different trails into the woods,

all marked with signs pointin' every which way: 'The Road
Not Taken.' 'The Path of Least Resistance.' 'The Lesser of
Two Evils.'"

I laughed. "Which one did you choose?"

I could have sworn he blushed, but maybe it was the way
the light grew rosier as the sun finally touched the horizon.

"Don't mock me, darlin', but there was one sign that
read 'This Way to the Faery Glen.'" He smiled, embarrassed. "It made me think of Granny. She used to love them
faery stories, I heard 'em over and over as a wee lad. Ye've
heard me complain about it, I'm sure!"

"Wait—so you chose the path to the 'Faery Glen,'" I
repeated stupidly. "On purpose?"

"Yes, Officer, I did." He smoothed the sand with his
fingers, an idle, nervous gesture. "The path went straight
into the woods. It was one of them tall, shadowy forests that
looks like it's been growin' there since the dawn of time. I
walked and walked, and soon I started hearin' somethin', a
deep and constant sound, like water rushin' through a
gorge. I thought I must be gettin' near the glen."

Then he paused. "But it wasn't water. It was hoofbeats.
There was a herd of wild horses in the distance, runnin'
through the forest, weavin' in and out o' the trees. At least
that's what I thought they were, until they got a wee bit
closer."

Colin hugged his knees and stared out at the sunset. I
knew better than to rush him. Finally he spoke, his voice
quiet and firm.

"They looked like unicorns, Mor. Beautiful creatures,

silver colored. Each with a long, spiral horn stickin' right out of its noggin'. 'Twas all dim and shadowy in the woods, but the horns were aglow, like they were lit from within." He turned to me. "Like those light-up thingamabubs yer sister likes to run around with at night."

"Glow sticks," I said blankly, while thinking, *Fek! Unicorns?* Leprechauns, gnomes, mermaids, faeries—these were old news to me. But even I had never laid eyes on a unicorn.

"What did you do?" I said finally.

He laughed darkly. "Well, to say I was gobsmacked would be an understatement. I figured I'd burst a brain artery and slipped off the beam somehow. I pictured meself droolin' in a chair for the rest of me days! But ye know me—I wasn't givin' up without a fight, so I made an effort to pull meself together. 'Reason it out, Colin, ye dumb ox,' I told meself. 'Yer mental operating system has crashed, so use yer brain and troubleshoot it like ye've been taught.'

"And then yer man had a brain flash: These aren't unicorns, fer St. Patrick's sake! It's Castell bloody Cyfareddol havin' some fun, that's all. The decorating committee probably leased a herd of costumed ponies from a circus and let 'em loose in the woods for effect. Another piece of whimsy to add to the carnival atmosphere."

"That makes sense," I agreed, while thinking, *If only it were that simple.*

"It does make sense." He angled his body back toward the water and looked at me. "In fact, I'd have no trouble at all acceptin' that explanation, if it weren't for what happened next."

Whoosh. Whoosh. Whoosh. The waves crashed and retreated. They seemed to be offering explanations of their own, but in a language I couldn't understand. Colin went on. "So, just as I'm convincin' meself that I've stumbled upon some poor circus ponies spray-painted silver and wearing illuminated headgear, one of the creatures trotted up to me. It looked me straight in the eye."

"Oh my God—did it say something?" I blurted.

"A talkin' horse? Even I'm not that daft, darlin'!" He laughed at his own joke. "But it did do a bit of a dance, ye could call it, stompin' its hooves and wavin' its tail. Then it pointed down at the dirt with its horn before runnin' off. Apparently there was somethin' on the ground it wanted me to see." He took out his cell phone. "Here, ye can read it yerself."

He flipped the phone open and pressed a few buttons. Then he showed me the screen.

The photo was small, but I could make it out quite clearly. Six words, scratched into the green moss of the forest floor. The letters were sharp and angular—as if they'd been scratched with the tip of a horn:

> MUST SAVE WORLD
> GET MORGAN
> NOW

I didn't know what to say.

Colin put the phone away. "Naturally I tried to get a shot of the beastie and its mates too, but they bolted back into the trees so fast I never had a chance."

We sat in silence. The sun was almost gone, and the beach felt suddenly cool.

"That's it, then." Colin shrugged. "I stumbled home like I was fluthered with drink. I've looked at the picture on me phone more times than I can count. Been drivin' the hotel clerks batty askin' if they knew of any ponies in the woods, but they just keep offerin' me ridin' lessons."

"But you didn't send me that e-mail?" I pressed.

He shook his head. "Why would I? So ye could've written me back sayin', 'ye've gone nutters, Colin, time for a visit to the happy ward'? Yet somehow ye've come anyway." He turned to me. "Under mysterious circumstances, to be sure. Do ye have any idea what it all means?"

"I don't know what that 'save the world' message means," I said carefully. "As for the unicorns—or whatever they are—there could be any number of explanations. I don't think we have enough information to know."

"That's a perfectly sane answer, and I agree one hundred percent." He brushed the sand off his hands. "Let's have a look at this blasted e-mail, then."

I pulled the folded up paper out of the pocket of my jeans. Colin read it, then read it again.

"See? It's from you."

"No it's not," he said, after a minute. "It does sound like me, which is bloody odd, but it's the wrong domain. I'm lovesdeathmetal at Dublin City University. This is from *fff*mail." He sounded like he'd sprung a leak.

"What's *fff*mail?"

"Well, I guess that's how ye'd pronounce it. It's spelled with a PH, look."

I read the FROM line:

FROM: Lovesdeathmetal@PHmail.com

PHmail? How could I not have noticed that?

"Somebody's hacked yer computer, that's obvious. It's just the who and why to figure out." Colin looked back at the page, then cocked an eyebrow at me, curious. "It says here I'll pay fer yer plane ticket, but obviously I didn't. How'd ye get here then?" He looked at me sternly. "Morgan! Do yer parents know where ye are?"

I made a face. "Not exactly."

"Well, they know ye didn't run out to the corner druggist to buy some sweets, don't they?"

I tried to laugh, but a stab of guilt stopped me. "They know I flew to England."

"But not that ye came to Wales?"

"No," I admitted. "Or that I'm with you. They think I'm taking a campus tour of Oxford." I bit my lip and waited for the reaction I knew was coming. *Five—four—three—two—*

"Oxford? Oxford *University*?" Colin hooted in disbelief. "Who'd believe a story like that? I mean, imagine, a perfectly nice person like you wastin' yer time at a snooty, Ivy-covered relic like that medieval pile of bricks! It's an antiquated shrine to the rich and obsolete. It's practically a thousand years old, ye know. It's a miracle the old junk heap is still standin'.".

"They think I'm on a campus tour of Oxford," I said slowly, "because I'm going to apply there to study mythology after I graduate high school, and the admissions office invited me to take a campus tour. Plane tickets included."

"Huh," Colin said.

Major. Awkward. Silence.

"Well, well," he said, after a moment. "Fancy that. I never knew ye were such a scholar, Mor. What else have ye been keepin' from me, I wonder?"

How about the fact that I'm a half-goddess from the days of Irish myth, with a human family in Connecticut and a Queen of Mean magic mom in the faery realm, and that I've been hopping back and forth between the two worlds on a regular basis ever since I'd bonked my head in Ireland last summer on the bike tour?

Or that I'd bet a pot of leprechaun's gold that those unicorns were real and the world must actually be in need of saving (by goddess-me, naturally)?

Or that the only "hacker" I had to worry about was undoubtedly Queen Titania herself?

Should I say all that, and spoil the beachy, sunset mood? Nah. Save it for another time. Like never.

"I thought guys liked mysterious women," I teased, avoiding the issue. "I bet I don't know everything about you, either."

"Ye know all the important stuff. Me fav'rite lunch is

shepherd's pie. Me fav'rite sport is rugby. And me fav'rite girl is you." He stood and reached down to help me up. "Well, we've got a pile of mysteries to solve now, don't we? But I'm sure we'll find a perfectly rational explanation fer all of it."

I got to my feet and surveyed the deserted beach. The moon hadn't risen yet, and the water, sand and sky were nearly indistinguishable in the dark. Above us, the lights of all the cottages and buildings of Castell Cyfareddol were twinkling cozily along the top of the cliff and on the hillsides.

Colin took my hand and warmed it between his own. "Look how dark it is! Grandpap'll be wonderin' if we washed out to sea. Here's what we should do: Tomorrow mornin', bright and early, we'll go back to the forest together. I'll take ye to the spot where I saw the message in the dirt. Maybe we'll find a clue of some kind to help us figure out what's goin' on. I bet we'll find silver paint rubbed off on the tree bark, or worn out glow sticks abandoned in the leaves, that sort of thing."

"That's a good plan." I put my arms around him.

"We'll have breakfast first, o' course. I'm a right whiz in the kitchen. Ye didn't know that about me, did ye?" He gave me a warm, tight hug. "See, I guess I do have a few secrets left."

Me too, I thought, squeezing my eyes shut against the truth. *Me too.*

ten

It took all our concentration to find our way back to the Seahorse Cottage in the dark. The path was uphill and slippery with sand, so we had to pay attention to each step we took.

Maybe it was just the everything-looks-creepier-at-night factor, but it seemed to me as if the surrounding shrubs and tall grasses had doubled in size since we'd come down to the beach. I was getting breathless from the climb—*gym class, Morgan, get some*—so I was really glad when I saw the lights of the cottage up ahead. There was something odd, though . . .

"Didn't the Seahorse used to be on the other side of the path?" I asked, panting.

"No luv, we're farther up," Colin replied. He was so fit from playing football (meaning soccer) and rugby that he could have climbed a sheer rock face without breaking a sweat. "That's the Tip of the Iceberg cottage, where Mr. McAlister lives. Ye hardly notice it in the day because of all the shrubbery, but when the lights are on it jumps out at ye."

He was right about that. At the moment the Tip of the Iceberg was impossible to miss. Unlike the Seahorse, it was spare and clean in design, with circular porthole windows in every wall, like you'd see in the side of a ship. In the dark, with lights streaming through the portholes, the effect was like a car with its high beams on, except it was pointing in all four directions at once.

"Looks like someone's home," I said, while thinking *I have to figure out why that McAlister guy looks so familiar. And obviously there's something he wants to tell me—or, correction, "Morganne."*

"Maybe I'll stop in," I said, veering toward the front door. "I'd love to hear more about the history of Castell Cyfareddol, and all that architecture stuff he was talking about earlier."

Colin looked perplexed. "Mor, are ye serious? Ye want to spend the evening discussing architecture? We've got kind of a big day ahead of us. And we still have plenty of catchin' up to do, don't we, darlin'?" he added, in a much warmer voice that almost made me change my plan.

But half-goddess duty called, even though I didn't know what that duty was yet. I stood in front of the door, my hand raised to knock. "Just for a little while. You don't see a bell anywhere, do you?"

The heavy wooden door, which also had a porthole in its center, swung open with a slow creak.

Mr. McAlister stood in the doorway. He wore an old-fashioned ankle-length nightgown and a nightcap. In fact, he looked exactly like Ebenezer Scrooge from *A Christmas Carol*. Not the made-for-TV version with the stupid Broadway show tunes, or the color version where Scrooge seemed more sad than mean. No, Mr. McAlister looked like the Scrooge from the old, spooky, black-and-white version my parents made us watch every holiday season. The one that used to scare the crap out of Tammy. Because it's good to give your kids nightmares about ghosts on Christmas, right?

"Miss Rawlinson. And Colin too, I see. How delightfully unexpected to find you here." Despite his words, Mr. McAlister didn't sound at all surprised.

"Good evening, Mr. McAlister." Colin was always polite, even when talking to a weirdo in a nightcap. "Hope we didn't wake ye. We're just on our way back from the beach."

"Wake me?" His hands flew to his nightcap. "Ah, of course! I do like to dress comfortably at home, but I'm hard at work, believe me. I'm trying to figure out how to provide adequate cell phone coverage on the grounds of Castell Cyfareddol without marring the authenticity of the architecture with unsightly towers. You may have noticed that it's a problem? I rarely have trouble getting a signal here myself, but of course, my phone is rather unusual . . ."

He held out something that looked like no cell phone I'd ever seen. It was about the right size, but it had the rustic, handmade appearance of something that had been hammered out of copper in a medieval forge.

As always, Colin was fascinated by anything technological. "What's that, an antique? Or did you stick some modern phone innards into an old tin can, like them steampunkers do?"

"Quite a beauty, isn't it?" Mr. McAlister displayed it proudly. "It's called the oPhone. For Oxford graduates only. A perk we get for making a substantial contribution to the alumni association. And," he added, looking at me, "the number is registered to Oxford University, so it makes quite a good impression when you call people."

I knew my mouth was hanging open, but I couldn't help it. "You mean, when you call someone on that phone, it says the call is coming from Oxford?"

"Indeed it does," he said with satisfaction. "Alumni relations have reached such heights of sophistication! Not like the old days, when they simply invited you to dinner once a year to get you drunk and ask for money." He started patting the sides of his nightdress as if he'd forgotten he had no pockets. "Ah, it's not here, it's in my breeches—but if I had my wallet handy I could show you my Oxford MasterCard, which generates a small donation to my alma mater each time I use it—"

I had to work really hard not to scream *Shut up, already, no one cares about your MasterCard*. "Mr. McAlister," I said through a forced smile, "do you think I could use your phone? I need to call my parents in the States. I will happily reimburse you for any additional charges incurred," I added, in my best pretentious Oxford-speak.

"No need for that! International calls are always free on the oPhone," Mr. McAlister said proudly. "It's the university's policy, promotes understanding between nations and so forth. If it helps build a bridge between parent and child along the way, so much the better! Of course you may use it, my dear. But you must come inside, it's getting chilly."

He stepped aside to make way for us to enter, but then paused. "Oh, Colin—I believe your grandfather was looking for you with some urgency. Perhaps you ought to run home? I'll make sure Morgan gets back to the Seahorse Cottage safely."

Colin jerked back in alarm. "Grandpap? Is he sick?"

"Hmm," said Mr. McAlister, with maddening vagueness. "I'm not sure what the trouble is, to be frank. He complained of a headache, then cut our card game short and said he was going to bed." Mr. McAlister let his voice drop in an ominous way. "He seemed rather eager for you to get back from the beach."

"I'd best run then." Colin leaned down to kiss me on the cheek, and whispered: "But make sure ye tell yer ma and pa what a moldy wreck the Oxford campus is. Tell 'em ye'd rather enroll at Dublin City University, where the good honest workin' folk go."

"It's a deal. And I do want to stay and ask Mr. McAlister a few questions about architecture," I answered lightly. "So I might be a while."

* * *

After Colin left, my host pulled the door closed. We looked at each other. I was full of questions. So was he, I could tell. But which one of us was going to go first?

"We do have much to discuss," he murmured, as if he were thinking the same thing. "But first, welcome to the Tip of the Iceberg! Won't you have a look around?"

I did, and all at once I couldn't make sense of where I was. I'd already noticed how the Seahorse Cottage looked bigger on the inside than it did on the outside. This was the opposite: The interior of the Tip of the Iceberg looked surprisingly small. In fact, it was a dead ringer for a ship's cabin. There was a single, narrow cast-iron bed. The walls and ceiling were painted a creamy white. Tall mirrors flanked the door, and there were a few pieces of antique furniture, including a white enamel pedestal sink and a small mahogany dresser.

"Is this supposed to be a ship?" I asked, dumbfounded.

"In a manner of speaking, we *are* on a ship," Mr. McAlister said proudly. "But not just any ship. Look!" He handed me an ashtray.

"I don't smoke. It's seriously bad for your health—"

"Read it," he urged.

The ashtray was heavy glass. On the bottom, in an ornate gold leaf script, it read: RMS *TITANIC*.

"What—what is *that* supposed to mean?" I stammered.

"Excellent question! People usually assume the RMS stands for Royal Majesty something or other, but RMS actually means Royal Mail Steamship. And *Titanic* simply means very, very large; I'm sure you knew that." He looked around with pride. "Everything in this cottage is a perfect replica of a second-class passenger cabin on the RMS *Titanic*, exactly as it was built in 1911."

Tip of the Iceberg, I thought. Already I was starting to feel seasick. *Duh. Now I get it.*

"Did you know the real *Titanic* was built at a shipyard in Ireland?" he went on cheerfully. "I'm sure your friend Colin is well aware of that fact."

"Mr. McAlister, the real *Titanic* sank to the bottom of the sea and thousands of people died." Part of me wanted to scrounge around for a life jacket. "I hope your cottage doesn't try to perfectly replicate *that.*"

"Well," he said cautiously, "authenticity has always been my passion. But one has to draw the line somewhere." He tucked his nightgown underneath him as he settled himself in a small wooden chair near the sink. "Heavens! We are forgetting your phone call. Please feel free to sit on my cot. There isn't much room in here for company, I'm afraid."

I did as he suggested, and he handed me the oPhone. If you looked closely you could see the Oxford emblem stamped in the hammered copper, but I was relieved to see that underneath the geeky World of Warcraft exterior it was your basic state-of-the-art touch screen phone. It even had a headphone jack.

"Does this thing play MP3s?" I asked, as I dialed.

"Em-pee whats?"

"Never mind." One ring. Two rings. It would be late afternoon in Connecticut. Dad was probably at work; Mom might be out if she had a client. And Tammy could be any-where. Home with a sitter, at a play date, out at the pool—

Three rings. I hoped nobody was home. I just needed to leave one reassuring message, let them see "Oxford Univer-sity" in the missed calls list, and I'd have bought myself some time. Would it be enough? Enough for me to save the world from whatever it needed saving from and maybe snag a little one-on-one with Colin?

Four rings. Five—

"Hello! You've reached the Rawlinson household. We're not at home right now, so please leave a brief, clear-ly ar-tic-u-lat-ed message. If you mum-ble, we may not know who you are!"

This was the way my mom talked on the phone. So em-bar-ras-sing.

"If you're calling for Morgan, please note that she is cur-rently on an *extremely* prestigious, invitation-only campus tour of Ox-ford U-ni-ver-si-ty, in En-gland. She will call you back when she returns from a-broad. Now wait for the beep!"

Beeeeep!

I faced away from Mr. McAlister to give myself some privacy, but he was sitting three feet away from me so it was kind of a futile gesture. "*Mom!* Oh my God, I can't believe you put that on the answering machine, that is to-tally humiliating. Look, I just wanted to call and tell you that I'm here at *Ox-ford*"—I couldn't help mocking her e-lo-cu-tion—"and everything's fine. Oxford is really . . . well, I would say it has a lot of authenticity."

I heard a snicker from Mr. McAlister, which I ignored.

"It seems like a great school and everything. I'm really busy so I'll call again in a day or so, and please, *don't* call me back at this number because I'll get in huge trouble for using the admissions office phone, we're not supposed to, bye."

Breathless, I hung up and tossed the phone back to Mr. McAlister like it was a very hot hammered-copper potato.

"So, your parents think you're at Oxford." He sounded rather smug.

"It's a long story," I grumbled. "Hey—did you already know that? Is that why you offered to lend me the phone?"

"Let me put it this way," he said, sounding totally full of himself. "Special Admissions Applicants are not chosen at random. As an Oxford alumni I sit on several important committees. Special Admissions is one of them. The truth is, I know a great deal about you, Miss Rawlinson."

"You do?" I felt my face turning red. "Enough to maybe tell me what I'm doing here? Because I really would like to know."

"It's difficult, I completely sympathize," he said kindly. "Not being able to tell your loved ones the whole truth. I often find myself in the same predicament; think of my little fib earlier about Colin's grandfather not feeling well. But I thought it best if we spoke privately."

He adjusted his nightcap then sat calmly, his hands folded in his lap. "But from now on I *will* tell you the truth, as plainly as I can. I fear it would be dangerous not to."

This was getting awfully confusing. "I wish I knew what

you're talking about, Mr. McAlister," I said firmly. "But I don't. Maybe you should start at the beginning."

He leaned back in his chair and smiled more broadly, revealing his yellowed teeth. "The beginning? Ah, dear Morganne! If you only knew how long ago that was!"

eleven

"let me ask you a question," Mr. McAlister said. "How old do you think I am?"

I wanted to grab him by the nightshirt and shake him to make him spill all this mysterious "truth" he'd just promised, but now that I knew he was actually on the Oxford admissions committee I figured I'd better play along.

I remembered that Colin's grandfather was eighty-two. Mr. McAlister seemed slightly younger, but really, who could tell with old people?

"I dunno." I shrugged. "Seventy-sixish, more or less?"

He laughed, a smug, "gotcha" kind of laugh. "Seventy-six years ago, when you imagine me as a newborn, I was a grown man at the height of my profession. In fact, I was overseeing one of the first major renovations to Castell Cyfareddol: the addition of the reflecting pool."

"Shut *up*!" I exclaimed. "So you're not the grandson of Devyn McAlister at all. You *are* Devyn McAlister!"

He nodded modestly. "Indeed I am. That little flourish of putting 'the third' at the end of my name is yet another example of a necessary, though I hope harmless, deception—in order to avoid confusion, suspicion, ceaseless medical examinations . . . You can understand that, can't you?"

"I definitely can." I did the math in my head. "No offense, Mr. McAlister, but shouldn't you be, like, dead by now?"

He sighed. "No doubt I would be, if my career as an architect had taken a more traditional route. Bank buildings, stately homes, the occasional monument to fallen war heroes—a nice, normal career followed by a nice, normal demise." He sounded almost nostalgic for the missed opportunity to croak. "But instead, I devoted myself completely to this."

He waved a hand loosely around, in a way that encompassed far more than the Tip of the Iceberg cottage. "Castell Cyfareddol was—and is—my life's work. But there came a fateful moment when the place took on what one might literally call a life of its own." He leaned forward, an excited gleam in his eye. "Have you noticed how reality seems so *fluid* around here?"

I frowned. "You mean, like the waterfall?"

"That?" He gestured dismissively. "Pure stagecraft. A fancy bit of plumbing, really. No, I mean how reality is heightened—almost to the point of feeling like make-believe."

I thought of the unicorns. "And how things that ought to be make-believe start to seem—or be—real?" I asked hesitantly.

"Precisely. Now, make no mistake: Even as I originally designed it, Castell Cyfareddol was unprecedented! A vision of all the architectural styles of the world, living together in peace and harmony, nestled in a veritable paradise of nature's glory, with a color palette so varied, so uninhibited—"

"It looks like a pack of Starbursts," I offered.

"Well put! I love Starbursts," he agreed. "But the critics scorned my creation. They called it 'McAlister's folly,' the vanity project of an overreaching architect who simply didn't know when to stop."

"I bet they wouldn't like Disneyland, either," I said, trying to be nice.

Mr. McAlister shrugged. "None of that bothered me. My vision was beautiful and strange, and the public appreciated it even when my colleagues failed to understand. But something happened when I added the reflecting pool. Something profound."

I thought of the disorienting way the hotel was reflected in the pool. "It's hard to know which one is which," I murmured.

"Yes. The world of reality, the world of reflections—the pool makes them interchangeable. To my great surprise, the pool revealed itself to be a kind of doorway."

"To where?"

He smiled indulgently. "Do you have to ask, Morganne?

The dimension of magic and dreams has many names, but I believe you know it best as the faery realm."

I shivered, suddenly cold. How did he know so much about what I knew? But he wasn't finished.

"When I realized what I had inadvertently done by adding the pool, I was frightened, but fascinated. I did countless hours of research trying to understand the properties of these types of places—places where the two worlds intersect."

Like me, I thought. *He's talking about me.*

"There are many other doorways, of course. Some are famous, like Stonehenge or the Bermuda Triangle. Some are known only to the local residents who still believe in such things: faery mounds, enchanted lagoons and so forth. Bodies of water and mirrors both tend to loosen the veil between the two worlds. So does any environment where the imagination has been allowed to run particularly free."

"Lucky Lou's!" I blurted, suddenly understanding.

He looked puzzled. "Lucky whose?"

"Lucky Lou's. It's a supermarket. A very imaginative supermarket," I explained, thinking of all the animatronic creatures in the store. "I had a kind of magical experience in there once."

"Interesting. And of course, because they live so much in the imagination, young children are often 'doorways' too, though generally in a minor, playful way."

Tammy in the bathtub, I thought.

He furrowed his silvery eyebrows in concentration. "Somehow, the pool, which is, of course, filled with water and designed to act as a mirror to the hotel, combined with the highly imaginative ambience of Castell Cyfareddol, and perhaps even the fact that we have so many children as guests—it's quite a popular family vacation destination, you know—created an 'open border' between our world and theirs. Or theirs and ours, depending on how you look at it."

I had so many questions I didn't know where to start. "But, Mr. McAlister—I mean, you were a normal human person, originally, right? So what happened? I mean, obviously you've aged, so it's not like you've become—"

"Immortal? Hardly!" He laughed. "Most portals to the faery realm are like doors: they stay shut except when someone or something is passing through. The reflecting pool is more like a window that's been left half-open. Because of it, the whole of Castell Cyfareddol is half-magic, all the time. If I were living in faery time, I'd be immortal. In normal human time, I'd be dead. But I've lived my whole adult life in this half-magic place—"

"So you're living twice as long as you should?"

"Exactly. You might have heard that celebrities like to vacation at Castell Cyfareddol? That's because they feel oddly refreshed by their visits here."

"Because as long as they're here, they're aging at half the rate they ought to be—is that it?"

He nodded. "The outward evidence is too subtle for the human eye to see, but the experience of aging at half-time creates an indefinable sense of well-being. The more sensitive ones have figured it out. Madonna comes twice a year," he confided.

"Whoa," I said. "And I thought she just used a lot of Botox."

This was a lot of mind-blowing information to take in. The idea of aging at half-time was kind of awesome to think about, but many creepy possibilities suddenly came to mind. For instance, what if I stayed here and Colin left? Twenty years from now I'd look twenty-seven, and he'd be forty, which (even though I'd still love him madly) would be slightly *ewww.* And how long would it take for Tammy and I to look the same age?

"The 'fountain of youth' aspect of Castell Cyfareddol is a strictly guarded secret, and it needs to stay that way." Mr. McAlister sounded stern. "Imagine the insanity—the tabloids—the hordes of desperate, youth-crazed people sneaking onto the grounds day and night!"

"Is that what the message was all about?" I said it without thinking.

"The one asking you to come here and save the world?" He smiled sadly. "No, my dear. I wish it were that simple. Controlling the publicity 'spin' of Castell Cyfareddol is a relatively simple matter. I have it well in hand."

My hands flew to cover my big, ginormous blabbermouth. "Wait. So you already know about the message Colin received?"

"I know what the message said. I don't know where it came from, or what it means." He saw the confusion on my face. "Morgan, I may be ridiculously old, exceedingly well-educated and occasionally deceitful, but I'm only human. I have no power to read minds. Or do magic," he added.

"Then how do you—"

"I saw the picture on his cell phone. Quite by accident, I assure you! I misplaced my oPhone while at the Seahorse Cottage to play cards with William and—oh dear, this will make me sound rather senile, I'm afraid—I wanted to call my own number so I could find the phone by its ring."

"It's not senile. I do that all the time," I confessed.

"Colin handed me his phone, I pressed the wrong button and, voila! There was the picture. Because of my long study of these types of phenomena, I recognized it at once as a message from the faery realm. And I knew who *you* were. I studied you at school, you know!"

My face started to feel hot.

"The half-goddess Morganne," he went on, clearly enjoying himself. "Heroine of myth and legend. When the faery realm is in danger, Morganne always comes back to save the day."

"There are other people named Morgan, you know," I protested lamely. "Morgan Fairchild. Morgan Freeman."

"Perhaps. But the way Colin spoke about you, I knew you must be no ordinary girl. And you fit every description I've ever read—and I've read them all."

He saw the puzzled look on my face. "My dear, you are speaking to an Oxford graduate! During my quest to become expert in the lore of faeries I have had access to the finest library of ancient and esoteric texts ever assembled on either side of the veil. Haven't you heard of the Bod?"

Now he was losing me. "You mean, J.Lo?"

"Heavens, no! 'The Bod' is what scholars call the Bodleian Library, at Oxford. Dear old Bod! It was always one of my favorite haunts on campus. The treasures it contains! Shakespeare's first folio. The Magna Carta. The Gutenberg Bible. And other, rarer books as well." He lowered his voice, though there was no one to hear us. "Books that are beyond ancient. Books that come from . . . the other side."

"So you're saying there are actual books from the faery realm in the library at Oxford?" *Try to beat that, UConn,* I thought.

He nodded. "It's called the Special Collection. Only a handful of students and faculty have ever been given access. You might be surprised to learn which of your favorite authors were 'inspired' by actual faery texts. Of course, there are many works attributed to humans—Shakespeare, for example—that experts believe actually did originate in the other realm. It's a fascinating topic of study."

All this information was making my head spin, so much so that I was starting to feel queasy. Or maybe I was getting seasick. But I couldn't be—I mean, we were in a cottage on land, not an actual ship at sea, right?

I took a deep breath to clear my head. "Mr. McAlister. This strange message, about me saving the world—can you guess what it means?"

He looked grim. "I regret to say I haven't a clue. But I will certainly assist in whatever way I can as you endeavor to find out. To be frank, it's a matter of professional interest! And now, if I may ask you a question, Morganne—or Morgan, if that's how you prefer to be known—how did Colin come across that message in the first place?"

"It was scratched in the forest floor by a, um, unicorn," I mumbled.

"A *unicorn?*" Mr. McAlister leaped up from his chair. "Oh my goodness! That is simply unprecedented. Things are getting out of hand. Something is wrong; very wrong indeed."

He paced around the tiny room, gesturing wildly. "The fact that you've been summoned at all indicates that this is truly a crisis. And unicorns!" Then he looked at me, quite grave. "You must go find them at once."

"I will, I promise. Tomorrow I'll go to the woods and—"

"Tomorrow could be too late!" He was so agitated, his Scrooge nightcap was bouncing up and down. "Understand this: No magical creatures are more passionate about keeping their existence hidden than the unicorns. They would never have revealed themselves to a human if it weren't a dire emergency."

"I'll go tonight, then." I stood up too. "I'll sneak out as soon as Colin and Grandpap are asleep."

"Good. And remember, all of us—the whole world—will be counting on you, Morganne," he said ominously.

I yawned in spite of myself. The thought of wandering the woods alone in the middle of the night was not making me happy, but Mr. McAlister was in a full-blown panic and I figured there must be a reason. "Yeah, I get that. I just hope these unicorns can explain what the fek is going on. Whoops! Sorry about the language, it's a bad habit."

"No need to apologize," he said. There was no mistaking the fear in his eyes. "I was thinking *precisely* the same thing."

Mr. McAlister offered to walk me back to the Seahorse, but once he pointed me in the right direction I could see the lights up the path. It wasn't very far. And, face it, the guy was like a hundred and fifty years old, plus he was already in his pajamas. What kind of bodyguard could I really expect him to be? I assured him I'd be fine.

I was worried that Colin would quiz me about my newfound expertise in mansard roofs and fluted whatchamacall-ems, but apparently I'd been at Mr. McAlister's a lot longer than I'd planned. By the time I got back to the Seahorse, Grandpap was snoring in the back bedroom and Colin was stretched out asleep on the living room sofa. I tried to be quiet and get to the stairs without waking him, but he rolled over and started mumbling.

"Mor? Everything okay?"

"Everything's fine." I knelt by the sofa and smooched him on the forehead. "How's Grandpap?"

"Couldn't find his glasses; lookin' at the cards was givin' him a headache, that's all." He rolled over to face me but his eyes stayed closed. "Tell me about the fluted thingies."

"I'll tell you in the morning. Go back to sleep."

"Right . . . bright and early . . . make breakfast . . . save world . . ."

"Sounds like a plan," I whispered. He was out cold

again. There was a crocheted afghan thrown over the back of the sofa—in a seashell pattern, of course. I tucked it around Colin's legs and turned off the light.

I knew I should grab some Z's too, considering what I needed to do that night. But there was something I wanted to check first. After I tippytoed my way upstairs I made a beeline for my suitcase.

The Oxford brochure was still tucked in the outer pocket, wrinkled from its travels but perfectly readable. The idea that there was a secret library at Oxford containing ancient faery books—books that mentioned *me*, no less—was so mind-boggling, I just wanted to see if there was a photograph of the building anywhere.

The Bod, the Bod, the Bod. I flipped the pages. *I could have sworn there was a picture . . .*

I found it. It was an old photo; judging from the clothes I'd say it was from the 1920s. The caption read:

Three Oxonians confer on the steps of the Bodleian Library.
From left to right: J.R.R. Tolkien, C. S. Lewis, D. McAlister.

There he was, third Oxonian from the left, chillin' with his soon-to-be-famous home skillets in those wild, wacky, pre-Narnia, pre-hobbit days at school, many decades before Orlando Bloom was even born. He looked younger, of course, but it was Mr. McAlister, no question.

That's why he seemed familiar to me, I thought. *I've been looking at his picture for the past two days.*

Then I finished reading the caption:

Also pictured: C. Phineas.

C. Phineas? *My* Mr. Phineas?

Wait—so Mr. Phineas was *also* at Oxford in the olden days? Was *also* somehow drinking the antiaging Kool-Aid? Had *also* failed to get the memo that men's pants had gotten significantly longer since 1925?

Or maybe that was his father in the picture, and the Mr. Phineas I'd met was really a "junior." Or maybe it was no relation, a different Phineas altogether. It was impossible to tell from the photo, since the guy identified as C. Phineas was standing behind the other three and holding a book in front of his face.

Fek. Another mystery.

I got in bed, still dressed, and set my travel alarm. Half an hour should be enough of a power nap to keep me going. All I had to do was make my escape without waking Colin or Grandpap.

The question briefly crossed my mind: What would Colin think if caught me sneaking out? Would he be amused? Puzzled? Furious?

I shoved the alarm under my pillow so only I would hear it. *Sorry it has to be this way, honey*, I thought, as I drifted off. *But I need to talk to the unicorns alone . . .*

twelve

My eyes flew open. My heart raced. What time was it? Had I overslept? Missed the bus? *Damn, now I'm gonna be late for school—*

I grabbed my watch off the nightstand and peered at it in the dark. It was four A.M. Then it came back to me: I was in Wales, and I was supposed to save the world, and the fekkin' cheap travel alarm never went off. Great.

Nobody said this saving the world stuff would be easy, I scolded myself, as I dragged myself out of bed. *Suck it up and pretend you're a superhero.* My mission: go wandering in a strange forest alone to look for unicorns in the dark, and be back in time for breakfast.

Of course, if I really were some kind of übercool superhero I might have some actual superpowers to rely on, or at least a few useful gadgets: designer sunglasses that turned into night vision goggles, or a personal GPS with a "find unicorn" setting. At this point I'd have been happy with an extra sweater, frankly, because it was freezing out and my hoodie was still draped over that creepy picture of Queen Titania. Which is where it was going to stay.

But I had no superpowers or gadgets. I was nothing but a shivering half-goddess, silently ransacking the kitchen drawers trying to find a freakin' flashlight in the dark without waking Colin or Grandpap. And I was having no luck whatsoever.

Fail! I closed the last drawer. Time to take a deep breath and give myself a pep talk. *I can do this blind,* I thought. I just needed to take it step-by-step: Follow the path to the boardwalk, follow the boardwalk to the forest, follow the trail marked "Faery Glen" into the woods. It'd be just like following the Yellow Brick Road to find Oz. If I steered clear of wicked witches and flying monkeys, I'd be fine.

But once I made it in to see the Wizard, then what? Would the unicorns be friend or foe? And was there any hope that I could deal with this faery-world emergency and still keep my half-goddess mojo on the down-low? Maybe then I could squeeze in a romantic summer vacay with Colin before my parents realized I'd gone AWOL and called Interpol to kidnap me and drag me home.

I deserve a final bit of fun, I thought grimly. *Because once I get busted about ditching the Oxford tour I'm going to be grounded for life. I'll only be permitted to leave the house to go to my deeply unsatisfying job as an X-ray technician.*

I let myself out of the cottage as quietly as I could and

looked around. The moon had already come and gone and the stars were doing their usual far-off twinkling thing, which didn't provide much help in the ambient lighting department. All the light switches in the various cottages and buildings of Castell Cyfareddol were in the OFF position. Their residents, unlike some miserable people I could name, were asleep.

I took a few steps and nearly tripped over the jockey-on-a-seahorse statue. I eyed his lantern with envy.

"Any chance that thing lights up?" I whispered.

No answer from the jockey. *Whoosh! Two points for reality,* I thought.

It would have been easy to get completely turned around in the dark, so I took a few experimental steps to make sure I was walking uphill, in the direction of the boardwalk. Soon I fell into a hesitant rhythm. Right foot forward, put my weight on it, step. Left foot forward, put my weight on it, step.

At this rate I figured it would be sometime next week before I found the forest. But I made progress, and finally the footing changed from cool sand to smooth planks of wood. The uphill slope flattened out. I'd reached the boardwalk. My eyes had adjusted to the darkness, and I could make out basic shapes—was that a curious glint in the eye of the dragon statue that guarded the path?

Maybe it would be smarter to wait for morning, my inner wimpy voice suggested. *What's a few hours one way or another? And why was this my problem, anyway? Didn't the unicorns have anybody else on speed dial?*

Wimpy voice was damned convincing, I have to say. And it wouldn't shut up. *All I have to do is stop. And go back to the cottage. And get back into my nice, snuggly bed.*

A streak of light whizzed by my face. Before I could catch enough breath to shriek I realized it was a firefly. It made me think of Tammy, who loved to chase the little light-up bugs and was always horrified when my dad suggested she put one in a jar.

"Wish there were a bunch more of you, pal," I muttered. I'd layered on three T-shirts but my arms were bare except for the goose bumps. Light and warmth—two great concepts that I had obviously failed to appreciate enough in my life until now.

Then I noticed another bug chasing after the first. *The firefly life cycle must be different in Wales,* I thought, shivering. *At home we usually don't see them until August.*

Another firefly. The three bugs flew in formation, making patterns in the dark that my eye was almost able to register before they disappeared. It was like when you try to write your name in the air with the tip of a lit sparkler by waving it really fast—your eye can hold the image for *almost* long enough to read the letters—almost, but not quite . . .

All of a sudden there were ten fireflies. Then twenty. Now I was getting anxious. Did fireflies swarm? Form angry mobs? Were they dangerous when provoked, like killer bees? Why hadn't I paid more attention in science class?

Think, Morgan! I vaguely recalled something about monarch butterflies migrating in groups. And I knew ladybugs swarmed, because we'd found a cluster of them on the wall of the garage one year and Tammy cried and begged my dad not to spray them with pesticide. "They're not nasty boy bugs! They're *ladybugs*!" she'd bawled.

I tried to stay calm. Despite the nerve-wracking example set by killer bees and flesh-eating ants, I decided it was highly unlikely that fireflies were capable of cooperative attack behavior. I mean, evolutionarily speaking, wasn't making your ass light up enough of an achievement? But I had to admit that the on-again, off-again phosphorescent glow of this particular flock—herd?—invasion?—was doing a pretty good job of illuminating the path. They circled and swirled in front of me, keeping pace as I walked.

I could only see ahead as far as the fireflies lit up for me, so I couldn't gauge how far off the end of the boardwalk was, and I had no idea how long I'd been walking. It came as a total surprise when, all at once, the wooden walkway beneath my feet ended and I found myself standing on mossy ground.

I breathed it in, a damp, foresty smell. I'd made it! The sign pointing to the Faery Glen must be just ahead.

I walked forward blindly, arms extended like I was playing pin the tail on the donkey. My firefly pals must have lost patience. Now numbering in the hundreds, they swirled, swooped and landed in a flickering border around the very sign I was looking for: "This Way to the Faery Glen."

For added effect, their butt-lights were timed like chaser lights around a billboard. It wasn't Vegas, but you had to appreciate the effort.

"Very impressive, bugs," I said.

"You think that's impressive?" a low, melodious voice whinnied back from the darkness. "You should see what we can do with our hooooooooorns!"

And then, as if someone flicked a switch, a hundred whorled glow sticks lit up in front of me. Some were held straight up, some were horizontal, some were angled and crossed against one another. It was like that stupid YMCA dance, where you stick your arms out in different directions to make the letters.

Except these were unicorn horns, and they spelled:

WELCOME MORGAN!

"Are you all right? Moooooorgan? Can you hear me?" A warm, soft muzzle pushed gently against my head.

"I'm fine," I mumbled. "Sorry, lost it for minute. I haven't slept much, and—that kind of sent me over the edge."

I was on my ass, on the moss-covered earth. A circle of worried-looking unicorns were standing around me, snorting steam and gently pawing the ground.

"Are you sure she's the right one, Epona?" a deep, horsey voice asked from the circle. "She seems pretty wimpy."

"Hush," scolded the unicorn that was nudging me. "Just because *you* can sleep standing up doesn't mean everyone can! She must be tired. She came a long way, remember? And without even knowing why she was needed." This unicorn's voice was warm, older, and definitely female. "That doesn't sound wimpy to me."

I struggled to my feet, using the friendly unicorn's mane as a support. "I'm fine. You took me by surprise, that's all."

To be honest, it wasn't just the cheer that had freaked me out. I'd seen plenty of magic, but come on—these were unicorns! How cool was that? They looked like incredibly beautiful silver horses, with glowing horns and strangely human eyes.

"We wanted to welcome you in style. Show her!" At which point the unicorns leaped into formation and did another bit of horn-spelling, accompanied by chanting—"Em Oh Are! Gee A En! Gooooooo, Morgan!"—followed by loud snorts and whinnies.

"Awesome," I said, trying not to keel over again. *Just my luck,* I thought. *Cheerleader unicorns.*

"I am Epona," the nice one said again. "Leader of the Herd. We have many chants and dances designed to embolden your spirit for the dangerous work that lies ahead! Would you like to see more?"

Quickly I held up a hand to stop them. "Actually, I would appreciate it if we could just skip ahead to the part where you explain to me about this 'saving the world' stuff," I said, brushing the moss off the butt of my jeans. The unicorns looked disappointed, so I added, "It sounds like the sooner I get started doing whatever it is you need me to do, the better."

"I take back what I said about her being wimpy," the

unicorn with the deep voice intoned. "Listen to how eager she is to face the terror that lies ahead! To fight the unbeatable foe! To run where the brave dare not go! To strive, with her last ounce of courage—"

"Excuse me, but I'm pretty sure that's from *Man of La Mancha*," I interjected. "My parents took my sister and me to see it in a dinner theater once."

"It's an old unicorn song." Epona reared up on her hind legs with pride. "'To Break the Unbreakable Horn.' Now and then our traditions slip into your world by accident. A little faery world spillover is no biggie, especially if it ends up someplace harmless, like in a Broadway musical. But it's been happening more often, lately."

"Too often!" one of the unicorns cried. Others shouted agreement.

At that there was a round of worried-sounding snorting and neighing. "Yes," said Epona, agreeing with whatever it was they'd said. "That is the problem, indeed. The veil is slipping. It's already begun."

The veil? Mr. McAlister had used that word too. "What does it mean, 'The veil is slipping'?"

"The veil is what separates our magical world from your human world," Epona explained. "And it's starting to disappear."

"I know about the reflecting pool," I said. "Is that what you mean?"

She shook her lovely silver muzzle from side to side. "There have always been portals. And the occasional bit of cultural exchange has benefited both realms. But for the most part, our worlds have remained separate, and this has been for the safety of all."

Epona lowered her head so her horn was pointing right at me. "Over time, your world has convinced itself that we of the magic realm do not really exist. We are called fiction, myth, fantasy, fairy tale. But our kind are all too familiar with the ways of humans. In fact, to some of us, what you call 'reality' has become a deeply addictive source of entertainment."

I was confused. "Reality? You mean, like *Survivor*?"

Epona stamped her hooves with passion. "I mean all of it! *Dancing with the Stars*, stiletto heels, Facebook! There are those in the faery realm who think that you humans are simply having more fun than we are." Epona's long silver lashes half-lowered over her soulful eyes. "There is one magical being in particular who believes this. Unfortunately, she is very powerful."

"You mean Queen Titania." It wasn't a question. As soon as I heard "stiletto heels" I knew where this was going.

"Unfortunately, you are correct." Epona's tail flicked with worry. "Titania's fascination with human civilization is out of control. She believes the time has come to undo the veil between the human and magic realms."

The unicorn's horn blushed pink, making Epona look almost embarrassed. "She claims she is sick of hiding from mortals. She wants to shop at Abercrombie & Fitch and work out with a personal trainer. She wants to attend the Teen Choice Awards and be on the cover of *Us Weekly*. And she wants to bring all of us with her. Faeries, mermaids, elves, trolls, giants, leprechauns, pixies—you name it."

"Even unicooooooooorns!" one of the herd whinnied in dismay.

"So Titania wants to turn the whole world into one big faery party, permanently?" I said dumbly. "But that would be awful! People would freak out. It would be a total mess."

"We fear it would be worse than that," Epona said. The rest of the unicorns nickered tragically. "No one knows better than we unicorns that your kind are not always tolerant of magical difference. Our species once ran freely on the earth but was nearly wiped out by the human tendency to destroy even beautiful things that they don't understand. If we had not confined our surviving members to the magical dimension, the unicorns would have become stinked."

Had I heard her right? "You mean extinct, don't you?"

"Indeed." She lowered her head. "You cannot imagine how hard it was for us to come through the pool and hide here in the forest. But it was the only way we could call for your help without Titania knowing."

"Extinct?" I thought of Tammy and her crackpot theories about math. "Do you really think that's what would happen?"

"We believe that if the human and magic worlds were merged again, the way they used to be in the long-ago times of myths and legend, it would mean the end not only of unicorns, but of faeries, trolls, leprechauns, pixies, mermaids and every other magical being you can think of. Santa Claus. Even the tooth fairy," Epona said sadly. "All gone."

I hated to think she was right—but inside, I knew that she was. When humans got scared, they came out fighting. No way could this be allowed to happen. And then I remembered why Epona was telling me all this.

Must Save World.

Me? There must be some kind of mistake.

"Epona," I said, trying to sound reasonable. "I totally see your point. And I agree that what Queen Titania plans to do would be a catastrophe. I'm just wondering what exactly you think I can do about it?"

"Simple, Morganne." Epona's big silver lips moved around her giant horse teeth with surprising delicacy. "Only the Queen of the Faeries has the power to lift the veil between the worlds—or to restore it."

For some reason my stomach was starting to ache, just like it did right before I took the SATs. "Okay, so only the queen can lift the veil—and your point is?"

"Titania has to gooooooo," she whinnied. "It's time for *you* to become Queen."

thirteen

the echo of Epona's whinny seemed to bounce around the forest for a really long time. Long enough for me to thoroughly freak out.

"Are you insane?" I cried. "I can't be Queen of the Faeries! For one thing, I'm not qualified. I have no idea how to run a realm. And anyway, I have my own career plans. Big plans!"

"Bigger than saving the world?" She snorted.

"To me they are." I was so flustered I was practically snorting too. "I'm going to apply to college. And get a job someday, doing, I don't know, something—I haven't really figured it out yet. And I'm kind of in a relationship, you know."

Epona tossed her head flirtatiously. "But your royal consort would be welcome in our world, of course!"

Colin? Royal consort to the faery queen? This was getting worse and worse. "Epona, you don't understand. Not only is Colin *not* going to be my royal consort, I don't want him to have anything to do with the faery realm. It's bad enough that you played with his head by scratching that message in the dirt." I scowled at her. "That wasn't keeping a very good separation of the worlds, now, was it?"

Epona hung her head until her long silvery mane touched the ground. "We were desperate. We thought it was the best way to get your attention," she confessed.

"Yeah, well—lucky for you, Colin doesn't believe in unicorns. He's convinced himself that you're some weird troupe of costumed circus animals. And that's exactly what I want him to think." My voice was getting stronger and more impassioned. "I believe in maintaining the separation of the realms. Some things are better left as mysteries."

At which point the unicorns burst into thunderous unicorn applause, blowing trumpet-calls out of their horns and stomping their hooves. I was startled, but then I thought, *Oh, fek. I've just given my first Morganne for Queen campaign speech.*

The unicorns murmured excitedly.

"Listen to her fiery spirit! Her conviction! She believes what we believe!"

"Morganne will keep the worlds separate! Morganne will keep the worlds safe!"

"Morganne for Queen! Morganne for Queen!"

Epona quieted the crowd with a trumpet blast from the tip of her horn.

"I'm serious," I went on, once the noise had died down. "Forget what I said. I can't do what you're asking. I wouldn't even know how to begin."

"The truth is, neither do we," Epona admitted. "Since faeries are immortal, the question of succession to the throne has never come up before. But the Rules of Succession do exist, and your first task will be to find out what they are."

"Wait a minute." Now I was getting mad. "You want me to take over as Queen of the Faeries, but you don't even know how it's done?"

The unicorns looked chagrined. Their horns started to glow a sad shade of blue.

"Unbelievable. I'm going back to bed. Fireflies, you're with me." I turned to leave, but blocking my way was a big sad-face chat emoticon made of twinkling firefly butts, hovering in the air an arm's length in front of me. When I tried to step around it, it just kept moving and getting in my face.

I should tell Tammy to add "phosphorescent" to the double-PH word section of her notebook, I thought, annoyed. *Bet she doesn't have many of those.*

"We do not accept your answer, Morganne." A tear glistened in the corner of Epona's practically human eye. "We cannot. Look at the world as it is. Then imagine how it would be if you refuse your duty. Come back to the forest when you find the Rules of Succession. We will be waiting."

Before I could think of anything else to say, the unicorns bounded off into the trees. Their horns streaked disappointed trails of blue light behind them, as they raced away from the wimpiest superhero ever.

the sun hadn't risen yet, but as dawn approached the dark of night was definitely getting a lot less dark. Soon I could see where I was going, and I started striding along the boardwalk in a desperate half-run.

The fireflies swirled around me like angry gnats. Did they just like the smell of my shampoo? Or were they trying to tell me *Stop, don't be a wuss, we need your help Morganne*—

"Shut up," I growled, even though no one was nagging me but my own guilty conscience. The bugs took it personally, though. As one, they zoomed into the air in front of me and formed a perfect rendition of a sticking-out-your-tongue emoticon. Then they turned off their butt-lights and scattered.

It was a snazzy (if rude) display of aerial pyrotechnics, sure. But, come on—what Epona had asked me to do was *so* completely out of the question. I mean, I'd never even run for class clown! Now some sparkly pony with a glow stick on its head wanted me to stage a coup and become Queen of the Faeries? How was I supposed to explain that sudden career change to my friends back home in Connecticut? Nope, nope and more nope.

But I had to admit that the other stuff Epona had said—about the veil between the worlds slipping for good—didn't sound so hot, either. My whole plan to keep magic-me secret from Colin was just not going to work if Titania gatecrashed the human world and brought her whole faery posse with her.

Not to mention the threat of a permanent fade-to-black of all magical beings. Including Santa.

Look at the world as it is. Then imagine how it would be if you refuse your duty. . . . I kept my head down as I walked, careful not to look anywhere but directly in front of my feet. Between the half-magic ambience at Castell Cyfareddol and this business about the veil slipping, I had no intention of making eye contact with any gargoyles—in case they had something to add to the conversation too.

I held my breath as I tiptoed past the jockey-on-a-seahorse outside the cottage—was that a whispered *Giddy-up, Seabiscuit!* I heard? Then I opened the front door as silently as I could.

Now that it was half-light out I found myself wishing for the dark again. I felt much too conspicuous trying to sneak across the living room to the stairs. But Colin still looked thoroughly unconscious on the sofa, and the afghan I'd tucked around him was now partially covering his face. If I could be totally quiet—and was totally lucky—

One step—two steps—the third step I was extra-careful on, because I knew it tended to *creeeeeeeeeak—*

"Colin, me boy! Are ye up?"

Fek! Grandpap and his superhuman hearing! Nothing to do but dash the rest of the way upstairs and slip under the covers. I listened carefully while keeping myself in pretending-to-be-out-cold position, in case anyone came up, but the sound of slippers scuffing across the floor stopped in the living room.

Colin's voice was rough with sleep. "No, I'm not up, Pap. Nor should you be. Go back to bed."

"I thought I heard a noise. I thought it was me old girl, comin' home."

"Ye mean Granny?"

I gulped. Colin's voice grew softer until I could barely hear. "There there, now, Paps. I think ye've been dreamin' again. Go catch yerself another forty winks and we'll talk about it later."

"Forty winks? All right, if ye say so, lad . . ." Grandpap sounded confused, but I heard him shuffle back to the bedroom.

Poor Grandpap! I felt awful about disturbing him. Maybe he would go back to sleep and forget all about it.

But what about Colin? Would he go back to sleep too? Or was dawn what he meant by bright and early?

I heard footsteps. Bathroom door closing. Various plumbing-related flushes and gurgles.

More footsteps, this time coming up the stairs. *Step, step, creeeeeak, step, step-step*—

Then a *tap-tap-tap* on the door.

"Hey, Mor. Ready to rise and shine?"

"Nnnnn."

"Sun's up. We said bright and early."

"Nnnnnnnnnnnn." Truly, it was an Oscar-worthy performance.

"Did ye get a good night's sleep?"

"Five more minutes," I mumbled, quite convincingly. I'd had lots of practice during the school year, of course.

"All right, make it ten." I could hear the fond smile in his voice. Also the impatience. "But then it's time for breakfast. And hunting for clues."

Considering that i was a severely sleep-deprived person who'd stayed up half the night arguing with unicorns, ten minutes was a dangerous amount of time to be left lying in a warm bed with my eyes closed, cozy blankets drawn over me and a soft pillow underneath my head.

Someplace between minutes six and seven I sank into a deep, exhausted sleep, the kind where your limbs go heavy as lead and no power in this realm or any other can make you move a muscle.

In my sleep I smelled bacon frying, but that was part of the dream I was having. It was one of those dreams that I knew was ridiculous even while I was in it: There was a unicorn, poking at a frying pan full of nice crispy bacon using the end of its horn. I was starving but the unicorn wouldn't let me have any food.

"Whyyyyyyyyyyy didn't you do any extra-curricular activities?" it whinnied. "If only you'd run for some kind of office! Treasurer! Secretary! Queen, even!" The unicorn speared a strip of particularly crisp-looking bacon on its horn but kept it dangling just out of my reach. "But nooooooooooo! I guess you couldn't dooooooooo that!"

"It's not that I couldn't," I mumbled in my dream. "It's that I didn't . . ."

"Didn't what? Didn't sleep well? Could've fooled me, darlin'. I've been shakin' ye for two minutes already."

What a nice voice, with its sexy Irish accent. It seemed familiar, but at that moment I didn't know where I was or whether I was awake or asleep; and if I was asleep, whether it had been ten minutes or ten hours since I'd conked out.

"Wake up now, love. Time fer breakfast."

With effort, my brain navigated an agonizing, zigzag path back toward consciousness. Toward Colin. Toward the real, wide-awake, human world. The world where unicorns didn't exist except in stories, and where Santa Claus and the tooth fairy would always be cherished figures of childhood make-believe.

The nice, familiar world that I—and I alone—was supposed to save.

"C'mon downstairs, love." I peeled my eyes open and saw Colin's face slowly coming into focus. "I've got some bacon fryin' up in the kitchen. Smells delicious, doesn't it?"

by the time i made it downstairs Colin was lifting the last strip of bacon from the pan and transferring it to a paper towel–lined plate. While he'd cooked I'd endured a fast and brutal, too-cold-on-purpose shower to wake me up. I still felt like I'd pulled two all-nighters in a row, but the shower helped, and I figured I could fake my way through the day with some effort. *It'll be just like finals week,* I told myself as I put on my Natalie Portman's Shaved Head band T-shirt and a pair of old jeans. *All it takes is coffee and determination.*

Colin, on the other hand, was so full of energy he seemed practically hyper. The brisk and efficient way he whipped up breakfast was like something out of a cable cooking show, but at the same time he was trying to be quiet because Grandpap was still in bed. The clock on the kitchen wall read six forty-five.

"I don't usually do too much food prep on vacation, but none of the local eateries'll be open this early." He grabbed another paper towel from the roll and gave the bacon strips an extra blotting. "Later on we can grab some lunch at the pub. Assuming the world's been saved by then, o' course."

I leaned against the kitchen doorway, watching him. I had to admit, he'd make a pretty sexy consort to the Queen of the Faeries. "It's nice to see you cook. Pretty cute, in fact."

"Not as cute as you sleepin'. Hey, love the shirt. Reminds me of the day we first met, back when your hair was all sheared off. Fine band too, if ye're in the mood fer cutesy electronica dance-pop, though it's all a bit eighties fer my taste."

I ignored the dig at my current favorite band. "I remember the day we met too," I said coyly. "It was in the airport at Shannon. I thought you were totally gorgeous and kind of obnoxious."

He grinned. "And I thought ye were pretty as a picture and bald as an egg. Speakin' o' which: scrambled or fried?"

"Scrambled."

"Comin' right up." He cracked a couple of eggs in a bowl. I heard birds twittering outside the cottage. How incredibly normal everything seemed. *How amazingly wonderful "normal" was,* I realized. *And how fragile.*

"Ye want salt, pepper?"

"I'll get it. Is there any ketchup?"

"In the fridge."

I had to squeeze right by him to get to the refrigerator door. Impulsively I put my arms around his waist.

"Hey," I said, giving a quick hug.

"Hey hey," he said, sounding nice and flirty.

Just my luck, I thought. *Our chaperone's asleep, and we're going to waste the morning searching for clues that I already know don't exist.*

I grabbed the ketchup from the fridge and sidestepped back out of the kitchen. Once I was out of the way, Colin took two warmed plates out of the oven and loaded them with eggs and bacon. Then we sat down at the tiny white-topped kitchen table to eat.

Colin usually gobbled his food like it was a race to the finish, but now he was eating slowly, one mouthful at a time.

"Mmm, this is so good," I said, to keep the conversation in a safe, food-related zone. "You have mad cooking skills."

"Glad ye like it. I must say it's a lovely time of day to be up. I could get used to this rising-with-the-roosters business." He paused to wipe his lips. "Too bad Granny and Grandpap sold off the farm. I miss it, now that it's gone. I might've taken a shine to that life. I'm a simple bloke at heart, ye know. Hey, luv—why are ye lookin' at me like that?"

Would it really be so bad if Queen Titania got her way? a dark, seductive voice inside me whispered. *Then everyone would know about the faery realm, including Colin. It wouldn't be your secret to keep anymore. Problem solved.*

"Earth to Morgan! Why the long face?" Colin tapped his fork on the edge of my plate to get my attention. "If it's not directly related to national security ye should let me in on it."

"I'm just out of it." I moved my food around on the plate. "Jet lag, probably. If I were a superhero my name would be SuperSnoozer."

"SuperSleeptalker, more like it. What were ye dreamin' about this mornin'?"

What had he heard? "Something . . . silly," I said hastily.

Come on, tell him, it won't be that hard: "Colin, magic is real and I'm a half-goddess, the faeries are about to take over the world but it's no big deal, could you pass the ketchup please?"

"Too silly to tell? Never mind then, maybe it's private."

Tell him tell him tell him tell him—

"Colin," I started, then stopped. "There is something I want to—it's kind of hard to—could I have the ketchup please?"

He shoved his last bit of bacon in his mouth and handed

me the ketchup. "Here ye go. Hey, speakin' of national security, I've been keepin' a bit of a secret meself."

I didn't know whether to be scared or excited. "It's not something bad, is it?"

Colin's eyebrows wiggled comically. "That depends on yer reaction, I suppose. Hang on a sec." He pushed his chair back from the table, stood up and left the room briefly. When he came back he was holding a small box.

"Oh my God." My heart was pounding. "Colin—what the fek—"

"Watch yer Irish, now. Especially in front of me granny's locket."

He opened the box. Inside was an absolutely beautiful heart-shaped locket on a thin gold chain. At the sight of it my eyes filled with tears.

Colin cleared his throat. "I want to make somethin' perfectly clear, Morgan Rawlinson. This is no ordinary bauble yer gazin' at."

"It certainly isn't." My voice felt stuck. "Colin, it's gorgeous. I don't know what to—"

"Hush, woman! I did a fair bit o' thinkin' last night, while ye were out havin' architecture lessons. Now I've got a few things to say to ye, and if ye get me all flustered I'll ferget me lines." He looked at me earnestly. The intense blue of his eyes seemed even more vivid than usual. "Morgan, I hope ye have some idea of what ye mean to me. I mean, I'm kind of a stupid bloke most of the time, makin' wisecracks and all. But I swear to ye, I'm not jokin' now."

He sounded so open and full of love—it made my own

tangle of unspoken truths seem that much more pathetic by comparison.

"It's a year now since we met, can ye believe it? And I know it's been hard to really know what we are to each other, what with you livin' in all yer Connecticut splendor and me toilin' away at me schoolwork in Dublin. But I thought, since the fates have seen fit to drop us on the same side of the ocean for a change—well, I'd be a right eejit not to take advantage of the chance to make me feelings plain."

A big pathetic tear was now snowboarding down my cheek. I wish I could say it was a tear of pure happiness, but it wasn't. It was mixed up with my guilt over all that I'd never told Colin about my true self, and my growing fear that whatever was about to happen in this fragile world we thought of as reality would drive us apart for good.

But Colin drew his own conclusions. He smiled tenderly and wiped the tear away with his fingertip. "Be my girl, luv. That's all I'm askin' fer right now. We can sort out the details later. If ye'll have me, o' course! Though how ye could refuse any bloke capable of whippin' up a fine Irish breakfast at such an ungodly hour is beyond me."

"Colin . . ." But this was not an occasion for words. It was too easy to lie with words. I threw myself at him so fast I nearly knocked over the table. He caught me and held me tight. We stood together in the tiny kitchen, arms wrapped around each other.

"Ye like it, then?" His breath was warm, right next to my ear.

"I do." Whoops. I hadn't really been planning to use those two particular words, but out they slipped.

Be my girl . . . Part of me felt as full of love and happiness as I'd ever been in my whole life. Me and Colin, together at last—officially, with a locket and everything. It was a dream come true. For half of me, at least.

But what about the other half? The goddess-half that knew the secret I was still keeping, and the urgent duty I was doing my best to ignore? Surely that wasn't a very important part? Not compared to that delicious-milk-shake-of-happiness feeling inside me, with the magic rainbows and glitter hearts, the pretty unicorns sprouting flowers and dancing, dancing—

Game over. I squeezed my eyes shut and held Colin so fiercely it was as if someone was trying to tear him away. *This is what I want, and nothing is going to screw it up. I am resigning my half-goddess gig as of now. If the unicorns are so freakin' worried about Titania, let them deal with her.*

"If ye hold me any tighter ye'll be breakin' a rib, there, sweetheart," Colin murmured in my ear.

"Sorry." I loosened my grip and didn't say anything more. But inside my head I made my very own Public Service Announcement. I hoped it was coming through loud and clear: *Attention, Faery Folk! Regarding Queen Titania, I have three words and three words only: Not. My. Problem.*

There was a knock at the door.

"Damn, and just when I was goin' to kiss ye. Well, ye know what they say: No Hallmark moment goes unpunished." Colin disentangled himself from my clinging and went to the door. "Who could it be, callin' at the crack of dawn? The milkman lookin' fer a tip, maybe?"

If only. But it was Mr. McAlister, dressed in old-fashioned tennis whites, a college letter sweater (with a big *O*, of course) and a tweed cap. It was like he'd just climbed out of his Model T. The sight of him in the doorway, leaning on his wooden-handled tennis racquet, made my milk-shake-of-happiness feeling curdle into cottage cheese.

We're all counting on you, Morganne. . . .

"Ye're up awfully early, Mr. McAlister," Colin said with automatic hospitality. "Care for some rashers and eggs?"

"At my age a man doesn't need much sleep. No sense wasting the time you have left snoring into a pillow." He gave me a wink to underscore the "at my age" bit. Then he gestured with his racquet. "Your invitation to breakfast is very generous, but I must decline. I have a tennis match scheduled for later, with a noted collector of architectural antiquities, no less! I've booked some practice time this morning to brush up on my serve. My sole purpose in stopping by is to give Miss Rawlinson a message."

Colin took a step back from the door so Mr. McAlister and I could see each other more clearly.

"A message?" It came out like a frightened squeak. "For me?"

"Normally I would have waited until a more civilized hour to deliver it, but the marvelous culinary aromas wafting on the breeze from your cottage to mine indicated that you were already up. In any case, I thought you'd prefer to receive it promptly."

All of a sudden the locket around my neck felt like it was burning a heart-shaped hole in my skin. I tried not to look as full of dread as I felt. "What is it?"

"It's a very simple message, so I do hope I get it right." Mr. McAlister took off his tweed cap and cleared his throat. "'Your mother called.'"

fourteen

"My mother?" I stared at him, hard. The question *which one?* was burning in my eyes. Had his research at "the Bod" included getting the scoop about my all-too-special relationship with Queen Titania?

"Yes, she left a message on my phone; she said her name was . . . hmm, let me think for a moment . . ."

"Helen!" I felt like the stooge in the audience feeding answers to a fake psychic.

"Helen, of course! She must have retrieved the number when you used the oPhone to leave her a message. These gadgets today! Simply astonishing. In my day, we had to ask the operator—"

I gave Mr. McAlister a major death glare, thinking, *With all due respect, sir, shut up. This is not the time to let Colin know how ancient you are.*

He stopped himself short with a nervous laugh. "But of course, in my day all kinds of things were different. Perhaps we ought to leave it at that. What a lovely necklace, dear. Is it new?"

"It's new on Morgan. It was me granny's," Colin explained. "I can pour ye some coffee to go if ye like. The pot's already made."

Mr. McAlister gave his tennis racquet a practice swing. "Some coffee would hit the spot, actually—provide a smidgen of extra energy on the court. I *am* hoping to make a good impression on this collector—"

"Mr. McAlister!" I interrupted, before a whole new round of chitchat could get started. "Did you happen to save the message from my mother? I'd like to hear it before I call her back." *So I can make sure it's really her and not the crazy Queen of the Faeries who I'm supposed to dethrone,* is what I was thinking.

"Yes, I believe I did." As I saw him start to reach for the pocket of his white pants, I mouthed a silent "nooooooo."

"Ah!" he exclaimed, folding his arms. "But how silly of me to leave my phone back at the cottage! I forget how portable everything has become. In my day, to make a call we had to physically enter these large enclosed booths—"

My *zip it, big mouth* facial expression must have been terrifying to behold, but Mr. McAlister simply shifted gears again and said, "Would you care to accompany me to the Tip of the Iceberg? I have a few minutes to kill before my court time."

I glanced at Colin.

"Go ahead. I've got a bit more thinkin' to do about those nasty computer problems ye've been havin'," he said with a sly look. "Go hear what yer ma has to say, and then we'll get started . . . with what we've got planned."

"I'll be back in a flash." I smooched Colin quickly on the cheek and touched the locket with my finger. "Thank you for this. I love you."

I dashed out of the cottage before Colin could answer, but I heard him calling—"Remember, Mor, it's the middle o' the night at yer parents' house—"

Mr. McAlister walked pretty fast for a guy who was well into his second century. When we were halfway to his cottage he turned, reached into the pocket of his silly white pants and retrieved the oPhone.

"I realize it's none of my business," he said, handing me the phone, "but if you and Colin are going to have a chance at real happiness together, you'll have to learn not to be so skittish about retrieving your telephone messages in front of him."

"Thanks for the advice," I muttered, fiddling with the phone's hand-forged cover until it opened. I stared at the touch screen, stumped. The icons didn't look like any I'd seen before. "How do you get messages on this thing?"

"Look for the picture of the ostrich quill pen."

"Got it." I tapped the icon and listened. *Please,* I thought, *let it be from my real mom and not Titania . . .*

"Hello, this is Hel-en Raw-lin-son speaking. I'm the

mother of Mor-gan Raw-lin-son, one of your 'Special Ad-missions Candidates.'"

Whew. It was Mom, using her sweetest, o-ver-ar-tic-u-la-ted voice. The ass-kissing voice, as I liked to think of it.

"I'm *so* incredibly sorry to use this number, I know we're not supposed to. However, my husband and I have reason to believe Morgan's wallet may have been lost or stolen."

My wallet? What was she talking about? My wallet was still in my suitcase, I hadn't used it since—since—oh, *fek*—

"You see, her father went online to pay the bills and found a charge on Morgan's American Express account that seemed suspicious. It was a rather expensive bus ticket to someplace in Wales; I won't even try to pronounce it! But now we're terribly worried, and we just wanted to make sure Morgan is all right and that her credit card hasn't been purloined."

Nice vocab word, Mom, I thought, rolling my eyes. *Just because you think you're talking to a college admissions office doesn't mean you have to whip out your SAT Word-of-the-Day desk calendar.*

"Please have Morgan call me back at our home number in the States. I would deeply appreciate it, since we don't have any other way of reaching her. Thank you so very kindly!"

I snapped the cover shut.

"You seem displeased," Mr. McAlister observed.

"No, I'm pissed!" I gave him back the phone. "It's not easy to keep your half-goddess identity secret when Ameri-can Express is ratting out your every move. Now my parents know I bought a bus ticket to Wales. How am I supposed to explain that?"

"That *is* inconvenient," he said sympathetically. "Perhaps you can tell your mother your campus tour included a field trip: 'Architectural Oddities of Great Britain.' As the world's leading, and in fact, only, expert on Castell Cyfareddol, I would happily write you a note."

"It's all Mr. Phineas's fault." I was too frustrated to listen to reason. "He's the one who got my parents all worked up about me going to Oxford—as if that's ever gonna happen. And basically I've been lying to everyone about everything, and when the truth comes out my family's going to hate me, and Colin's going to hate me, and I don't even know who this Phineas guy *is*. Plus, I blew off doing my community service hours at the SmartYCamp!"

I knew I was getting off-topic, but I was so aggravated I just kept ranting. "Not that I really *wanted* to do them, but without them I won't be able to get in to even the lamest of the lame schools, so now I'm going to end up being an X-ray technician and my parents will be so embarrassed they'll probably move to New Jersey."

I stood there, breathless and pouting. Mr. McAlister looked at me like I was a toddler having a tantrum, which was pretty close to my state of mind. Finally he spoke. "My dear girl, if you really want to apply to Oxford, no one is stopping you."

"I've *already* stopped me, that's what's so pathetic! My grades suck and I have no extracurriculars. And get this: Last night the unicorns told me I had to get rid of Titania and become the Queen of the Faeries so I can save the human realm from getting all smooshed together with the magic realm."

"Hmmm," he said. "So that's what they meant by saving the world. It's quite a task."

"Like I have time for that." I threw up my hands. "It's just nuts."

"No doubt it is." He twirled his tennis racquet thoughtfully. "But consider this, Morgan: In your heart, you don't want the magic world to get 'smooshed together' with the human world any more than the unicorns do, correct?"

I touched the locket and thought of Colin. "Correct. But that doesn't mean—"

"And you *are* still interested in pursuing higher education at a prestigious university of international reputation, are you not?"

"Well, yeah, but I don't see where you're going with this—"

"Morgan, think! Saving the world—surely *that* would have to count as community service hours, don't you agree?"

I shrugged. "I don't know. Would it?"

He shrugged right back. "I don't know, either. Personally I think it would be a rather impressive 'extracurricular,' as you call it."

Okay, now he had me completely mixed up. "So, wait. You're saying there's still a chance that I could get in to Oxford?"

He looked at me kindly. "Morgan, if there's one thing I've learned in my ridiculously long life, it's that 'unlikely' does not mean anything remotely like 'impossible.' But your intentions must be clear—do you sincerely wish to attend? If offered a place in Oxford's freshman class, would you enroll? Assuming a suitable financial aid package was made available, of course."

Pull it together, you doofus, I told myself. *He's on the admissions committee, remember?*

"Well, yeah, sure." I felt kind of dumb all of a sudden, talking about my college plans when the world still needed saving. "I mean, why not? Oxford would be awesome."

"And would you be willing to first perform this difficult yet urgent task that the unicorns have requested?" he pressed. "Community service, leadership, self-sacrifice—I do think it would make a significant difference in how your application is received."

It was an interesting question: Could saving the world be any worse than teaching long division to Monstrous Marcus at the SmartYCamp? Probably not.

And, since I was here in Wales and the SmartYCamp had already started without me in Connecticut, what choice did I really have?

"But Mr. McAlister," I protested weakly, "I don't even know how to do what the unicorns want me to do. Even *they* don't know how I'm supposed to do it."

"That's what makes it such a challenge! But you really ought to have a campus tour before applying; it's protocol.

Let me make some inquiries." He stroked his chin. "Perhaps something can be arranged. . . ."

Mr. McAlister left for his tennis practice and I went back to the Seahorse. Colin was already nearly finished cleaning the kitchen. "How's yer ma?" he asked, wiping his hands on a dish towel. "Everything okay on the homestead? They still think ye're at Oxford, don't they?"

No point getting Colin worried about stupid parent stuff. "Yeah, she's just obsessing. I'll call her later when they're awake. Hey, you did all the dishes! You should've waited for me."

He gave a low chuckle. "I'm not takin' any chances with the housekeepin'. If Grandpap wakes up to dishes in the sink there'll be a hue and cry like a thousand banshees wailin'. I can do without that, thank ye very much."

"What's a banshee?"

He looked startled, then laughed. "More Irish faery clap-trap. In the old stories the banshees were beautiful faery women who'd come screechin' and howlin' around the house. If the banshees showed up, it meant someone was about to die."

He folded the damp towel neatly and draped it over the faucet. "Now ye see why I never believed in any o' that stuff. Most of it's silly, and the rest is bloody morbid, if ye ask me. All right, we've got a big day ahead. Let's have a cuppa and sketch out a game plan."

Colin poured fresh coffee and we sat at the table. I half listened as he made flow charts diagramming the three different but possibly related mysteries we were allegedly trying to solve: a strange message scratched on the forest floor, a sighting of animals that looked suspiciously like unicorns and an e-mail received by me from Colin that apparently he'd neither written nor sent.

I say *allegedly* because the first two weren't mysteries at all—at least not to me. But I did have a couple of burning questions of my own. The first: What were these Rules of Succession that the unicorns were so sure existed?

The second? *When is Colin going to discover that I've been lying worse than a cheap rug from Ikea, and how much will he hate me when he does?*

"The e-mail's the easy one; I'll get to the bottom of that sooner or later," Colin explained briskly. "It's shockingly simple to hack someone's account. When I'm back at the computer lab at school I might be able to figure out who did it, or at least where the server's located. Most of the serious hackers are based in Russia and China, but this could've been done anywhere." He shook his head. "They did a decent job of writin' in me own distinctive prose style, I'll give 'em credit for that much." He gave me a meaningful look. "They must've had a good time readin' our mail."

I blushed. The e-mails Colin and I had been exchanging during the past few months were noticeably steamier than they'd been before I turned seventeen.

"But—hmmm." He frowned in concentration. "Even if they did read all yer mail, I hadn't yet written ye about me trip to Wales. But I booked the ferry and cottage from me cell phone . . . I'd best give the company a call and see if the line's been compromised. As fer Mr. Hacker pretending to be me tellin' ye that something weird happened—well, that's a generic thing to say. Probably just a coincidence."

"Wow." For a guy who didn't believe in faeries, Colin had some wild imagination.

"Identity theft is serious business. I don't mean to alarm ye, love, but there might be some con artist out there right now taking out student loans using your personal identification. Ye have to promise me to follow up on that. I'll talk to yer da about it if ye like."

"Oh, he works at a bank, I bet he knows all about that stuff," I said quickly. "But I'll definitely tell him."

"Now, about the message in the dirt." Colin smiled. "Let's assume, fer the moment at least, that despite how warped the situation appears there's nothing supernatural involved."

I nodded, trying not to spit out my coffee.

"One theory I've been considering: Maybe it's the work of a graffiti artist, 'save the world' bein' yer basic feel-good type of message. And 'Morgan' could be a tag of some kind." He gave me a teasing look. "A tag, ye know, that's what them graffiti types call the names they sign on the walls."

"I know what a tag is, silly." Trying to follow Colin's

theory was like watching a game of Twister being played by a contortionist, though I was impressed by how many of the dots he'd managed to connect. "So you think there might be a graffiti artist on the premises who tags his work 'Morgan'?"

"Why not? Ye're not the only person named Morgan in the world, ye know."

I rolled my eyes. "I know! Morgan Fairchild. Morgan Freeman."

"How Grandpap loved him in *The Bucket List*," Colin reminisced. "Though I preferred his work in *The Dark Knight* meself. Ye know, I might have it bollixed up, but now that we're makin' a list of Morgans, I could swear me granny used to tell stories about some old fairy-tale character named Morgan, or Morganne or some such. Wonder what she's all about? P'raps we should look her up on Wikipedia."

I almost upchucked my breakfast at that remark. Luckily Colin moved on to other topics. "Graffiti's a common thing in Dublin. Some of it's bloody artistic, in my opinion. But I'll tell ye one thing—if there's a tagger named Morgan wanderin' Castell Cyfareddol, he—or she, I suppose!—is not goin' to be content leavin' his mark in the woods where hardly a soul will see it. It'll be showin' up other places as well."

"In that case," I said, thinking fast, "I propose that we take a look around and see if we spot any other marks or messages anywhere on the grounds of Castell Cyfareddol."

I liked this plan for two reasons: It would keep Colin

busy while I tried to figure out where the Rules of Succession might be written. And it kept us away from the forest, which at the moment was inconveniently infested with unicorns.

"Deal," Colin said after a moment. "And later on we can head back to the forest and look for any unusual activity there."

"Sounds good," I said, while thinking, *Would a herd of unicorns performing a halftime show count as "unusual activity" in Colin's eyes?*

Or would he find a way, no matter how convoluted and improbable, to explain that away too?

fifteen

Colin puttered around gathering pencils and graph paper, and wrote a quick note to Grandpap telling him where we were going. Now that we had a "game plan," Colin wanted to proceed in a scientific and methodical fashion, starting back at the hotel so we could survey the grounds of Castell Cyfareddol thoroughly, from one end to the other. Together we'd mark down everything we found that might have some relevance to the mysterious Morgan message in the woods.

We left the cottage, passing the jockey and his trusty steed (whom I now thought of as Seabiscuit, of course), and headed toward the boardwalk. Soon we reached the dragon statue. Colin stared at it curiously.

"How do they manage the iridescence in the scales, I wonder?"

"Scales?" Last time I'd seen the dragon it had been carved out of stone.

"I never noticed it before either, but there's some kind of finish on the stone. Makes it look like the scales are catchin' the light." Colin reached up and ran his hand over the dragon's enormous back. "See how it shimmers with all the colors o' the rainbow? Must be the angle of the early mornin' sun that's makin' it visible now."

"Must be," I said, while thinking, *This is what the unicorns meant when they said the veil-slippage had already begun.* Colin stroked his hand over the scales again. A deep rumble shook the ground where we stood.

Oh fek, I thought. *The dragon is purring.*

"Wow." I forced a weak laugh. "Earthquakes in Wales, who knew?"

Colin shook his head. "Probably some eighteen-wheel lorry makin' a delivery to the hotel." The rumble subsided. We walked on, and I glanced back over my shoulder. The dragon's eye was the size of a basketball, with a feline metallic sheen.

As if someone had drawn it with a pen, an ink-black vertical slit opened down the center of the eye. The pupil widened slightly. Then the dragon blinked.

I whipped my head around so fast it was like I'd walked in on my parents making out. *It's already started,* I thought in a panic. *I've got to find these Rules, fast.*

"If it's feedin' time at the conservatory we might want to stop in," Colin remarked, as we waited for the waterfall to let us pass. "Watching the plants eat is bound to attract crowds. Perfect lure for a chap cravin' attention, like our hypothetical tagger."

I didn't get it. "Why would feeding plants attract crowds? I've seen my dad do it. It's just like watering, except you sprinkle Miracle-Gro in the water. Totally boring."

Colin smiled. "Not at Castell Cyfareddol. It's a carnivorous plant conservatory. The place is brimmin' with blood-thirsty petunias."

"Carnivorous? What do they eat, cheeseburgers? Oh my God, look!"

"What's the matter?" Colin asked, worried.

"Oh, nothing." I waved it off. "Just noticed the gargoyles had been moved, that's all." Up and down the board-walk, the stone pillars were empty. Damp reptilian footprints led from the boardwalk into the shrubs beyond.

"Huh. They probably took 'em off fer cleaning and re-pairs." Colin kept walking, a little faster than before.

I followed, but I couldn't help glancing into the shadows underneath the bushes. If the gargoyles weren't on their perches, where were they? Would we soon see them skittering around the boardwalk like stray cats?

And if we did, what kind of scientific explanation would Colin come up with for that?

"Careful, Mor—see, I told ye to keep yer hands in yer pockets!"

I snatched my hand back from some creepy-looking flower that was visibly salivating at my presence.

Colin moved methodically through the conservatory, examining the walls, the floors, and—very carefully—the containers that housed the bloodthirsty vegetation. "It's a fascinatin' notion, innit? Shrubbery that eats meat. See any graffiti yet?"

"No," I said, preoccupied. I was still thinking about the gargoyles. And the dragon. And these fekkin' Rules of Succession that I needed to locate, pronto.

I tickled the mouth of a Venus flytrap with a twig I'd found lying on the floor, and watched in fascination as it closed. "I guess photosynthesis just isn't enough for some plants," I remarked.

"It turns the whole food chain concept on its arse, if ye ask me. Imagine if all the green grass of Ireland developed a taste for bangers and mash! There'd be a general panic, not to mention a run on the pubs. What's this, then?" Colin's voice had suddenly dropped half an octave. I moved to join him, but he gestured at me to stay back.

"Did you find something?"

Colin stood staring at the door that led out of the conservatory. Using his foot, he slowly pushed it open. He looked, and then stepped through. "Bloody hell," I heard him mutter. Then he started to chuckle.

"What is it?" I pleaded.

"Yer man's losin' it. See fer yerself."

Stenciled on the door in bright silver paint was the unmistakable silhouette of a unicorn.

"It's not graffiti. It's just a sign," Colin explained, dragging me to the arrow-shaped marker in the center of the tiny courtyard. "Leadin' visitors from one exhibit to the next. See? Go ahead, read it."

This way to the Unicorn Tapestry Garden

I vaguely recalled what the unicorn tapestries were; I'd seen them in a museum in New York on a middle-school field trip. They were enormous wall hangings, woven many centuries ago when people had time to do stuff like that. And they told a story—a bloody, violent story about humans hunting a unicorn.

I remembered that the museum had looked exactly like a castle, and that, once our class arrived, Sarah and I made a pact to talk in English accents for the rest of the day. The task absorbed all of our concentration. As a result, I didn't retain too much information about the tapestries—like why someone would plant a garden because of them.

Or whether the unicorn was killed in the end.

Colin squeezed my shoulder reassuringly. "Just goes to show: If ye keep yer wits about ye, there's always a rational, scientific explanation. Shall we have a look?"

i followed Colin in the direction indicated by the sign. We passed through a curtain of vines and into a larger, square garden. In the center was a gnarled tree laden with strange-looking red fruit. Every remaining square inch of ground was planted with flowers, all in full bloom. The effect was dizzying.

A tour guide stood at the far end of the garden with her back to us, chatting happily into a wireless lavalier microphone that fit snugly over her head. The mike seemed like overkill to me. The garden wasn't that big, and there were only a half dozen visitors standing around listening to her spiel to begin with.

"More than a hundred different plants are depicted in the unicorn tapestries! A *hundred*, can you imagine? Honestly, I didn't even know there *were* that many types of plants!"

What made the microphone even more out of place was that the tour guide was dressed in medieval style, in a floor-length, high-waisted dress. Her hair was piled high on her head, with a flowy, princess-style train pinned to the back.

"Let me see: We have wild orchids, and some thistle, and this skah-*rumptious* pomegranate tree, and ooh, just *so* many others! Great care has been taken to reproduce the plants shown in the tapestries *exactly*! Though I couldn't for the life of me tell you why someone would bother. I mean, who cares, really? I'd much rather be out clubbing. But wait, we have some new arrivals."

The tour guide wheeled and faced the newcomers— meaning, Colin and me. "Better late than never, I suppose! You just missed the part where I explained how this garden strives to reproduce the unicorn tapestries *exactly*, down to the last stitch. And of course, that includes the one-horned star of the show—that mysterious, mythical creature herself. Let's hear it for . . . the unicorn!"

She clapped loudly and whistled right into her mike. The sound was so piercing I had to cover my ears. My eyes were wide open, though, and as I looked at the all-too-familiar face of Queen Titania, with that ridiculous microphone curved around her gaunt cheek, just like Madonna, I got angry. So angry that I could barely tear my eyes away from her mocking gaze to see the blinking, terrified creature that now stumbled reluctantly into the garden.

I heard Colin gasp.

"Holy moly!" one of the tourists exclaimed, reaching for her camera. "That is so realistic-looking!"

"Ringling Brothers used to have a unicorn," her companion scoffed. "They do it by grafting a goat's horn onto the middle of its head. I saw it on *Mythbusters*."

The woman with the camera hesitated. "You mean—it's a goat?"

"They shave it so it has a mane and tail. But, yeah, it's a goat."

We all stared at the graceful, silver-hued creature trembling before us. The ridiculous rhinestone-studded collar around its neck was attached to a long, sturdy-looking tether. Electric sparks zapped frantically along the spiraled edge of its horn, as if the animal were short-circuiting with fear.

"No way that's a goat," someone finally said.

"Well, what is it then?"

"I don't know, but it's not a goat."

"I know what it is." I found my voice and pushed to the front. "It's a living creature that's being mistreated. May I have a word with you privately, Titan—Tour Guide?"

"And you are?" she said haughtily. "If we've met before I apologize *profusely* for blocking it out. Obviously the experience was much too unpleasant to remember."

"I am Special Admissions Candidate Rawlinson," I declared, improvising like mad for the benefit of the tourists. "A representative of the newly formed Society for the Prevention of Meanness to Things That Are Alive."

Titania yanked the mike off her head and hissed at me. "Morgan, honestly. SPMTTAA? What a perfectly *appalling* acronym; you'll never get anywhere with a name like that." Then she held the microphone to her mouth. "All right, tour's over. Everybody have fun looking around the garden. And don't make eye contact with the unicorn! It's vicious and easily provoked." She stared laser beams of rage at me as she spat out the words.

Obediently, the crowd scattered. I could sense Colin close behind me, but I didn't dare turn to look at him. I had a sinking feeling that whatever was about to happen might be impossible to write off with one of those rational, scientific explanations he liked so much.

"Well, look who's here." Titania sounded just as nasty as I remembered. "Aren't you on the wrong continent, dear?"

The unicorn nickered nervously.

"Let the unicorn go," I said, glancing its way. "Now."

"Unicorn?" Titania sneered. "Why, I thought it was a

goat! Or are you implying that unicorns are *real*, Special Candidate Rawlinson?" She glanced at Colin. "Surely you wouldn't want your all-too-human *boyfriend* here to think you believed in something as ridiculous as unicorns? What a humiliating revelation that would be!"

Colin stepped next to me. "Do ye know this woman, Mor?"

Titania exploded in icy laughter. "Does she know me, he says! That is high-*larious*. How I would love to dawdle long enough to hear you answer that *fascinating* question, my dear! But right now I have to run-run-run; I have a previous sporting engagement." Then she turned to Colin. "What's your name again, champ?"

"Colin."

"Colin! Of course—but we've met before too, how could I forget? Be a love and go get my tennis bag. I left it behind the tree. Just thataway, tiger, that's right, can't miss it."

Throwing me a concerned look, Colin went to get the bag.

As soon as he was out of earshot, I got right in Titania's grill.

"The veil is slipping, Titania."

She cackled. "Like I didn't know that."

"Are you making it happen?"

"What if I am?"

This was like arguing with Tammy. "The veil is slipping." *No, your face is slipping!* "Are you making it happen?" *No, your face is making it happen!*

"Undoing the veil is a huge mistake," I said. "It's not too late to stop it."

"Stop it? I've barely started. I am sick and tired of this 'reality is off-limits,' 'don't spill the beans to the humans' crap. Anyone who believes *that* is nothing more than a party pooper!" She leaned down and snarled right in my face. "And if some deluded four-legged pep squad has given you the impression that you can somehow stand in my way, trust me: They are dead—and I mean *dead*—wrong."

Colin returned with the bag. "Found yer bag, ma'am," he said gruffly. "But your racquet's in no shape to play tennis. It needs to be strung."

A slow, evil smile spread across Titania's face. "What a literal-minded person you are! Strings are only necessary if you believe they are. And please don't call me 'ma'am'—I *much* prefer 'Your Majesty.'"

Then, in a foul-smelling puff of smoke like something out of a bad magic act, she disappeared.

sixteen

i stood there like an idiot. the lavalier mike lay on the ground at our feet.

"Where'd she go?" Colin coughed and waved away the smoke.

Don't be such a party pooper, a voice inside me urged. *Tell him tell him tell him—*

The unicorn let out a pathetic, practically goatlike bleat. Without thinking I moved to unsnap the hideous collar from its neck. Colin stopped me.

"Careful, there. Don't ye think we ought to call a vet? This unigoat, or goaticorn, or whatever it is—it might need medical attention."

The unicorn looked at me in horror, but I didn't know if it was because of the vet idea or because Colin had called it a unigoat.

"It looks perfectly healthy to me." I petted the unicorn's neck, and it stamped one hoof in agreement. Using my mother's patented o-ver-ar-tic-u-la-ted vocal technique to get my message across, I added, "I bet it can easily *find-its-way-home*." Then I pointed the unicorn's nose in the direction of the forest with one hand and undid its collar with the other.

The collar slipped to the ground, and the tether with it. The freed unicorn gave itself a relieved shake, from muzzle to tail. It briefly dipped its horn in my direction.

You're welcome, I thought.

Taking only a few steps to gain speed, the unicorn leapt over the rear hedge of the garden in a high, graceful jump, then galloped away so quickly we lost sight of it within seconds. Only a trail of sparks from its horn remained. Then those faded as well.

That was one problem solved—but now I had to deal with Colin. What could he possibly be thinking, after seeing what he'd just seen? Feeling more scared than the unicorn had looked, I turned to face him.

"Must be a mountain goat to jump like that." Colin was pale and his voice quivered slightly, but he kept bravely spinning the facts to fit his view of reality. "And that woman—I bet she's done time in the carnivals too. Of course I've seen magicians perform the same tricks dozens o' times. Guessin' people's names, disappearing into thin air. Bit o' smoke and mirrors is all it takes." Now he sounded somewhat less sure of himself. "Funny—did ye notice how she looked a bit like that hideous painting in yer room back at the cottage? Let's be on our way, then."

Dear, logical, high-tech Colin. Was there any impossible occurrence sufficiently freaky to make him believe in magic, once and for all?

And if there wasn't, I thought, fighting back a sudden rush of tears, *how would he ever be able to believe in me?*

the rest of our walk to the hotel revealed nothing out of the ordinary. The topiary shrubs looked firmly rooted in their planters. The boardwalk seemed steady underfoot.

Look at all the happy humans, I thought miserably. Budget-minded couples on second honeymoons. Rock stars on iron-ically low-brow vacations. Would they be able to get along peacefully with faeryland run amok? Or was some kind of horrible human-faery bloodbath the only possible result of Titania's need for fun-fun-fun, reality style?

We were on the piazza now, near the reflecting pool. Colin unpacked his messenger bag of pencils and graph paper. He used his stride to measure off the length of the pool so he could mark the precise locations of any "evidence" he found.

Meanwhile, I stared into the water. Everything was reflected there: me, the hotel, all the nice, normal, family-on-vacay–type people wandering around the piazza, snapping photos, perusing their maps of the grounds—

"Hey, do you have one of those maps?" I asked Colin as he marched by me.

"Twelve, thirteen fourteen—not with me, no. Might be one back at the cottage. Why?"

"I was wondering where the tennis courts might be."
Mr. McAlister had said he had a tennis game scheduled with
some collector of antiquities, then Titania claimed to have a
"sporting engagement" and had tennis gear in her bag.
What were the odds, I thought, *that they're planning to play
each other?* I made a mental note to check in on Mr. McAlister later, just in case.

Colin kept marching and measuring, and I kept staring.
The water in the pool was spookily clear. It was like looking
through air. In fact, when a stream of tiny bubbles rose to
the surface of the pool it came as a shock. I peered deeper
into the water to find the bubbles' source—were there fish
swimming around? Or did the pool have a filter pump, like
in an aquarium?

More and bigger bubbles came to the surface. Then,
caught by a sudden gust of wind, one of the bubbles broke
free of the water and rose slowly into the air.

Another bubble did the same thing. Then another. I
watched, amazed. These were not slimy toxic waste bubbles;
they were nice, clean, soapy bubbles.

As the bubbles floated past my face, I inhaled.

They smelled like Mr. Bubble.

Colin had finished his measuring walk around the pool
and was now standing behind me again.

"Colin?" I tried to sound calm as I batted aside the dense
cloud of bubbles that now surrounded me. "Would you go
inside the hotel and ask for one of those maps?"

"Sure." He stared at me. "What's up with the bubbles?"

"I'm not sure." I blew some away from my face. "They're coming from the pool."

Colin looked at the pool, which was now covered with sweet-smelling soapy froth. It looked like a giant bubble bath. He frowned. "Must be some reflux from the laundry drains. Let me go notify building services; they can send the plumbers to check."

"Awesome," I said, spitting soap out of my mouth. "I'll wait here."

Filled with purpose, Colin headed for the hotel.

As the breeze from the ocean picked up, the bubbles floated everywhere, much to the delight of the younger tourists on the piazza. The kids chased after them, squealing and trying to catch the bubbles on their fingertips.

I leaned over the side of the pool and scooped away the surface foam with my hands so I could see what was going on. Deep beneath the surface of the water, standing in the reflection of the piazza, were two figures. They held drippy wet bubble wands and were happily blowing away.

One was a guy about my age, fair-haired, dark eyes, chiseled features, boy-band handsome in a completely otherworldly way. In other words, Finnbar.

The other was my sister, Tammy.

As I watched, Finnbar tapped Tammy on the shoulder and pointed in my direction. At first she looked puzzled. Then she saw me. A big smile broke over her face, and she waved.

I didn't stop to think. I just dove in.

*   *   *

Ow. Ow.

Soap in my eyes, ow ow ow—

Owwwwwwww—

I was on my feet, on solid ground, slap-fighting my way out of a blinding swarm of bubbles. Finally I opened my eyes.

On my left was a picturesque, winding river, bordered by a sloped meadow. Medieval church spires rose above the trees. The setting seemed weirdly familiar.

Finnbar sat cross-legged on a felled log at the river's edge. Tammy stood next to him, still blowing bubbles. They were both dressed in Ye Olde Timey costumes, but the bubble wands were ordinary modern plastic. When she saw me, Tammy squealed and hurled herself in my direction, wrapping her arms tightly around my waist.

"Hey hey hey, Tamster—are you all right?"

Tammy gazed up at me. Then she stuck out her tongue. Oh yeah, she was fine.

"Took you long enough, Morganne!" Finnbar stood up, bubble wand still in hand. "We have been waiting and waiting and *waiting* for you! Put away the soap, Tammy. Your sister's here, and we have an appointment."

"Look, Morgan!" Tammy said proudly, waving a plastic bottle of dishwashing soap in my face. "Faery soap! It makes the bestest bubbles."

"I can see that," I said, extricating myself from her boa constrictor grip. "Tam, what are you doing here?"

Finnbar leaned over and whispered to me. "Remember, it's still rather early in the morning in that unspellable place where your family lives."

"Connecticut?"

He made a face. "Precisely. The child's asleep, but don't tell her. If she wakes up it spoils the fun."

"Finnbar, I *need* some of this super-awesome bubble soap!" Tammy jumped up and down. "Where can I get some?"

Finnbar wiped his soapy hands on his tweed trousers. "There's nothing 'super-awesome' about Fairy Liquid; you can buy it at any supermarket. At least, in Great Britain you can." He struck a pose with the bottle like a spokesperson on a commercial. "'When it's time to do the washing-up, choose Fairy Liquid, the brand trusted by millions. In regular or lemon-scented. It's *so* easy on the hands!'" He shoved the bottle in his pocket. "Now come along! We don't want Morganne to be late."

I looked around, still unsure where we were. "Late for what?"

Finnbar put his hands on his hips as if he were going to scold me. "Truly, it boggles the mind: after *so* many people have gone to *so* much trouble on your behalf, and still you have no clue! Late for your campus tour, silly!"

"You mean, this is Oxford?" I spun around, taking it all in. "*The* Oxford University?"

"That's the one," Finnbar said proudly.

"And I'm coming too," Tammy chirped.

"Yes, but only if you stay quiet. This is regarding your sister's higher education and you must behave." Finnbar peered at his watch. "Whoops! It's time. The campus tour is about to begin. Wait for it—five, four, three, two, one—"

He snapped to attention. "Good morning, Special Admissions Candidates! I mean, Candidate. And sibling!"

"Good morning!" Tammy parroted cheerfully.

Finnbar looked at me, waiting.

I caved. "Good morning."

He smiled angelically. "It is with enormous pride and pleasure that I now introduce you to the one of the great universities known to humankind, non-humankind and several other kinds as well. My tour will be both entertaining and informative. Feel free to ask questions but only when I call on you; look but don't touch and please, please, pretty *please*"—he scowled at us sternly—"stay with the group!"

Tammy and I looked at each other.

"We will," I promised. Tammy took my hand and squeezed.

"This way!" Finnbar proceeded to walk backward, slowly waving his hands in the classic tour guide follow-me gesture. "First stop—the Bod!"

So this is Oxford, I thought, as we walked across the quad. *Medieval Times theme park meets college campus. Kewl.*

Students wandered around and lay on the grass, chatting and reading. It was college, all right. But I saw no jeans, no hoodies, no skateboards, no Frisbees. In fact, the wardrobe choices seemed to involve a lot of breeches. And, other than Tammy and me, there were no girls, anywhere.

"Finnbar—"

"Raise your hand if you have a question, please!"

I raised my hand.

"Yes! Special Admissions Candidate Rawlinson?"

"I can see we're at Oxford, I recognize it from the pictures. But *when* are we?"

He shrugged. "Does it matter? So little changes around here. We might be in the 1400s—oh, that would be fun! You could meet Sir Thomas More. A bit later there was Dr. Samuel Johnson. He was just like you, Tammy, always making lists of words. More recently we've had Indira Gandhi and that Lawrence of Arabia fellow. And Lewis Carroll—now he was an odd duck."

"He wrote *Alice in Wonderland*." Tammy spun around, showing off her little blue frock with the sash around the waist. "That's what Mommy was reading to me at bedtime."

Finnbar pressed his lips together in disapproval. "I knew there was an explanation for that dress. Not your color, dear." He turned back to me. "Now, I'm not very good with numbers, but if I had to guess I would venture to say we've landed someplace between the Dark Ages—*loved* them!—and the invention of the sitcom. If you want to narrow it down further, we'll have to ask someone."

A youngish man, too old to be a student, sat with his back against a nearby tree. Finnbar walked briskly over to him and cleared his throat. "*Ahem!* Sir?"

The man didn't seem to hear; he was completely engrossed writing in a journal of some kind.

"Sir? Might I trouble you by asking a question?" Finnbar

touched him lightly on the shoulder. The man flinched, obviously startled, and scrambled to his feet when he saw us.

"Ah, how are ye, Finnsie? Forgive me for not noticing ye at once; I'm in the midst of a bit o' work, here." He bowed in my direction. "I'm Professor Lewis to me students, Clive to me mum. But ye must call me Jack."

He had a pleasant Irish accent, which made me like him right away. "I'm, uh, Morgan Rawlinson. Nice to meet you."

Tammy pushed herself in front of me. "Tammy Rawlinson, how dooooooooo you dooooooooo?"

Finnbar clicked his heels together and bowed with a flourish. "Very sorry to disturb you while you're working, Professor. But do you happen to know *when* it is?"

"Certainly." Professor Lewis checked his pocket watch. "'Tis nearly half past eleven."

"There you have it!" Finnbar looked at me, quite satisfied with that answer. "Shall we continue with our tour?"

"What are you writing?" Tammy tried to sneak a peek at the professor's notebook.

"Don't be such a nosy-pants," I scolded, but he smiled.

"Not much of anything yet, miss. I'm trying to think of a title. It's fer a book I plan to write someday." He flipped back a page. "So far I have: *The Lion, the Witch and the Chest of Drawers. The Lion, the Witch and the Shoebox. The Lion, the Witch and the Tippy Old Armoire*." He put his journal down in frustration. "Unfortunately, none of those sound quite right."

Tammy giggled madly. "That's because it's 'Wardrobe.'

The Lion, the Witch and the Wardrobe. W-A-R-D-R-O-B-E."
Then she curtsied. "I did Fun with Phonics, can you tell?"

Finnbar cradled his head in his hands as if he were getting a migraine. "Tammy, please! You and your books and your spelling words! And at your age! Really, would it be so hard to play with twigs and leaves for a few more years?"

But Professor Lewis seemed intrigued by Tammy's suggestion. "A wardrobe? You mean, in the sense of—a closet? How interesting . . ."

"It *is* interesting!" Tammy hopped with excitement. "Would you like me to tell you what happens? There are four children, all named Pevensie, and Lucy is the smartest, and—"

I slapped my hand over her mouth. "Maybe we ought to let Professor Lewis work in peace."

"Yes!" Finnbar tapped his foot with impatience. "Our campus tour is falling behind schedule, and it's really stressing me out! Next stop, the library. Good day, Professor."

"Good day! If ye see our friend Ronald, tell him to come 'round and see me." Professor Lewis was already scribbling fresh notes in his book. "I'm eager to get his opinion on this new title. . . ."

We'd made it halfway across the campus when Tammy abruptly sat down on the ground. "I'm tired," she announced. "I don't want to look at old buildings anymore."

Finnbar threw up his hands in frustration. "Honestly, Tammy, it was your idea to come! And now you want to leave when we've just gotten started?"

Tammy yawned. "But I'm sleepy. Really, I just wanted to surprise Morgan. Now I want to go home and"—*yawn*—"finish sleeping and then get up and watch *SpongeBob*."

Finnbar sighed. It amused me to see that not even a faery could stand up to Tammy's persistence. "Fine, off with you then. How would you like to travel?"

"Bubble ride, please."

Then she and Finnbar did an elaborate handshake, involving palm slides, hip shimmies, shoulder bumps and wiggling fingers. When they were finished Tammy looked up expectantly.

From an altitude far above the clouds, a shiny soap bubble gently floated down from the sky. It was enormous—big enough to contain Tammy's own bed, rumpled Disney princess comforter and all.

Covering her eyes to keep out the soap, Tammy stepped inside the bubble. She climbed into her bed, gave me a tiny wave and was instantly sound asleep. The bubble made one lazy rotation in place before it floated up, up and away.

"This is how it always goes with children," Finnbar said, sounding wistful. "They start out believing in faeries, then before you know it they'd rather watch television and learn to spell."

The bubble was already no bigger than a speck. I knew Tammy was fine, but it made my heart race to see her floating up into the sky like that. "The bubble ride thing is cute,"

I said to Finnbar, trying not to sound anxious. "Very *Wizard of Oz*."

He giggled. "Glinda was one of ours, you know. She was a lot like Queen Titania, now that I think of it—seduced by the glamour of 'reality.' *Had* to go to Hollywood! *Had* to be in the movies! It was quite a scandal when she defected to the human realm to appear in that film. You would not believe the cattiness!"

Together we watched as Tammy's bubble disappeared from sight.

"Half the leprechauns in Ireland showed up at the munchkin auditions just to yank Glinda's chain," Finnbar reminisced. "Not all of them got cast, either. 'Not the right type,' is what they were told. That nearly started a riot! But now—on with the tour!"

seventeen

Now that Finnbar and I were finally alone, I had a million questions for him. To my extreme annoyance, he kept walking backward and made me raise my hand every time I wanted to speak.

"Finnbar, we need to talk. There's something serious going on—"

"Whoopsie, I didn't see a hand!"

I stuck my hand in the air.

"Yes?"

"What do you know about Titania's plan to undo the veil between the realms?"

"Very little."

"Is there any way—"

"Wait until I call on you, please! That's better. Yes?"

"Is there any way to stop her?"

"Yes."

"Well, what *is* it?"

"We're out of time, I'm afraid! Please save the rest of your questions until the end of the tour."

I thrust my hand in the hair and jumped up and down. "Come on, just one more!"

He rolled his eyes. "One more, but that's it. We do have a schedule to keep to, you know!"

Okay, obviously I wasn't going to get anywhere asking him direct questions about Titania. After all, not only was she a bitch, she was his mother, and that meant Finnbar was twice as scared of her as everybody else was. Instead, I asked him about something that'd been bugging me ever since the last time I'd looked at my Oxford brochure. "Finnbar, do you happen to know a guy named Cornelius Phineas?"

He giggled. "'Certified to Give Advice'? *That* Cornelius Phineas?"

"That's him."

"Never heard of him! But it wouldn't surprise me if he'd heard of me. I'm rather well-known around here, in fact."

As if to prove his point, a man walked toward us eagerly, waving a lit pipe as he approached.

"Oh dear, it's Ronald," Finnbar muttered. "He can be tedious, although he does know how to swear in Old Icelandic."

"Finnbar, my friend! I've been looking for you; I need

your opinion." The man nodded in my direction. "How do you do, miss?"

Finnbar hesitated before making an introduction. "This is Special Admissions Candidate Rawlinson. Candidate Rawlinson, may I present John Ronald Reuel Tolkien." He shot me a warning glance. "He's just another professor here at Oxford, Morganne, don't burst a vein."

Tolkien? *Lord of the Rings* Tolkien? I tried not to shriek. "You're—oh my God! I'm—I mean, wow! I'm awesome, thanks," I said, while thinking, *Stop acting like a dork.* "It's kind of amazing to meet you."

Finnbar turned back to Tolkien. "Professor, before I forget: We just ran into Jack Lewis on the quad. He's eager to speak to you. It's something to do with his books."

Tolkien rolled his eyes. "Oh, not Jack and his talking animals again! When is that man going to grow up? I have problems of my own to worry about." He dug into the leather satchel that was slung over his shoulder. "Have a gander at this, would you, Finnsie? I'm still trying to crack the elf problem; the physical characteristics have me stumped. I've been sketching—am I getting warmer?"

He held out a sketch pad to show us. It was a very good drawing, but the creature it depicted was short and plump, with a pointy hat and beard. Totally garden-gnomish, in my opinion. Without meaning to I made a face.

"You hate it?" Tolkien looked hurt.

"No!" I said quickly. "It's great. I mean, who knew you could draw? But if it's supposed to be an elf . . ." I handed the sketch back to him. "Sorry, it's not even close. That looks like a department store Christmas elf. Real elves are totally hawt. Think of Legolas."

Finnbar started tugging at the back of my T-shirt, but I ignored him. Tolkien took a puff on his pipe and looked at me with sudden, deep curiosity. "Pardon me, but who is Legolas?"

What a joker this guy was! "From the books! *Your* books. You know, *Lord of the Rings*."

"I don't believe he's written it yet," Finnbar whispered.

Tolkien's eyes darted from me to Finnbar and back to me again. His charcoal drawing pencil seemed poised to take notes.

"Oops. Never mind." I tried to look clueless. "I'm just saying, in my opinion, I think elves in general would be really good-looking."

"Fascinating," Tolkien murmured. "This is precisely what I've been trying to decide." He turned to Finnbar. "Which reminds me: Finnbar old man, were you able to get the materials I requested?"

"The materials?" Finnbar went blank for a moment, then starting patting his pockets. "Of course! You filled out a request for anatomical illustrations, if I recall."

Tolkien turned to me to explain. "This is all research for a rather ambitious project I hope to write someday. Finnbar has been an invaluable help."

"In addition to serving as a campus tour guide, I work part-time as a librarian," Finnbar admitted modestly, as he continued searching. "You've heard of the Special Collection?"

I nodded.

"That's my department. Interdimensional library loans, my specialty—huzzah! I knew I had it somewhere."

Finnbar reached into his inside jacket pocket and produced a page torn from a magazine, folded in quarters.

Tolkien took the page and smoothed it open. I nearly choked.

It was a glossy, gorgeous, full-color photograph of Orlando Bloom, torn out of *Teen People*. I knew this because it was the same picture Sarah kept taped inside her locker. At the bottom-right-hand corner of the page you could even see my locker combination scrawled in pencil, in case I forgot it. I kept a copy of Sarah's combo in my locker too. If we ever forgot our locker combos at the same time we'd be screwed, but so far it hadn't happened.

Tolkien stared at the photo in awe. *"Aiya Eärendil elenion ancalima!"* he exclaimed. "I see what you mean by 'hawt'! This changes my thinking completely." Suddenly antsy, he quickly tucked the page in his satchel. *"Lord of the Rings*, you say? It has possibilities, yes . . . but to make it work I'd have to add in something about a ring . . ."

Tolkien wandered off, mumbling to himself and stroking his chin. *How twisted is this?* I thought, amazed. *If Sarah only knew that the picture in her locker was the reason Orlando Bloom got the part in the first place!*

Finnbar waited until Tolkien was out of earshot before he started whining. "Here we are, wasting time on all this literary chitchat, and we haven't even seen the dining hall yet. Or the dormitories! What an awful tour guide I'm turning out to be."

"Now, now," I soothed. "You're doing an excellent job. You've already introduced me to two faculty members."

His mood brightened instantly. "That's very kind, thank you. I would happily introduce you to more, but of course most of them will be dead by the time you enroll."

"Most?" I said, surprised. "Not all?"

His hand flew to his mouth. "Perhaps I shouldn't have let that slip. But it's true—in exchange for Oxford housing the Special Collection, 'our side' occasionally lends the university an 'expert' to teach a course in mythology, folklore, 'The Faery Tale as Literature,' that sort of thing. . . ."

Listening to him talk about the Special Collection was giving me an idea.

". . . of course it's all about tenure in the halls of academe; adjunct faculty never get any respect. Especially if they're trolls . . . the giants tend to fare somewhat better . . ."

"Finnbar," I interrupted, "is it really your job to help people do research about faery world stuff? Like finding that picture of Orlando Bloom for Professor Tolkien?"

He assumed a straight-backed, military posture. "Of course! It's my sworn duty as a librarian."

"That's awesome," I said, trying not to sound sneaky. "Because I have a research project of my own to do. Maybe you could help me."

He looked surprised and very pleased. "But of course. All Special Admissions Candidates are eligible to use the library and its services for thirty days following their campus visit." He reached into his jacket pocket once more and took out a pair of wire-rimmed glasses.

"Hello! And welcome to the Bodleian Library," he said, as he put on the glasses. "I am Finnbar, your devoted and efficient part-time librarian, Special Collection department. How may I help you?"

As calmly as I could, I said, "It's no big deal. I just need to know the Rules of Succession of the Faery Realm."

"The Rules of Succession? Hmm." He tapped his index finger to his lips. "No one's ever requested those before. I believe they're written in the *Book of Horns*, which is part of the Extra-Special Materials subcategory of the Special Collection. That means it's a non-circulating item, I'm afraid. Would a photocopy be adequate for your needs?"

"Absolutely." I couldn't believe my luck.

He took out a pen and an index card. "Excellent. The first step is to fill out an official interdimensional library loan request. It's just a few short questions. Now, is your information request for academic, practical or commercial purposes?"

"Practical," I answered without thinking.

Wrong answer. His eyes grew wide, and the index card in his hand started to shake. "Oh dear! Oh no! Is someone actually planning to—do they really think they can—does Mother have any idea . . ." His voice trailed off in terror.

"No one's going to hurt your mother, I promise."

"Oh, I don't care about *that*. She's a repellent monster even on her best days. But she's going to be very angry, that's all. Mum's always been queen, you see. Always! And if she found out I was involved in any way . . . oh my! This is most upsetting!"

I laid my steady hands across his two shaky ones. "I wouldn't ask you to do this if it weren't really, really important. I mean, literally, the future of the whole world could depend on it."

Then I put on my most serious, talking-to-authority-figures voice, which I guess was loosely based on my mom's ass-kissing voice. "Finnbar, I appeal to you in your official capacity as a part-time librarian. *Please* help me find the information I need!"

That did the trick. Slowly getting hold of himself, Finnbar pushed his glasses up his nose, puffed out his chest and spoke in a deep, authoritative voice. "Well, since you put it that way, I will be honored to fulfill your request, Library Patron Rawlinson! If the Rules of Succession are what you need to know, then the Rules of Succession are what I will find." His voice quavered a bit, but he held firm. "Let the chips fall where they may!"

Impulsively I gave him a hug. "Thanks, Finnbar. You're the best."

He blushed. "I should warn you—there's a reason the *Book of Horns* is rarely requested."

"What?"

"It's written in unicorn. No one can read it. The verbs are very irregular."

That made me smile. "Just get me a copy. I'll take care of getting it translated."

"Fair enough." He handed me his pen. "Now, if you

will finish filling out the request form, I'll get right on it.
Please print clearly in blue or black ink. Thank you for your
patronage!"

i filled out the card as best i could, using Castell
Cyfareddol as my home address. As I wrote it down I realized that I had no idea how much time was passing in Wales
while I'd been touring Oxford. Usually my faery world ex-
cursions took next to no time in the human realm, but the
sooner I got back, the better.

"Before you go, would you mind filling out this brief cus-
tomer survey evaluating your tour? It's multiple choice; it'll
only take you a minute." Finnbar looked at me earnestly. "If
I get enough high marks I become eligible to win a vacation
package. Just so you know."

"Sure." I filled in all the "Excellent—exceeded expecta-
tions" bubbles and handed it back to him. He gave an ec-
static squeal when he saw what I'd written, but quickly
regained his professionalism.

"Congratulations, Special Admissions Candidate! The
Campus Tour portion of your application process has been
successfully completed. Please await further instructions,
and on behalf of Oxford University I wish you the best of
luck in your future educational endeavors. Now, how would
you like to go back?"

What *was* the best way to zoom through eighty-plus
years and a couple hundred miles in the blink of an eye?

There weren't that many options. I shrugged. "Bubble ride, I guess."

"It *is* the fastest. And extremely fuel-efficient too. I'll have to make you a new one, though; the old ones must have popped by now." He reached into his pocket, took out his bottle of Fairy Liquid and plastic bubble wand, and proceeded to blow a very impressive stream of bubbles my way.

It wasn't exactly like Glinda the Good Witch from *The Wizard of Oz*, but it worked. The bubbles surrounded me until all I could see was a field of shiny rainbows. At the last minute I remembered to close my eyes against the soapy sting. Then I felt myself being lifted up, and I floated gently away.

Whoosh!

A sharp, swirling wind whisked the dense cloud of bubbles away from me so fast it was like someone yanked the covers off while I was sleeping. Cautiously I opened my eyes. I was standing by the reflecting pool, exactly where I'd been before. The water in the pool was clear as glass. Not a bubble in sight.

I looked up in time to see Colin stride back out of the hotel, now with something under his arm. He did a double-take when he saw the crystal clear water in the pool.

"Bloody hell, that was quick!" he exclaimed. "I just spoke to the super a moment ago about the soap problem.

Must've been an easy fix. I got the map ye asked fer, but I couldn't find any tennis courts and I looked it over twice. See fer yerself. But here's an odd thing: There was some mail for ye." He handed me two envelopes: a large yellow one and a business-sized white one.

Mail? I was confused, but Colin seemed triumphant.

"Good news, eh? Ye know what they say—every criminal secretly wants to get caught." He rubbed his hands together excitedly. "Seems like we came out to look for clues, but the clues have found us instead. Yer hacker bloke is the only person who knew ye were comin' here, after all—it must be from him. Aren't you going to see who it's from?"

I turned the envelope over and saw the familiar Oxford crest. Rubber-stamped in block letters, the envelope read:

The Materials You Requested Are Enclosed.
Thank you for your patronage!

Regards,

The Bodleian Library
Department of Special Collections

The Rules of Succession from the *Book of Horns*! I gave a mental shout-out of thanks to Finnbar for the super-fast service. But no way was I going to open this envelope in front of Colin. I didn't know what unicorn writing looked like, but it was bound to raise questions.

I shoved the yellow envelope under my arm and turned my attention to the white one. It was addressed to my house in Connecticut, with a handwritten "Please Forward" scrawled next to the address. There was no return address. *Please,* I thought, as Colin watched me open it, *be something halfway normal.*

Inside were two pieces of paper: a cover letter and a form that I was obviously supposed to fill out. The letter read:

Dear Special Admissions Candidate Rawlinson,

 Congratulations! Our office has been notified that your Oxford campus tour was successfully completed.

 In order to continue the application process you will be required to attend an interview with one of our distinguished Alumni. At this time we also ask that you provide detailed information regarding your recent or planned community service activities. Please fill out the enclosed form and return it in the envelope provided.

 Note that you must choose from the times/dates listed on the form for your Alumni Interview. List choices in order of preference. We cannot guarantee your first choice can be accommodated, so please list at least three. You will be notified of your appointment time when it is confirmed.

Remember to dress appropriately for your interview! First impressions count!

Regards,

Cornelius Phineas

Cornelius Phineas, C. G. A.
"Certified to Give Advice"

I could feel Colin's bewilderment reaching massive, blood pressure–raising proportions.

"Dress appropriately?" I said weakly, knowing there was no way to explain all this. "But all I brought with me is jeans and band T-shirts. What the fek am I going to wear?"

eighteen

"What are you going to wear?" he repeated incredulously. "That's the least of yer worries, don't ye think, Mor?"

"I know, I'm just being dumb," I said lamely. "It's just all so weird, right?"

"It's bloody bizarre." He snatched the letter away from me and held it up to the sun. "Look at that watermark—this is real Oxford stationery, all right. But how did they know you were here? And what does that mean, 'Your campus tour was successfully completed?' And—bloody hell, look at yer three choices for the interview time: 'Now,' 'Soon,' and 'Later.' Ye'd think Oxford could do better than that." He gave the letter back to me. "Hey, ye didn't open the yellow envelope."

"What yellow envelope?" I kept the large envelope with the Rules of Succession in it pinned under my arm. "Oh, that! More college stuff, probably. *Fek!*" I shrieked, out of nowhere. "I just thought of something horrible!"

Colin jumped back. "What? What is it?"

Think of something horrible, quick, I urged myself. "Um . . . my parents! All the computers in our house are on a network my dad set up so we could share the printer. If someone is hacking my computer, couldn't that person get into my parents' bank accounts and stuff too?"

"It's a risky situation, to be sure. But don't panic—"

My attempt to change the subject through the use of extreme drama (also known as the Tammy Technique) was working. "And my dad *works* at a bank! What if they hack into his work account? This could cause, like, a worldwide financial disaster of really large global proportions!" I backed away from Colin. "I have to find Mr. McAlister and call them on the oPhone right away."

Colin looked bewildered. "They have courtesy phones right inside the lobby, Mor; if ye're that upset ye should call them right now—"

"I can't!" If I'd known how to make myself froth at the mouth I would have. "They still think I'm at Oxford! I'll just say my wallet was stolen and they should cancel all the accounts and change all the passwords on everything. That should do it. I'll see you later. I'm going to find the oPhone."

"I'll come with ye—"

"*Noooooooo!*" I was practically whinnying. "You stick to the game plan! Look for clues! That's more important."

Before he could argue with me any more, I turned and

ran full speed toward the boardwalk, in the direction of the forest.

Crunch. Crunch. Crunch.

Pant. Pant. Pant.

Ba-boom, ba-boom, ba-boom—

Surely the unicorns could hear me crashing through the trees like a drunken elephant? Where were they?

"Epona!" I was so winded from running I could barely get the word out. My heartbeat hammered in my ears. "Unicorns! Show yourselves, already!"

In the distance, thunder. The ground shook. Then, a trumpet blast—the kind that might come from a long, whorled horn—

"Em Oh Are! Gee A En!

"Morgan has come back again!

"Goooooooo, Morgan!

"Neeeeiiiigh!"

It was the unicorns, galloping through the trees like a four-legged halftime show on steroids.

"You've come back!" Epona circled me once and pranced in place excitedly. "Did you find the Rules of Succession?"

"Yes!" Still panting, I waved the envelope. "I have them right here."

"Sweeeeeeeeeet!" Epona whinnied. "Give it up, unicorns: one more time!"

"Goooooooo, Morgan!

"Neeeeiiiigh!"

OMG, I thought wearily. *Headache. Rapidly. Coming. On.*

"Where were the Rules hidden?" one of the unicorns asked.

I was tempted to say *in my underwear drawer, of course.* But this was no time to wisecrack. "In the library at Oxford. They were written in the *Book of Horns.*"

Awestruck whinnies filled the air. When the noise subsided, Epona explained, "The *Book of Horns* is the most important book in all of Faery, written by the unicorns at the beginning of time. It contains various rules, regulations, points of etiquette, tax codes, the Faery Bill of Rights, emergency phone numbers, that sort of thing."

Now I was confused. "So, wait—if it was written by the unicorns, how come you guys don't have a copy?"

"We did, once, eons ago." Epona hung her head. "But we lost it." There was some background bickering from the herd—*You lost it! No, I gave it to you—did not—did so—*

These unicorns are pretty to look at, I thought, *but not what I would call geniuses.* "Well, it doesn't matter now. The Rules of Succession are in this envelope." I held it out to Epona. "Go ahead, open it."

"Not so fast! We've prepared a ceremony to mark the occasion."

I thought of the gargoyles, lurking in the bushes. "No offense, but we don't have time. The veil is already slipping—"

Epona blinked at me. "We like to put on a show. It's a unicorn thing."

Then, right on cue, the unicorns did a big light wave

with their horns. Two of them, including the little one I'd rescued from Titania, bounded up to me and put wreaths of flowers in my hair.

"Close your eyes, Morganne."

Fine, let's get this over with, I thought. I closed my eyes.

"Destiny is written in the stars, but it also must be chosen. Do you choose yours, Morganne?"

"Uh, sure."

I felt warm horse-breath on my neck, as Epona whispered, "Say 'Yes, I choose my destiny.' That's the way we practiced it."

"Yes, I choose my destiny." Why did I suddenly feel like a Pokémon master? "But—wait—I still have a few questions about this Queen of the Faeries gig—"

But it was too late. Epona blew a little trumpet call through her horn. "Summon the *Book of Horns!*"

Eyes still closed, I offered the envelope again.

"That isn't a book," someone complained.

"I know," I said, annoyed. "It's a photocopy. The *Book of Horns* is non-circulating. It's the best I could do."

"Photocopies are acceptable!" Epona assured the unicorns. "And now, for the first time anywhere, at least that we can recall: the Rules of Succession!"

Epona slit open the envelope with her horn, which also served as a handy booklight. She speared the single sheet of paper it contained and lifted it high.

"What does it say?" I asked.

"Hmmm." She stared at it some more. "It's a bit inscrutable, I'm afraid."

"Can't you read it?" I was getting antsy. "I was told it was written in unicorn."

"Oh, it is, it is. But my vision is not what it was." She shook her horn a bit so the paper slid farther away from her eyes. "There, got it!" she cried. "It's—drat, it's a prophecy."

"A prophecy, a prophecy!" The unicorns stamped their hooves and flicked their tails in excitement. One of them tried to start a spontaneous cheer: "Pee Are Oh! Ef Ee See!"

"It's not Ef, it's Pee Aitch," another unicorn interrupted. Then the cheer degenerated into a heated debate about how to spell prophecy.

"Please, can you just read what it says?" I begged. "The dragon statue on the boardwalk looks ready to take off."

The unicorns quickly pulled it together with a deafening "Goooooo, prophecy!"

Epona returned to the paper and gave a little clearing-her-throat whinny. "It says here: 'The Rules of Succession are contained in 'The Prophecy of the Three Clowns,' which is as follows:

To win the throne is easily done;
The throne is yours when the throne you've won.
The Fey and the Folk are safe at last,
When the Day of Three Clowns is safely past."

All those earnest, shining unicorn eyes were locked on me, filled with hope.

"Clowns?" I blurted. "You've got to be kidding."

"Hang on, hang on." Epona made her horn light a little

brighter and squinted. "My bad. It's not clowns. It's *crowns*. Sorry about that. Oh! Underneath the prophecy it reads: 'P.S.—You'll understand once you're Queen.'" Epona looked kind of embarrassed. "That's it. The Rules of Succession. Any idea what it means?"

I didn't even try to hide my grumpiness. "No. But I guess I'm going to have to figure it out, aren't I?"

Apparently the unicorns took my sarcasm as a resounding yes. "Out! Out! She's going to figure it out! Goooooooooooo, Morgan!"

Several more whinnied cheers and some elaborate pyramid formations later (complete with flying stunts), and the party finally broke up.

Now I was on my own, stomping back through the woods and trying to make sense of this mysterious "destiny" I apparently had no choice but to choose.

After all that, and the Rules of Succession were nothing but a joke. To find out how to become queen I had to understand the prophecy, but before I could understand the prophecy I had to be queen. Brilliant. It reminded me of the way my dad complained that you could only buy health insurance if you weren't sick.

"Typical faery logic," I muttered aloud in frustration. And then I heard a crack, like a tree branch snapping. There was a muffled cry. Directly in front of me, something substantial fell with a loud thud to the forest floor.

Correction: some*one*.

Someone about six feet tall, to be precise. Someone I loved more than anything, who was also the very last person I wanted to see sprawled on the ground in a pile of leaves and broken branches, staring at me as if—*as if*—

"Fek," Colin said, rubbing his head.

I didn't know whether to help him up or run away screaming. "Colin! Are you okay?"

"I'm fine. It wasn't a very high branch. Or a very strong one, apparently. I don't suppose ye'd believe me if I said I was up there pickin' apples."

His tone was light, but he was staring up at me with the strangest expression on his face. Like he was looking at a ghost—*or a half-goddess from the land of faery claptrap*—

Quickly I reached up and yanked the flowers out of my hair.

"Colin—how much did you see?"

"Just—ye know—the bit with you and the uh, unicorns." He sounded like he was about to choke.

"Oh *fek*!" I buried my face in my hands. "Fek fek fek fek *fek*!"

"That last flyin' pyramid routine was damned impressive," he added, his voice strained. "They're very agile beasts, I must say." He scrambled to his feet. "I shouldna followed ye, I know. But I couldn't stand not knowin' what was really goin' on."

"Colin—"

"I knew ye were keepin' something from me, Mor, I could tell. Ye were actin' fairly daft there by the pool.

But, holy cow, girl! Queen of the Faeries? It's a bit much to take in."

"You weren't supposed to see all that," I said helplessly. "I'm sorry." I stepped toward him, but he took a step back. "I'm so sorry you had to find out this way."

"Ye mean ye're sorry I found out, don't ye? Were ye never planning on tellin' me, then?" His voice was flat, but there was a flash of feeling in his eyes. Was it anger? Hurt? Or something worse?

"I-I don't know," I stammered. "I was afraid you wouldn't believe me."

"I'm not sure what to believe, to tell ye the truth."

He stretched out his hand. For a moment I thought it might be a gesture of forgiveness. But it was my hair he was reaching toward, and he came away with a sprig of violets.

He held it in two fingers, as if it were a strange and possibly dangerous object. "Is this part of yer faery princess getup, then?" His voice was thick, almost a sob.

Clearly he was too freaked out to say more, but it didn't matter. Everything I needed to know was written on his face. Confusion. Betrayal. Disbelief. Colin's eyes were a transparent blue pool that reflected only the truth. I could see myself mirrored in them with perfect clarity.

I was a stranger, not the person he'd once stupidly thought he loved.

I was something freakish, even repellent. Something that wasn't supposed to exist.

I was something he didn't—*refused to*—believe in.

It was over. We'd been, literally, too good to be true. And now that the truth was out—

Without thinking, my hand went to the locket around my neck.

He noticed the gesture. "Keep it," he said, his voice cracking.

Then he turned and ran, bashing his way through the forest like he was running for his life.

nineteen

howling, blubbering noises echoed through the forest, and they were all coming from me. I felt like a lead basketball had lodged itself in my chest. All I wanted to do was stay curled up on the ground and scream into the dirt.

Every soap bubble of happiness in the world had popped. At the end of each magic leprechaun rainbow was nothing but a steaming pot of misery.

Colin had discovered the truth of who I was, and now he hated me. Who could blame him? I was a lying weasel of a human being and a completely wimpy excuse for a half-goddess.

While he was the greatest, funniest, sweetest, not to mention hottest guy in the world.

Face it, Morgan, my inner voice sneered. *He deserves someone much better than you anyway.*

Gulping deep breaths, I made the heroic effort to uncurl from fetal position, and rose to my hands and knees on the damp ground. *Yes, he does,* I agreed.

I tried to take some comfort in that realization. Now that he was rid of me, at least one of us would eventually get a chance to be happy. Of the two of us I'd much rather it was him.

Colin deserved nothing but happiness. He'd never lie about who he was to someone he loved. He wouldn't be capable of it. His proud Irish heart was as true-blue as the color of his eyes. Even if I lived to be a hundred and fifty, I knew I'd never find anyone like him again.

If he were lucky, he'd never find anyone like me again, either.

Guess I might as well become Queen of the Faeries, I thought bitterly, as I finally dragged my sorry half-goddess self upright. *There's nothing left in the human world for me.*

Then I took a deep breath, and something weird happened. Extremely weird. Even weirder than cheerleader unicorns.

I felt relieved.

Heartbroken. But relieved.

It was because I wasn't lying to Colin anymore. Sure, I'd lost the only guy I would ever love, but for the first time in ages I wasn't living in *fear* of losing him. I was free. Free to tell the truth, piss people off, screw everything up and not worry about the consequences. Because really, the worst had already happened, right?

Or had it? I did a quick mental review of my to-do list:

I couldn't stay in the Seahorse Cottage anymore; that much was obvious. I'd have to get my stuff out somehow without having to face Colin or Grandpap.

And as long as my own life was ruined, I might as well figure out how to de-throne Titania and save the world. Once I did that I didn't really care what happened to me. X-ray technician? Bring it on.

And I needed to call my parents and spin some plausible explanation for that bus ticket to Wales, so they didn't sic the local constable on my runaway ass.

The fact that *Option Three: Deal with Parents* seemed like the least horrifying item on my list just proved how insanely bad my choices were. But this new, who-cares-what-the-fek-happens attitude of mine made it all strangely easy.

My decision was made: The first act of my miserable, loveless, post-Colin life would be to go to the Tip of the Iceberg cottage, find Mr. McAlister, borrow the oPhone and call my parents.

With his expertise in faery lore, maybe he could help me unscramble those stupid Rules of Succession too.

It'd been less than twenty-four hours since my last visit, but as soon as Mr. McAlister opened the door it was clear that conditions inside the Tip of the Iceberg had gotten shockingly worse—or a lot more "authentic," depending on how you looked at it.

The floor now sloped at a sharp angle. All the furniture had slid from one side of the cottage to the other. At the low end there was water seeping up through the floorboards.

I looked out one of the porthole windows. I saw rising water, dotted with chunks of ice.

"Mr. McAlister!" I had to brace myself in the doorway to stay upright. "I don't want to alarm you, but I think your cottage is sinking."

"I know, isn't it marvelous? It's as if you're actually on the *Titanic*!" He pulled himself hand over hand, clutching curtains and wall sconces to maneuver around the lopsided room. "Authenticity, Morgan! It's my obsession. Why travel the world to see all the things one dreams of? Too much *shlepping*, as they say nowadays. Now, thanks to my new business partner, Castell Cyfareddol can offer all the wonders of the world in one convenient location."

"Sounds like Epcot Center." I grunted, trying not to slide downhill. "What do you mean, your 'new business partner'?"

"The collector whom I met for tennis today. A most regal lady. She proposed a charming wager: If she won, I'd have to do her a special favor upon request. But if I lost, I'd have to perform an important service for her when the time came." He looked at me like this made sense.

"Did she win?" *As if there were any doubt,* I thought.

"In straight sets! She has a powerful net game for a creature so graceful and feminine. But she made me a generous offer nevertheless: In consideration for the favor I am now obligated to perform—and how I wish I could remember what it was!—she promised to assist me in my quest for architectural authenticity here at Castell Cyfareddol. In effect, she is my new partner."

The portholes were completely underwater now. It was like being inside a washing machine. "You mean, she's the one who's making your cottage sink?" I gasped, trying not to panic.

"Yes!" He sounded delighted, even as he lost his balance and slipped across the floor. "And that's only the beginning. All I need to do is tell her I've been pondering ancient Greek column design and, presto! She acquires the Parthenon and transports it here. Really, it's almost like magic. Madame Titania Royale is her name. Quite a handsome woman." His watery eyes were all a-twinkle. "I confess, I am a smitten man."

"Mr. McAlister, I hate to burst your bubble"—for some reason it was the first expression that came to mind—"but that's Queen Titania. She wants to undo the veil between the realms, remember? We have to stop her."

Icy water pooled around his feet, but he just smiled. "Yes, I recall she mentioned something about this veil business. 'Mingling,' she called it. Like at a cocktail party. Personally I think it's a marvelous idea. Why keep people apart? Why can't we all just get along and be friends?"

The cottage gave another sickening lurch, and so did my stomach, but Mr. McAlister's ridiculously old eyes were filled with joy. His smile was positively loopy. I recognized that vague, happy, yet undeniably stupid expression.

"Group hug!" he sang out, beaming and throwing his arms around himself.

Mr. McAlister was under an enchantment.

Fek. I was hoping for his help in figuring out the prophecy, but if he was under Titania's spell I couldn't trust him as far as I could throw one of her magical Manolos.

"The group hug plan sounds awesome," I said with a sigh. "Mr. McAlister, could I use your phone? If it's not underwater, that is."

"The oPhone is completely submersible!" he said proudly. He fished it out of a sodden pocket and tossed it to me. "Rustproof too!"

Mom believed my story about the "Architectural Oddities of Great Britain" field trip, especially when I started spouting off about fluted pilasters—as if I knew what they were. And my strategically edited report about the Oxford campus tour was music to her ears (naturally I left out the part about meeting C. S. Lewis, J. R. R. Tolkien and future literary superstar Tammy "Bubble Ride" Rawlinson).

Luckily my parents had waited to hear from me before calling AmEx, so my credit card was still valid. I'd be able to book myself a room in the hotel for however long it turned out I had to stay at Castell Cyfareddol. But I did have to muster the courage to go back to the Seahorse Cottage and get my stuff. The idea that I might run into Colin was so upsetting that, frankly, I'd rather be sinking on the *Titanic*.

I made it as far as the jockey. Then fear took over, and I

stood, paralyzed. Did I really *need* my clothes and my wallet and my two toothbrushes? Couldn't I just live in the woods and forage for food, like a contestant on one of those reality TV shows that Titania loved so much?

"Giddy-up, girlie! The old man's up to something."

At "giddy-up," the seahorse started bucking up and down by curling and uncurling its long, knobby seahorse tail.

"Not you, Seabiscuit! Easy, boy," the jockey soothed.

"What's the matter with Grandpap?" I didn't bother being surprised that the statue was talking to me. Conversing with lawn jockeys was all in a day's work at this point.

"The geezer's up to something, that's all I'm saying." Wild-eyed, the seahorse reared up high on its tail but the jockey held tight to the reins. "And pick up the newspaper on the way in, wouldja, girlie? Nobody's takin' care of this joint anymore! It's a shame if you ask me. No wonder Biscuit here is so upset."

My heart did flip-flops as I ran to the door of the cottage. The day's paper was still folded burrito style on the doormat. I picked up the paper, pushed the door open and stepped inside.

The first thing I noticed was the smell.

It wasn't a bad smell, though it definitely had overtones of petting zoo. If Glade offered a plug-in air freshener called "Fresh from the Farm," this is what it would have smelled like. Cow poop, horse poop, new-mown hay, damp earth, bread baking, a whiff of smoke from a chimney—all mixed in a base of fresh, clean country air.

A breeze blew through the cottage as if someone had left all the windows wide open. "Hello?" I tapped on the door to Grandpap's bedroom. "It's Morgan. Grandpap, are you up?"

"Give it a push, lass, it isn't locked."

I pushed. I looked. Then I gasped.

I was at the top of the hill overlooking Grandpap's old farm in Ireland. The farmhouse nestled cozily at the far end of the meadow, a ribbon of smoke curling up from the chimney. I half-expected to see a grubby five-year-old Colin come bursting out of the woods. Instead, I saw a man walking toward me across the long sloped meadow, now dotted with wildflowers. He was tall, blue-eyed, maybe in his early thirties, dressed in overalls.

With him was a pretty, auburn-haired woman, in an old-fashioned floral print dress and apron. They held hands as they walked.

"Sorry to keep ye waiting, Morgan!" the man called. "As ye can see, me wife and I are in the middle of celebratin' our anniversary." He grinned, and the familiar twinkle in his eye was unmistakable.

"Grandpap?" I choked out.

"Nobody starts out old, Morgan." He laughed. "Though we all end up that way, if we're lucky."

"Oh my God! I didn't mean to interrupt." I was clutching the doorknob so hard my knuckles were turning white. "I'll go. Do you want me to, uh, close this door?"

"Don't go, dear, not yet!" The woman's voice was warm. "It's lovely that ye've stopped by. I've been achin' to meet ye."

It's Colin's dead granny, I thought in amazement, though that description hardly suited her at the moment.

"This is me wife, Nan," Grandpap said, squeezing her hand. Nan smiled. She was the picture of a young farm wife, clear-skinned and apple-cheeked. Her thick hair was tied back in a loose, long braid.

"What a sweet thing ye are! I can't tell ye how glad it makes me to know Colin has found the right girl." She gazed lovingly at her husband. "Makes all the difference in yer life, ye know. When ye find the person yer meant to share it with."

They looked as happy together as I'd ever seen two people be. That's all it took to make my frozen heart melt. I started to cry.

"Why, what's the matter dear?" Nan looked at her husband worriedly. "Have I spoken amiss?"

"Maybe she's taken a bit of shock, seein' us together like this," Grandpap observed. "She knows yer dead, after all. Or will be someday, as will we all." He handed me a clean cotton hankie from the pocket of his overalls.

"No, that's not it." I blew my nose. "Colin and I had a fight. He found out I'm a-a—"

"Ye're a lass of the old ways, aren't ye?" Nan said, as if it were a perfectly ordinary thing.

"What Nan means is that ye talk to the faeries, and they talk back," Grandpap explained helpfully. I had to smile through my tears.

"Yes." I sniffed. "But it's even more than that."

"Why, she's some kind o' faery princess, William. Any fool

can see that just by lookin' at her." Nan pursed her lips. "And ye know what a thick stubborn head Colin has when it comes to believin' in the old ways. Is that what happened, dear? Did he find out about yer magic ways and run off in a huff?"

I nodded, still blubbering. "He hates me now, I know he does."

"Hush, now! I'm sure he doesn't hate you." She smiled gently, and her eyes came to rest on the locket hanging around my neck. "See, look at that! I doubt he'd have given ye me old locket if he wasn't sure in his heart he'd be lovin' ye forever and a day, no matter what surprises fortune had in store for ye both. It might take a while for common sense to take up residence in that thick skull o' his, that's all."

Grandpap put an arm around his wife's shoulders. "Thick skull, eh? It's a bit of a family trait. Remember our first fight, Nan?"

"Do I! It was on our honeymoon. Happened right where ye're standing, Morgan, there in the Seahorse Cottage. We were six hours into our first full day o' bein' married, and already I'd been tormented by so many bad jokes and God-awful puns I knew I'd made the mistake of me life marryin' this rogue."

"I thought I'd be spending the rest o' me days sleepin' in the barn." Grandpap chuckled. "Though the chickens enjoyed me sense o' humor just dandy, ta very much!"

"There's a reason they call 'em dumb clucks, Billy." She elbowed him fondly. "Anyway, dear, when people love each other they learn to put up with all manner o' quirks. Ye're the girl fer him, that's clear as the River Shannon. Have a little faith in each other. Go talk to him."

"He's probably drownin' his regrets at the pub right now, and preparin' his apology," Grandpap assured me.

Their warm conviction that everything would work out was contagious. If there was a possibility—however slim— that Colin could change his mind and find a way to love me again, that was all I needed to hear.

"I will talk to him. Thanks for the advice." My hand lingered on the doorknob. Curious, I swung it back and forth slightly. It was an ordinary, squeaky-hinged door.

"Grandpap?" I glanced up and around the frame. "This shortcut, let's call it, from the Seahorse Cottage in Wales to your old farm in Ireland half a century ago—how long has it been here?"

"Just since this mornin'. Ye can imagine how happy I was to discover it. I'd been hearin' faraway bits of birds singin' and cows mooin' and even me Nan's sweet voice callin' to me, ever since Colin and I checked in. But this mornin' I went to the lav in the hall to wash me face, came back to the bedroom and look where I found meself!" He stood behind Nan and wrapped his arms around her in a cozy embrace.

"It's Queen Titania's doing. She's trying to mix up the two worlds, and it's getting worse by the minute. I'm going to try to stop her." Then I had a disturbing thought. "If I succeed—I'm not sure what will happen to this doorway."

Grandpap gave the door an appraising look. "Don't worry, lass, the frame's sturdy and it hangs nice and plumb too."

Nan rolled her eyes. "She's sayin' ye might get stuck on one side or t'other, Bill."

He rolled his eyes back at her. "I understand what she's sayin', Granny Nanny! I may be old, but I'm not deaf."

She turned and twined her arms around his neck. "You don't look so very old to me, William O'Grady."

Oh, my. Could interdimensional time-traveling smoochy-woochy be far behind? Time for me to leave. "I'm going to the pub to look for Colin. Thanks for all the advice."

"You just keep wearin' that locket round yer neck, dear," Nan murmured, but she was still looking adoringly at her husband. "It'll remind ye what's important when all else fails."

"And I'll stay here—just a while longer." Grandpap gazed at his wife with a tender smile. "Nan and I've still got some catchin' up to do."

twenty

In the ripley's believe it or not! *department, get-*
ting relationship advice from Colin's deceased granny is going
to be hard to top, I thought, as I collapsed into one of the
chairs at the kitchen table to regroup.

I was a mess. I'd been up for most of two nights in a row.
I had dirt all over me from rolling around in misery on the
ground. I'd worked up a sweat sprinting back and forth to
the forest and was starting to have BO. And now I kind of
smelled like a farm too.

I checked my shoes for cow dung. Was there time to take
a shower and change? Not that I'd be getting that close to
anyone, but still, it was kind of gross.

Then I flipped over the local newspaper I'd tossed
onto the table when I'd arrived and glanced idly at the head-
line.

BIZARRE EVENTS AT FAMED WELSH
RESORT PROMPT INVESTIGATION

Southwest Wales, U.K.—Numerous calls to the authorities from guests at the popular Welsh vacation spot Castell Cyfareddol have prompted an investigation of what a government spokesman will only describe as "escalating occurrences of unexplained phenomena."

Filed complaints include the appearance and disappearance of famous architectural landmarks (one woman claimed that the Eiffel Tower, the Roman Coliseum and the Taj Mahal were all briefly visible outside her hotel room window). Also reported was an infestation of numerous gargoylelike creatures on the grounds, and a "bloody lifelike unicorn," according to one man who identified himself as a psychiatrist but refused to give his name, due to concerns about losing his license.

The most alarming incident reported so far was an encounter with what a witness claims was "a real live dragon." "At first I thought it was an animatronic display," explained Eleanor Cranbrook, a certified X-ray technician and mother of two who was a guest at the resort until she left in a panic yesterday after the alleged dragon incident. "So I held the baby up to see it, and the nasty beast started breathing flames at us! This certainly isn't what I had in mind when I put the deposit down on the room! We were hoping for a budget-minded family holiday, not scorched diapers. I'll be asking for a refund, you may be sure."

Teams of investigators and safety officers have been dispatched from Scotland Yard and are now en route to Wales. Calls to the resort's management office had not been returned by press time. . . .

So long, veil, I thought grimly. How long would it take for the slippage to spill out past the grounds of Castell Cyfareddol? A few more days, maybe? A few more hours?

The needle on the weirdness meter was now firmly pinned in the red zone. The swarms of journalists would be followed by engineers, scientists, the crew of *Mythbusters* and eventually, the locked-and-loaded military forces of NATO and probably most of the rest of the world too.

Time's up, I thought in despair. *It's already all over the papers, the radio, the telly—*

Wait—the telly? Where was Colin?

I felt a goddess-sized dose of adrenaline pump through my body. *He's going to completely freak out when he sees this. And I'm the only one who can explain.*

My hand flew to the locket. The world needed me. True.

Colin needed me more.

I threw down the newspaper and ran.

"Go, come on, go, go, *run,* ye lazy bastards!"

Grandpap knew his grandson well. Under severe mental and emotional stress, Colin had instinctively retreated to the safety of the mothership—in this case, the Achin' Head,

Castell Cyfareddol's very own pub, located off the hotel lobby.

Colin stood in front of the plasma TV at one end of the bar with a remote in one hand and a pint of Guinness in the other. On the screen, sweaty men in colorful uniforms and brutal-looking cleats ran up and down the field, throwing an egg-shaped ball back and forth.

The pub was crammed with people, but Colin watched the game alone. Everyone else crowded at the other end of the bar, their frightened eyes fixed on an even larger TV screen tuned to *BBC World News*. The lead story was the strange goings-on at Castell Cyfareddol.

"Which team are you rooting for?" I snuck up behind him and spoke just loud enough to get his attention. He spun around so fast you'd think a bee stung him.

"If I had me druthers, both teams'd lose. Why shouldn't everyone be miserable?" His face was hard to read. "Did ye come here to watch rugby, or are ye savin' the world one pub at a time? I'd order ye a beer but ye're still not old enough to drink."

"I came to apologize, Colin," I said as gently as I could. "There's so much I need to explain."

"It's not that much, really," he said darkly. "In fact there's only one thing I want to know, Mor—exactly how many lies have ye told me since the day we met?"

"A lot—but only about this one thing, Colin. Only about—well, you know." I glanced at the anxious crowd huddled around the other television. "And soon that secret'll be out too."

He put his drink on the bar and muted the rugby match with a click on the remote. "Forget about all that. How many lies have you, Morgan, told to me, Colin, just today?"

I thought back to the morning. "Well, I didn't actually forget my toothbrush."

"Ye know I ran all the way to the gift shop to buy ye a new one while ye were sleeping?" he exclaimed. "Why in bloody hell would ye lie about a toothbrush?"

"It was because of the painting," I explained desperately. "It was Queen Titania's face!"

And what the fek does that have to do with a toothbrush? The hurt in his eyes spoke louder than words could.

"Ye know I love ye, Mor," he said, his voice breaking. "I love ye like I never expected to love anybody. And I've felt that way for a whole bloody year. And now I find out that ye're not even the actual person I thought ye were. It's fekkin' upsetting, is what it is. I can't even imagine how ye did it. I'm a straight-shootin' bloke, Mor. I could never go through me whole life keepin' a secret from the whole world." His blue eyes burned into me. "I mean, you've even got two names, haven't ye? This 'Morgan, Morganne' business—it's no accident, is it?"

"But it's still *me*!" I wailed. "The name thing is just, you know, *spelling*—"

He threw up his hands. "And here I am like a dunce, worryin' about identity theft! But it's not yer bloody AmEx card or e-mail password that's been nicked. It's *you*. Ye're the girl I love. And *your* identity has been stolen. And mine too somehow." He looked at me, agony on his face. "Because now I don't know who I love. So who does that make me?"

The rugby players on the screen raced back and forth in muted silence. The people at the far end of the bar were talking in urgent, frightened tones. If it hadn't felt like the end of the world before, it sure did now.

I turned to him. "You're the same person you've always been," I said heatedly. "You're Colin. The smart, stubborn, wonderful guy I fell in love with a year ago. I'm sorry for not telling you the whole story about who I am. I'd convinced myself that I couldn't. I thought if you knew the truth about me you'd think I was crazy, or a freak."

I felt myself starting to slide into the blubbering danger zone, but I forced myself to go on. "I was afraid you'd run away from me. I didn't trust you enough. That's my fault. I should have taken the risk. Colin, I made a mistake, and I'm sorry for that." I held his gaze. "But I'm not sorry for who I am."

He fell silent, and his face softened. "Well, I did run away, didn't I? So I didn't deserve yer trust in the end."

At the other end of the bar, a woman screamed. Hysteria spread through the crowd as breaking news headlines crawled across the bottom of the screen. Someone adjusted the volume higher, but there was too much cross talk to hear. The news crawl was enough, though:

Winged fire-breathing dragon sighted in the skies over London—

That did it. A few people raced out of the pub, yelling

into their cell phones. Someone at the bar fainted, which caused a fresh round of pandemonium.

Colin looked at me with new understanding. "This is it, then? This is what ye're supposed to become Queen of the Faeries to save the world from?"

I nodded.

"What is it, some kind of invasion?"

"Not exactly." I took a deep breath—it was time to spill the beans. "Magic is everywhere, all the time, but there's a barrier between the human world and the faery realm. They can see us, we can't see them—at least, most of the time we can't. Unless you're a little kid, or someone who's extra imaginative, like a writer or an artist—"

"Or ye've downed a few too many pints," he said thoughtfully.

"Right." I gave him an ironic look. "It's been that way for ages. But now Queen Titania is removing the barrier, bit by bit. It's just going to be random weirdness everywhere from now on if I don't figure out how to de-throne her and put things back the way they were."

"Titania—ye mean that hatchet-faced wench with the unicorn?" That logical, problem-solving glimmer flashed in his shockingly blue eyes. "D'ye have any clues? Is there a game plan, or what?"

"Not really. Just a prophecy that I can't make sense of. It starts like this:

> *"To win the throne is easily done,*
> *The throne is yours when the throne you've won."*

I shrugged. "Useless, right?"

He looked thoughtful. "In programming that's what we call an infinite loop. Ye need to find the exit. Or rewrite the code." He shook his head. "Sorry I can't be more help, Mor. But ye've got my vote, for whatever it's worth."

It was worth plenty. The world might be rapidly slipping into chaos, and I still had no clue what to do about it, but at least Colin didn't hate me anymore. "Thanks," I said. I even managed a smile.

"No need to thank me; it's pure self-interest," he said wryly. "All me technical trainin' at DCU's not gonna be worth much if we transition to a new faery-world economy."

Together we turned and looked at the large screen. The news anchors were pale and disheveled, and the headlines just kept rolling in. . . .

Blurry cell phone pictures of what look to be living gargoyles appearing on the Internet . . . panel of experts to debate their authenticity after the break . . . stay tuned for live coverage from Castell Cyfareddol . . .

Colin let out a whistle. "Reality's bloody banjaxed, innit? I've spent me whole life believin' the world worked in a rational way, and now this. Everything's changing so fast." He looked at me with a trace of the old tenderness, and my heart quickened.

Then he turned away. "Listen to me! I sound just like Grandpap did when I tried to teach him how to use the cash machines at the bank." Worry clouded his face. "I ought to go back to the Seahorse. If Grandpap turns on the telly he'll get an earful of catastrophe, and who knows what he'll do?"

"Colin," I said quickly, "I should warn you: If you go back to the cottage you're in for another surprise."

"What?" He tensed. "Is something wrong with Grandpap?"

"No, it's just more magic stuff. A portal opened up in the cottage this morning. It's like a doorway—in fact, it *is* a doorway. Anyway, Grandpap went through it, and—"

"A doorway? What, into faeryland?" He looked wild. "I've got to go get him back!"

"Colin, he's fine, really—"

"Tell the barkeep to charge me Guinness to the Seahorse. If anyone still cares about such things, that is." He ran out of the pub before I could say another word.

Should I chase after him? I knew I'd never catch him. Colin was as fit and fast as the tireless rugby players who were still racing around on the screen above my head, as if this were just a normal day and not the beginning of the end of the world.

Or, who knows? Maybe the game was a rerun.

At the far end of the bar the newscasters continued barking out their dire announcements in hoarse, frightened voices to the rapidly emptying pub—

. . . *rash of unexplained phenomena has sparked a national frenzy . . . incidents of looting are being reported . . . citizens advised to stock up on bottled water and canned goods . . .*

* * *

Infinite loop is right, I thought wearily, spinning on the bar stool. *It just goes around in circles.*

The pub was clearing out as people scurried to track down their loved ones and stockbrokers, though maybe not in that order. I was thirsty and jonesing for a Coke, but the bartender had disappeared too. For a moment I considered chugging the remains of Colin's beer. Bad idea. I needed a clear head to work this out, and I knew from past experience that Guinness and I didn't mix that well.

> *To win the throne is easily done,*
> *The throne is yours when the throne you've won.*

I repeated the prophesy for the billionth time. It was clear about one thing and one thing only: I had to *win* the throne from Titania. Not steal it, or take it or trick her out of it. *Win* it.

But how? I grabbed the cocktail napkin from under Colin's beer, and a pen that was rolling around the bar. Across the top of the napkin I wrote *Things a Person Could Win.* Then I made a list:

1. *A rugby match.* Non-aerobic me? Not likely.

2. *A heart.* I'd won Colin's, once. But the jury was still out on whether I'd be able to win it again.

3. *A bet.* Titania had won a bet with Mr. McAlister over

their tennis game, but it was rigged. A real win had to be fair and square, like when Sarah won that free-throw bet. Too bad I couldn't shoot hoops to save my life.

4. *A card game.* Like Grandpap and Mr. McAlister. But I didn't really know how to play cards. I just built houses out of them, which Tammy always blew over before I was done.

5. *A prize.* From a Cracker Jack box, maybe.

6. *An election.* Right. Senior Class President Morgan. Ha, hah, double ha.

You've got my vote. Colin's voice echoed in my brain. Wait—an election?

It kind of made sense. I had to win the job of being the leader of a realm. Isn't that what elections did?

But could I win? Possibly. I spun around again, thinking. In a competition that required skill or endurance or talent I'd be hopeless, but running for office didn't require any of that. You just needed petitions and buttons and slogans, and maybe the chance to make a few speeches.

I wasn't Raphael's ex-girlfriend for nothing. I knew all about elections. I'd watched him run for student council from a ringside seat my whole sophomore year. I was the one puttering around quietly, the decorative girlfriend photocopying flyers as he strategized with his posse and made deals—like the time he traded the onetime use of his new

Infiniti FX50 on a Saturday night for the endorsement of
the school's top jock.

I mean, come on—could winning the throne of the
Queen of the Faeries be *that* different than winning president of the senior class?

Find the exit, Morgan, a voice inside me whispered. *Or
rewrite the code. It's now or never.*

I flipped the cocktail napkin over. First I wrote:

> *To win the throne is easily done.*
> *The throne is yours when the throne you've won.*

I thought hard. Then I added:

> *To win the throne, just do what I wrote:*
> *The winner's the one who carries the vote!*

I stuck the napkin in my pocket.

As poetry goes it's definitely lame, I thought, taking a last
triumphant spin on the bar stool. *But for a First Amendment
to the Rules of Succession, it's not bad. Not bad at all.*

twenty-one

to make it official, i figured that my cocktail napkin amendment should to be added to the *Book of Horns*, since that seemed to be like the Dungeon Master's rule book of Faerydom. And I knew the *Book of Horns* was at the Bod, under Finnbar's care.

So to the reflecting pool I ran. I didn't have any bubble juice handy, so I folded the cocktail napkin into a tiny boat and wrote H.M.S. *Bod* on the side. Then I tucked a pebble in the boat for ballast and carefully placed it in the water. I gave it a nudge to get it started.

It sailed halfway to the center of the pool before it sank— first tipping sharply to one side and slowly going *down, down, down*. Just like the *Titanic*.

I knew Finnbar would find it. He could be flighty about

some things, but so far he'd proven himself a very efficient part-time librarian.

Now it was time to launch my campaign. I didn't have any buttons or bumper stickers. Nor did I have much of a plan, exactly. But I did know what I believed in and what I wanted to say—shouldn't that be enough? And I was standing in a perfect spot by the reflecting pool, where the impact of my words would be doubled.

Better just do it, I thought. *That fire-breathing dragon is probably halfway to Connecticut by now.*

I climbed on top of the low wall surrounding the pool and took a deep breath. "Attention, citizens of all realms!" I yelled. "I, Morgan Rawlinson, hereby declare my candidacy for Queen of the Faeries!"

Strangely, that's all it took. The mere act of stepping out in front of the crowd and declaring myself was more than enough to make people pay attention. Call it a powerful yet totally democratic kind of magic.

First, a clique of tourists who'd been taking pictures of the ocean view put down their cameras and approached, shy but curious. Then another group wandered across the piazza to listen. The members of the second group were uniformly tall and good-looking. At first I thought they might be a bunch of supermodels on vacation, but then I realized they were elves. *Or maybe they're both,* I realized, thinking of Orlando Bloom.

Soon a dozen gargoyles flew in and arranged themselves neatly along the edge of the reflecting pool, as if they'd been carved there. They flexed their bat wings and stared at me with wide, slow-blinking eyes, awaiting my next utterance.

I wondered how long I should stall before making a speech. The bigger the crowd, the better, and I had a feeling that more people (and faeries, and trolls, and pixies and giants) would soon be arriving. And maybe a ticked-off faery queen too.

"Pardon me, make way, please! Part-time librarian coming through!"

It was Finnbar, laboriously making a path through the gathering crowd. Grunting with effort, he pushed an old-fashioned wooden library cart on squeaky casters. It held a cardboard box on the lower shelf and a single, massive volume on top.

"Sorry for the"—*huff*—"delay!" He parked the cart and braced himself, hands on knees, to catch his breath. "What a workout! I had to take the"—*huff*—"land route. I didn't want the *Book of Horns* to"—*huff, huff*—"get wet."

"I thought the *Book of Horns* was non-circulating," I said, grinning.

He nodded in between huffs. "The paperwork to get it out of the Bod was endless! But I thought it might come in useful under the circumstances."

"Thanks for making the trip, Finnbar. I'm really glad to see you." And I was. As faery half brothers went, Finnbar was all I had.

He beamed. "*De nada*, sister! Always glad to pitch in. Now, the faery realm has never had an election before, so remind me: Are beheadings involved? Because I think the

Tower of London just showed up on the croquet lawn behind the hotel."

"No beheadings," I said quickly. "The candidates give speeches, and there are buttons and signs and that kind of stuff. And then everybody votes, and the candidate who gets the most votes wins."

He looked relieved. "That shouldn't take long, then. We'll have it all wrapped up by teatime. Here—these are for you."

He dragged the cardboard box off the bottom shelf of the library cart and proudly showed me its contents: campaign buttons, bumper magnets, T-shirts, baseball hats, you name it. The sayings on the T-shirts were very creative:

No More Mean Queens: Vote for Morganne! This shirt had a picture of Titania's head in a circle with a slash through it.

Meet Morgan: "A Breath of Fresh Air in Faery Queens!" It showed an illustration of me, but with my long, flowing goddess-hair and wearing a faery princess dress right out of a Disney movie.

Whether You're Human or Faery, Morganne Understands! In this one I was pictured holding hands with a leprechaun on one side and Miley Cyrus on the other. Or maybe it was Hannah Montana; I could never remember which wig was which.

"I hope it was all right to put that singing girl on the shirt," Finnbar said worriedly. "I found out later she has two names, just like you. She's not another half-goddess, is she?"

"No, she's human. As far as anyone knows." Amazed, I poked through the contents of the box. "I can't believe you got all this done. But Finnbar, speaking of two names: half of this stuff says Morgan and half says Morganne. Isn't that confusing?"

He put his hands on his hips as if he were going to scold me. "Spelling, spelling, *spelling*! Honestly, Mor-Mor, what difference does it make? It's still *you*."

Whoosh. That was exactly the point I'd tried to make to Colin. Score two points for Finnbar. But I smiled at the nickname. "Nobody's called me Mor-Mor since Tammy was a baby."

He folded his hands over his heart nostalgically. "I know! And she used to call me Bar-Bar. Your mother always thought she meant the elephant from those French picture books." Then Finnbar gestured proudly to the massive tome that sat on top of the cart. "And speaking of books, may I present: the *Book of Horns*! Though after pushing it all the way from Oxford I think they should call it the 'Book of Lead.' This thing weighs a ton."

He patted the cover with pride. "*Love* the amendment, by the way. 'Wrote' and 'vote,' that's so clever and rhymey! I've copied it into the third appendix and it's cross-referenced and footnoted in eleven different places." He flipped through the book. "Would you like to see?"

I shielded my eyes from the sun and scanned the piazza. While Finnbar and I had been talking, hundreds of people and magical beings had gathered. Some were standing, some were setting up portable folding chairs, some were unpacking picnic lunches. The humans and the magical types eyed one another with suspicion. Some got close enough to snap photos, others just looked grim. But for the moment at least, they were waiting peacefully for whatever it was that was about to happen.

In contrast to this low-key milling about, a tight formation numbering a few dozen human-looking types appeared at the back of the crowd and strode purposefully toward us. They gestured animatedly with small notebooks and pencils and were closely trailed by another group, armed with video cameras and boom mikes.

"I'll look at the footnotes later, Finnbar." I gulped at the sight of the cameras and quickly tried to brush the dirt off my ripped jeans and my stinky Natalie Portman's Shaved Head T-shirt—*at least the band'll get some free promo out of this,* I thought. "Right now I think I have to uh, meet the press."

Finnbar turned and saw the reporters approaching. "Oh, goody!" he squealed. "The media have arrived! Now we can begin." He heaved the *Book of Horns* off the library cart and into the cardboard box. Then he flipped the cart on its side, turning it into an instant podium. One of the reporters ducked forward and stuck a microphone on top.

Finnbar stepped forward and tapped the mike.

"Testing, testing, check check. Am I on?" He cleared his throat. "Greetings, journalists! I am Finnbar, your friendly neighborhood librarian-turned-campaign manager, press secretary and now—television personality!" He blew a kiss to the cameras and went on.

"It is my distinct pleasure to introduce this remarkable candidate for Queen of the Faeries. Your questions have not been pre-screened, and the candidate's answers will be spontaneous and unscripted. It's possible they may make no sense whatsoever! We're really just winging it here, so fingers crossed."

He pulled a large stopwatch out of his pocket. "I will permit one minute for questions, one minute for answers, thirty seconds for follow-ups, fifteen seconds for clarifications, five seconds for denials, two seconds for shouted objections—"

"Finnbar, thanks," I interrupted. "But I think I can handle this."

"You're the boss, boss!" he said agreeably, then turned back to the mike. "Meet the next Queen of the Faeries— Morrrrrrrrrrgan Rawlinson!"

There was some polite, lukewarm applause as Finnbar relinquished the podium. Hesitantly I stepped forward. Flashbulbs popped. The boom mikes were lowered until they hung right in my face.

"Hello." Through the mike I sounded like a scared kid, even to me. "I'm Morgan Rawlinson, and I'm running for Queen of the Faeries."

The questions flew at me rapid-fire.

"Ms. Rawlinson! What made you decide to run for queen?"

"What are your qualifications for the job?"

"As queen, how will your policies differ from Titania's?"

"Do you believe in keeping the human and faery realms separate?"

"Is it true that you're only a half-goddess?"

"Some of the old myths refer to you as Titania's daughter. Can you comment on that?"

"Hang on a minute!" I held up a hand and waited for them to be quiet. "I can answer all your questions if you just let me talk. No, it wasn't my idea to run for Queen of the Faeries. I haven't even finished high school yet. But the unicorns told me that Titania was going to undo the veil between the magic realm and the human realm, and I knew that would cause chaos. As, obviously, it has."

At that moment a cold, winged shadow swept over the crowd. We all raised our eyes to the sky. It was the dragon, swooping and circling overhead, leaving a shower of sparks in its wake. Even the magical beings looked nervous.

"I do think the realms should stay separate. It's not that the human realm and the magic realm are enemies. In fact, we need each other." I thought of Tolkien. "Without the faery realm, humans would have a lot fewer cool books to read, for one thing. And human kids would be really bummed if there were no Tooth Fairy or Santa Claus. But humans get scared easily too. Humans like to know what the rules are and how things work. That's why we invented science, and multiplication, and stuff like that. It helps keep our lives organized. I mean, my mom's whole job is keeping people's closets organized and drawers decluttered. People like my mom serve a vital function in human society!"

That last improvised bit about my mom's personal organizer business had put me in real danger of cracking myself up. But I kept going. "Take it from a teenager: I know that having too many rules is a drag. But you have to have some if we're all going to be able to live in peace and harmony."

Ugh. Now I was starting to sound like a folk song. The reporters were copying down my words at a furious pace. The red lights on the cameras indicated they were on, and they were all pointing at me. And the crowd was growing larger by the minute.

If I'd known I was going to be on TV I definitely would have changed into clean clothes, I thought. At least I was still wearing the locket. If Colin was watching this on TV somewhere he might see that, anyway.

"How does this affect your plans for college?" one of the reporters called out.

"I don't know," I said truthfully. "I might have to sacrifice my own plans for the good of everyone. But the way I see it, if the world gets completely wrecked by Titania, none of us will get the chance to do what we want with our lives. The human realm is already freaking out because of her meddling." I glanced upward again. "And you guys in the faery realm don't seem too happy, either."

There were many nervous looks skyward and cries of *Ow! Ow! Ow!*, as sparks from the dragon's fire breath floated down and landed on people's heads.

"But isn't it too late to change course?" a gnarly-looking troll yelled from the back. "Do you honestly think a messy, smelly, half-grown half-goddess like you can fix this mess?"

I ignored the smelly part—especially coming from a troll. "You're right: some problems are too big for one person to fix, but that just means we all have to do our part. Right now, my part is taking the throne away from Titania and restoring the veil between the realms. Your part might be something different." I leaned in closer to the mike, just the way I'd seen Raph do at the graduation ceremony. "That's why they call it community service. If everybody *in* the community contributes something *to* the community, then the world keeps working. That's really all I have to say."

"Ask them to vote for you," Finnbar whispered in my ear.

"Oh, right! And I hope you'll vote for me. Thanks, everybody."

"Save the world! Vote for Morganne!" Finnbar yelled, pumping his fists in the air. "Save the world! Vote for Morganne!"

Scattered portions of the crowd took up the chant. The reporters had all turned to face their cameras and spoke intently into handheld mikes as they glanced down at their notes. I was curious about what they were saying, but mainly I felt relieved. My first press conference was over. I hoped it would be my last.

Among the reporters, I spotted one guy who seemed familiar. Buff, prematurely gray, kind of too good-looking to be true. "Hey!" I turned to Finnbar, realizing where I'd seen him before. "Isn't that the anchor dude from CNN? Oh my God, my mom has such a huge crush on him."

"You mean Anderson Cooper?" Finnbar leaned over to me and spoke confidentially. "Actually, he's one of ours. He's a student at the Elven School of Journalism. The cable gig is just an internship. I think he gets interdimensional extra credit."

Finnbar rummaged inside the cardboard box, found a banner that read "Campaign HQ" and draped it over the podium. As people came by to get a closer look at me he handed out leaflets and signs, buttons and bumper stickers. I shook hands and waved.

Somebody handed me an adorable tiny pixie baby to kiss. *This running for office thing isn't so bad,* I thought, as the flashbulbs popped. *Who knows? If I ever get to finish high school, maybe I'll even run for student council.*

the first sign of titania's arrival came moments later, when the water in the center of the reflecting pool began to churn. It sprayed upward, only a few feet at first, and then a few feet more, until there was an actual geyser erupting from the center of the pool.

Then, what looked like a scaled-down version of Johnny Depp's ship from *Pirates of the Caribbean* came rising out of the geyser, nose-first. The carved figurehead on the front of the ship was the spitting image of Titania. You could easily spot the resemblance because the queen herself stood at the helm of the ship, waving and blowing kisses at the crowd. She was dressed piratically, I guess you could call it: black lace-up bodice, a diamond-studded eye patch and a sword slung around her hip.

"Hello, fellow beings!" she yelled, peeking out from

beneath her eye patch. "How do you like my campaign boat?"

There were pockets of cheering. The press, who only a few minutes before had been completely fascinated by my every comment, abruptly turned their backs to me so they could capture shots of Titania's highly theatrical entrance.

"I am *so* ready for my close-up, darlings!" she cried, as she stepped daintily onto dry land. "Now let the worshipping—oops, I mean the campaigning—begin!"

She preened and posed as the cameras whirred and clicked, until a firm voice from the back of the press corps called out: "Your Majesty! How did you end up having to defend your throne after all these years as queen?"

She dropped the beauty pageant act and grabbed the nearest mike. "You know, Anderson," she crooned, "that is an excellent question, and I think all of us deserve to hear the answer. Especially me, so I can dish out the appropriate punishment." She narrowed her eyes and surveyed the crowd. "Somebody, anybody, *please* tell me: Where did this ridiculous *amendment* about letting the people choose their own queen come from?"

I stepped forward. "I wrote it."

"There's no rule that says you can do that." Her voice dripped with ice, but her eyes were throwing off more sparks than the dragon.

"There's no rule that says I can't." I turned to Finnbar. "Is there?"

He placed one hand on the *Book of Horns.* "There is not," he said, sounding shaky.

Titania clucked her tongue. "*Et tu*, Finnbar? I'm so disappointed." I saw his lip tremble, but he said nothing. Titania wheeled to face the crowd. "Fine, then. Let's get this nonsense over with. Miss Queen Wanna-Be here already gave her *tediously* sincere speech. I mean, get me some insulin, quick!"

That got a few mean-spirited laughs from the trolls. She smirked. "Now I'll give my far superior speech, which will be short and to the point. Then you'll all vote for me, and I'll continue the magnificent job I've done all these years of being your queen. This embarrassing election episode will be forgotten for all eternity. Are the cameras rolling?"

The cameramen nodded. A gargoyle swooped down and powdered Titania's nose as she yanked off the eye patch. "Come in nice and close, fellas—watch the claws, please!— I'm going to connect with my subjects now." The gargoyle flew off, and the cameraman counted off on his fingers— *five, four, three, two*—

"Ahem! My fellow Faery Folk," Titania purred, gazing wistfully into the lens. "You know me as your loving, wise, compassionate and enviably chic ruler, Titania! I have always been queen. I'm queen right now. And rest assured, I will always be your queen."

She batted her eyes and smiled sweetly. "Given that no one else but me has ever occupied my throne, I feel almost silly saying this. But ask yourselves: Who is more qualified for this position? Me! Who throws the most fabulous parties? Me! And if that isn't enough to earn your vote: take a moment to reflect. Look deep in your hearts. Do you remember how kind and generous and compassionate I've been to you all these many, many millennia?"

As one, the crowd shivered in fear.

"I can see that you do." She smiled icily. "Remember that cozy feeling of gratitude and terror when it's time to cast your vote. And, cut."

She tossed back her hair. "Any questions? No? Then let's get the formalities over with—"

"I have a question," I called. I heard Finnbar suck in his breath, but I was too pissed off to be afraid. "Titania, removing the veil between the faery realm and the human realm will throw the world into chaos. How can you possibly justify your actions?"

"It's an offensive stereotype to assume that mortals don't want magic in their world. There's nothing humans love better than hocus-pocus and mumbo jumbo. Look at the stock market, for heaven's sake!" She scowled. "I know the poor ignorant mortals will be upset for a while, but they'll get over it. A teensy bit of rioting, famine, bloodbath, revolution . . . so what? It'll pass."

"But not without a fight—and humans have been known to defend themselves to the death when they feel threatened," I argued. "This could be the start of a human-faery war that would destroy everything!"

"Hear hear!" Finnbar applauded wildly. "That makes good sense!"

Titania's hand moved to the hilt of her sword. "I'm afraid I don't agree. Humankind will absolutely adore my plan to 'unveil' the world; you'd have to be crazy not to. And I can prove that I'm right!"

There was a loud reaction from the crowd. Titania waved her sword in the air.

"Quiet down, everyone! The 'Queen Titania 4-Evah Campaign' will now present a completely voluntary endorsement—from a human!" Titania gestured behind her to the pirate ship. "Don't mind his appearance; I just fished him out of the sea."

From the hold of the pirate ship, through a trapdoor on deck, Mr. McAlister emerged. He was soaking wet, with frost on his hair and icicles hanging from the ends of his sleeves. He wore a life jacket stamped RMS *Titantic*, but the *c* was crossed out and an *a* was written in.

"Now, Devyn dear, step up to the mike and tell everyone how even *humans* prefer me as queen!" Titania held the microphone to his lips. "Go ahead, just do it like we practiced."

Through chattering teeth, Mr. McAlister recited: "I am Devyn McAlister, the original designer of Castell Cyfareddol. In the past I could only build replicas of different architectural styles. But thanks to Titania, soon I'll be able to offer authentic buildings for my customers to enjoy! The Tower of London! The Taj Mahal! Castell Cyfareddol will grow faster and better than I ever dreamed of. My accountant predicts that this will increase our number of visitors by twenty percent a year. It's good for me, it's good for the economy and it's good for humans everywhere. Thank you."

Titania snatched back the mike. "Thank you, soggy

human! I am Queen of the Faeries, and I endorse this message!"

As phony as it was, the crowd seemed swayed by McAlister's speech. I heard snatches of comments—*wow, endorsed by a human . . . twenty percent a year is a lot . . . I've always wanted to see the Taj Mahal but I hate to fly . . .*

"But Mr. McAlister is under an enchantment, can't you see that?" I yelled over the hubbub. Nobody was listening. "He doesn't know what he's saying!"

"Silly girl," Titania growled in my ear. "A person doesn't have to know what he's saying to get on TV. And you call yourself a half-human! You're just mad you didn't think of it first."

She put the mike back to her lips. "Now, come on, everybody! Let's stop wasting time and get on with this ridiculous vote. I've got a realm to rule!"

twenty-two

Vote! Vote! Vote!

The piazza overflowed with human beings and magical beings. They spilled out onto the boardwalk and the beach. Pixies perched in the branches of the trees, and leprechauns rode on the backs of the topiary rabbits, hopping here and there trying to get a better view.

As the rock stars on ironically low-brow vacations, couples on budget-minded second honeymoons and disgraced members of the royal family shrieked and got out of the way, a pair of giants lumbered back and forth through the crowd, carrying really big signs that read "Titania Rules" and "Stick to the Queen You Know!"

Where was my support? Where were the unicorns? Where, oh where, was Colin?

Vote! Vote! Vote!

The chant was insistent. There was no way to wait any longer.

Finnbar took hold of the podium microphone and announced in a solemn voice, "All right, time for the election! First we register eligible voters, ballots will be distributed, filled out in number two pencil, then sealed and transported in armored cars to the offices of Price Waterhouse . . ." He paused and saw the *enough, already* look on my face. "Never mind, we don't have time for all that. If you're here you can vote! How about a show of hands? All in favor of Queen Titania staying queen, raise your hands!"

About half the hands I could see went up. To my eye it seemed that Titania easily took the gargoyle vote, and most of the trolls. But there were literally thousands of votes to count.

Finnbar was overwhelmed. "I'm going to need a little help, please," he cried. Obligingly, the swarm of fireflies appeared from nowhere and whizzed around the crowd, counting. Then they formed a blinking numerical scoreboard directly over our heads.

Finnbar waited until the figures stopped tabulating. He whistled in admiration at the total. "What a big number! That's going to be hard to beat. All right—now raise your hand if you want Morganne to take over as queen!"

More hands went up. I seemed to have strong support among the pixies, humans and elves. The leprechauns looked evenly split. The fireflies scattered and re-formed, new numbers flickering until the tally was final.

My total was two votes short of Titania's.

"I win, I win!" Titania danced around, waving her pirate sword in victory. "What will I wear to the coronation? Must go shopping, must go shopping—"

There was a sound like distant thunder. The ground shook beneath our feet.

"Stop the tally," Finnbar yelled.

From the back of the press pool I heard Anderson Cooper's steady voice: "Election still too close to call; more voters are arriving at the polls, stay tuned for updates—"

As it got closer the sound grew more distinct. It was the sound of hooves, rhythmically pounding the earth. In the nearby hills I saw a mass of dust racing along the ground toward us, shot through with flashes of light and the glint of silver.

The unicorns were here! They leaped from the hillsides onto the boardwalk and then to the piazza. The crowd parted and the beautiful animals galloped through. They were led by Epona. Her silvery tail waved behind her proudly, like a flag of liquid metal.

On her back, white as a sheet and clutching her mane for dear life—Colin.

"Bloody hell," he cried, as he slipped off her back and nearly fell to the ground. "That's a bit different than riding a bike, I'll tell ye that much." He gave me a shaky grin and almost lost his balance again. Epona nimbly blocked his fall with her horn.

A moment later, Grandpap trotted up on another unicorn. He was his real age again but looked as hearty and vigorous as I'd ever seen him. Unlike Colin, he was perfectly comfortable on horseback.

"Whee!" He jumped confidently to the ground. "Haven't had a good gallop like that in years! Makes a fella feel young all over again." He gave me a broad wink.

I'd never been so glad to see anyone as I was to see these two. I threw my arms around Colin. "How did you know to come?"

"Are ye kiddin', lass?" Grandpap gave his mount a hearty muzzle-rub, which the unicorn seemed to appreciate. "Yer famous! This election business is all over the telly. We would've got here sooner but we were lollygagging on the farm; the news got to us a wee bit late."

Colin gave me a wry look. "Ye were right about the surprise, Mor. Though it was a happy one, once I picked me jaw up off the floor. But it was surely good to see Granny— well, Nan, again."

"Aye, that it was." Grandpap's voice was full of emotion. "Lucky these fine ponies here came by and picked us up, or we'd still be walkin'. But enough jibber jabber, we're here for the votin'. Where do I put me mark?"

"Sorry, you're too late," Titania barked. "Polls are closed."

"No, they're not," Finnbar said, hands fluttering nervously. "We haven't declared a winner yet."

"Well then," Grandpap declared, "I vote for Morgan here."

"I do too." There was an unmistakable glow shining in

Colin's eyes. "I know this girl as well as I know anyone, and I know ye could have no finer queen than she'll be."

Titania howled with contempt. "'Knows her well'? Please! He didn't even find out she was part goddess until today!"

"That's not entirely true," Colin said firmly. "I may not have understood it, but I always knew there was something special—something *magical*—about Morgan. Ye'd have to be blind not to see it."

He took both of my hands in his own. "What a stubborn-headed fool I've been, Mor. When I think of what ye must've gone through, having to keep such a big secret from everyone—even from me—just so as not to upset the world the way this selfish biddy seems eager to do. That takes a kind of courage that few people have."

"His grandmother talked some sense into him," Grandpap said to me as an aside. "Told him some of the old stories about the half-goddess Morganne too. Shoulda seen the look on his mug!"

Colin turned to the crowd. "The truth is, Morgan Rawlinson's always been a goddess in my eyes. And I'd be proud and happy to see her as Queen of the Faeries."

It may not have been very queenly, but I couldn't help it. I jumped up and kissed him, right on the lips. The fireflies obligingly formed themselves into a blinking heart shape encircling our heads, which made us laugh so hard we had to stop smooching.

"Don't look so happy, chickie," Titania snarled. "Even with these two highly questionable votes counted, it's still a tie. And I'm already queen, so in case of a tie I win. That's a rule."

"Really? I don't recall seeing that in the *Book of Horns.*" Finnbar hoisted the book into his arms and ruffled through the pages in a panic.

"Call it the Second Amendment," she said with a sneer. "I just thought of it."

"But what about the unicorns?" I laid my hand on Epona's warm neck. "They have to vote too."

Epona half-lowered her long lashes. "We voted absentee. You know how shy we are."

"Ha! The unicorn vote has already been counted! Now, about my coronation . . ." Titania's evil chuckle was the only sound to be heard.

"Wait a second," I said suddenly. "Finnbar! *You* haven't voted yet!"

"I can't." Finnbar was practically twitching with anxiety. "I'm holding the book, see?"

Colin held out his strong, reassuring hands. "No worries, pal. I'll hold this tome while ye cast yer ballot. It's yer right and yer duty, as a citizen."

"And as a librarian," I added.

Trembling from head to foot, Finnbar handed the book to Colin. He looked at me, and then at Titania. All the television cameras were trained on him. A dozen microphones were suddenly in front of his face.

"Oh my!" He giggled nervously. "I feel very, very important right now. I feel like what I say next will actually make a difference in the world. Like humble, ordinary me has the power to affect the course of history!"

He stopped shaking, and his voice gained strength. "In fact, I feel so important that I'm not scared anymore. And since I'm not scared anymore, I cast my vote for—" He paused for effect, then pointed at me. "Morganne! Let's hear it for Queen Morganne!"

"Nooooooooo!" Titania screeched, before the crowd could react. "Look at him! He's not old enough to vote! His vote doesn't count."

"He's fekkin' immortal!" I shouted. "How could he not be old enough?"

My supporters took up the cry. Finnbar tapped his chin thoughtfully, but now there was a gleam of mischief in his eye. "Hmmm. If you're going to judge solely by appearances, then Mother dear does have a point. But that problem is easily fixed."

And then, right before our eyes, Finnbar changed. First he made himself younger, until he was about Tammy's age.

"Oops!" he squealed, in his little boy voice. "Wrong direction, hang on."

Then he made himself older.

And older.

And older.

Until he looked like—

Correction: until he *was*—

"Mr. Phineas?" I croaked.

* * *

the crowd finally got to go wild. there was cheering, yelling, more firefly pyrotechnics, and revved-up unicorns doing a victory wave with their light-up horns. But all I could do was stare at Mr. Phineas—I mean Mr. Finnbar—oh, *phek it*—Phinnbar!

"You?" I still couldn't believe it, but there was no mistaking that shiny bald head surrounded by wild gray frizz. Even the ear hair was visible.

He chuckled. "You have to admit it was very clever, that bit with the 'check your e-mail at 8 P.M., follow instructions exactly!' Ha-ha! But I did *so* want you to come for a visit! It'd been ages since we'd seen each other!"

Only then did I notice that Colin and Grandpap were staring at Phinnbar too—Colin in amazement, Grandpap with a look of fond recognition.

Colin sputtered. "B-but—when you were a little boy there, a moment ago—that was you too then?"

"They're all me, Colin, old pal." Phinnbar grinned, revealing his yellow teeth. "Don't you remember me?"

"Bloody hell!" Colin cried. "Of course I remember ye! Ye're Finn; ye were my imaginary friend when I was just a wee boy-o. And then I went to school and I told ye to be gone, because I was too old for such babyish ways." I could swear Colin was blushing now. He stuck out his hand to Phinnbar. "What a rude dolt I was. I feel like I owe ye an apology, there, Finn."

Phinnbar took Colin's hand graciously. "No need. It

happens all the time with you mortals. And as you see, old friends never disappear for good."

"He used to come visit me and Nan too, after ye were grown," Grandpap added, crossing his arms. "She made him cups o' tea; oh, he'd tell us marvelous stories, marvelous! We always enjoyed yer visits immensely, Finnsie. Do ye know, it was Finnsie's idea for me to come back to Wales on me anniversary to begin with! Ye stopped by the house just last week, didn't ye? We had a long chat about it. Ye stuck the idea in my head like gum to the bottom of a chair."

"Ye daft old thing, why the bloody hell didn't ye tell me that a faery told ye to come here?" Colin sputtered. "I gave up a weeks' work for it, ye know!"

"Didn't tell ye?" Grandpap cuffed him on the side of the head. "How many times did we tell ye about the wee folk livin' in the fields and the forests? And did ye ever stop mockin' us long enough to listen?"

"All right, settle down, Paps—"

"Ye wouldn't believe in *him*, a faery lad ye'd seen with yer own eyes," Grandpap jerked his head toward Phinnbar, "but ye have no trouble believin' in them bloody Gloogles and Internets, and I defy ye to show me where those thing-amabubs live. So which one of us is daft, then, tell me that?"

Titania, meanwhile, was crumpled on the ground like a broken pirate doll.

"Don't *any* of you want to change your vote?" she whimpered. "Just a few people, that's all it would take. Anyone? It would really cheer me up!" But now that Titania was powerless her former supporters seemed to have evaporated.

She clambered to her feet and went over to Grandpap. "How about you, you adorable old man, you?" she pleaded. "Surely you can appreciate how the charms of experience *deserve* to triumph over the callowness of youth?"

"Sorry dear, but I've met yer type before, when I was in the service," Grandpap said, not unkindly. "Morgan's got my vote. I'll have none of ye, thanks."

An evil shadow crossed her face, which she quickly covered with a phony smile. "But if I'm queen again, I can make it so you can live on that adorable little farm forever, frozen in time with your charming deceased bride, back when she wasn't so deceased," she cooed. "There's no need to be old and lonely, is there?"

Grandpap hesitated, and my heart crawled halfway into my throat. Finally he spoke. "No thanks, lady. I'll be buyin' the farm on me own steam, soon enough. Though I must say, it was a glorious anniversary—well worth the trip." Maybe it was a trick of the light, but it looked like there was an actual twinkle in Grandpap's eye.

"Ah, ah—*achoo!*"

I'd forgotten all about the poor enchanted architect. The ice had melted and now he was standing in a puddle, shivering and sneezing. I handed him a crumpled but mostly clean tissue from the pocket of my jeans. "Bless you, Mr. McAlister. Maybe we should get you a blanket or something."

"As you wish, Your Majesty!" Before I could say another word, a team of elves dressed like medics had wrapped Mr.

McAlister in foil blankets, like he'd just finished running a marathon. A winged pixie, looking like Tinker Bell in a nurse's uniform, fluttered around his head and spooned hot cocoa into his mouth. He gave me a thumbs-up and talked between spoonfuls.

"Congratulations, Morgan dear—*yum*! Not enchanted"—*mmmm*—"anymore! Sorry for my"—*slurp*—"embarrassing remarks earlier, I don't know what got into me. More marshmallows, please!"

I'm gonna have to be careful giving orders from now on, I thought.

Phinnbar now held a clipboard and was busy ticking items off a list. "Throwing a coronation on such short notice, *tsk tsk*! But I'll do my best. Your Majesty?"

It took me a minute to realize he meant me. "Uh, what?"

"Will you be bringing a royal consort to the coronation? I'm trying to do a seating chart." He tapped his pencil on the clipboard. "For dinner we have beef, chicken and vegetarian options."

"I'll be her date. If she'll have me, that is." Colin put his arm around my waist. "And chicken suits me fine."

I turned and slid my arms around his neck. "One chicken, one vegetarian," I said, as romantically as I could.

Phinnbar clucked his tongue and made marks on the clipboard. Colin held me tightly. "My girlfriend, the half-goddess," he murmured. "And now ye're Queen of the Faeries! Ye must have had some wild adventures. I want to hear all about 'em. If ye choose to tell me, o' course."

"No more secrets," I whispered in his ear. "Hey, would you like to know why you were so sleepy when you came to Connecticut? There was this enchantment, see, and—"

"At the moment I'm just curious about what it'd be like to kiss royalty," he said, cutting me off. "But if that's classified information I'll completely understand."

"Classified . . . ?" I was going to make some kind of wisecrack but somehow we were already too busy locking lips for that.

"Ahem! Your Majesty? Royal Consort? Enough with the tonsil hockey." Phinnbar clicked his heels together officiously. "It's time for your coronation!"

Colin and I slowly floated back to earth. I looked down at my grubby jeans and T-shirt. Colin's outfit wasn't much better, plus his pants were covered with unicorn hair.

"I feel like a slob," I confessed to Phinnbar. "My first coronation, and I'm a total fashion disaster."

"No worries, Your Eminence! We have people to take care of this kind of thing. Bring on the royal stylists!" No sooner did he say it than luxurious scarlet robes were draped around our shoulders. Somebody did something fancy with my hair, and a golden crown was placed on my head. And a handsome medal reading "Royally Excellent Boyfriend" was pinned to Colin's robe.

"I feel like the bloody prom king now," Colin cracked. I made sure to hang my locket on the outside of the robe, where everyone could see it. Grandpap looked ready to burst with pride.

"Spectacular!" Phinnbar declared. "Now, it's been so long since the last coronation, nobody really remembers what the ceremony is supposed to include. Even the *Book of Horns* is vague on the subject; it merely says that 'appropriate revels should ensue.' But the unicorns have offered to do a little something, and in the absence of any other entertainment I say let's go with it." He pointed. "Cue unicorns!"

The unicorns proceeded to perform the halftime coronation show to end all halftime coronation shows. Formation gallops, synchronized leaping, gymnastic tricks and elaborate unicorn pyramids. They ended by spelling out LONG LIVE QUEEN MORGAN(NE) with their twinkling horns, as the fireflies provided a laser light-style display overhead and the sea of onlookers cheered.

"They're bloody fantastic," Colin whispered to me. "Beijing Olympics pales in comparison. So much better to see these large-scale spectacles in person too, the television cameras can never really do 'em justice."

Which made me start to hyperventilate, as I suddenly realized—*television cameras*?

I looked around the piazza. The cameras were still rolling, filming the festivities. Reporters wandered everywhere, gathering on-the-spot reaction from spectators and blathering all the usual self-evident commentary into their microphones.

"Phinnbar?" I tugged on his sleeve. "Where exactly is all this being broadcast?"

He looked at me like I was dense. "Everywhere, of course!

It's the biggest news story ever, practically. According to the latest Nielsen data, ratings are through the roof."

"Everywhere?" I gulped. "Meaning, in the human realm too? Even in Connecticut?"

"*Especially* Connecticut!" he crowed. "I mean, how often does their very own hometown girl get elected queen?"

twenty-three

Oh, phek.

How could I be so stupid? Of course all of this was being broadcast. My campaign speech was probably a YouTube sensation by now.

I thought of Tammy, glued to the TV. Except instead of *SpongeBob*, she'd be watching *My Sister, the Faery Queen*. On every channel.

Imagine the princess outfits she's picking out right about now, I thought. *She'll be mighty pissed off to have missed the coronation.*

And what about Sarah, and her boyfriend, Dylan, and all my other friends from school? Would being Queen of the Faeries boost my chances at winning senior prom queen next year?

And—oh yeah—my parents. I could just picture Mom,

white-knuckled, clutching the coffee table and fanning her-self with a Princeton brochure, while the voice mail picked up call after hysterical call from her astonished friends. At least I'd given a major shout-out about how declutter-ing was vital to human happiness. That had to score a few points.

And, nearby: my dad, taking up smoking again twenty years after he quit.

I even thought of Raph. I had to admit, it would be pretty satisfying to see his smug face seething with envy. Ruler of a realm totally pwned valedictorian.

But really—this was an *epic* fail! After all my obsessing about keeping goddess-me secret, now every single person within remote-control reach of a TV set was in on it. My fantasy of freelancing on the down-low as part-time Queen of the Faeries while faking my way through another year as Morgan Whatshername, third Senior from the left, had just popped like a Mr. Bubble bubble that floated too close to a ceiling fan.

But it isn't about you anymore, my inner get-your-act-together voice reminded me. *It's time to save the world, re-member?* Messing with the heads of the mortals was exactly what I'd been supposed to prevent, and in fifteen minutes as queen I'd wreaked more havoc in that department than Titania ever had. Was there any way to undo the damage? It was time for Queen Me to find out.

"That was so cool, everybody, thanks!" I yelled, waving to the crowd. Then I turned to Phinnbar and Epona. "The 'appropriate revels' were awesome, and I really appreciate all the fuss. But I want to get to work fixing stuff, like I promised during the campaign."

"Now?" Phinnbar looked hurt. "What about your dinner? I thought we might have a little dancing after."

"That would be fun." I was pretty hungry, to be honest. "But think about those poor mortals. They must be getting more freaked out by the minute. I want to put the veil back right away. So, stupid question: What do I do?"

"It's very simple," Epona explained. "As Queen of the Faeries, you have unimaginable powers. If you decree that the veil between the realms is restored, it shall be restored."

I glanced at Titania, who was sprawled on a nearby bench having a weepy fit while Mr. McAlister patiently handed her tissue after tissue. "And what about the magic stuff that's already gotten loose?" I asked. "All those gargoyles and the dragon—and these television broadcasts!" I thought of my family and cringed. "Can I decree that everybody in the world forgets what happened?"

"Your powers are vast, Your Majesty, but not *that* vast," Epona said thoughtfully. "Erasing the memory of the whole human race is a big job. But you can certainly make the mortals a bit foggy about what's happened. Rest assured, they'll come up with some perfectly rational explanation for whatever memories remain."

"Sounds like it's up to you, love." Colin gave me a supportive wink. "Just say the word."

"Okay." I took a deep breath. "I want the veil between the realms restored. I want everything put back the way it was before Titania started to mess it up. And I want the human realm to forget all the magic stuff that's happened, or at least not be freaked out by whatever it was they think they saw. Let no evidence remain."

I did a z-snap in the air, just to give my first act of queenly authority some oomph.

An icy wind blasted across the piazza. My robe and Colin's billowed outward like red velvet sails. A strange buzz traveled up my spine until my scalp tingled. It was like the static shock you sometimes get from touching a balloon, only much, much weirder.

Whoosh. The topiary bunnies were shrubs once more.

Whoosh. The gargoyles resumed their rightful positions along the balustrade.

Whoosh. Whoosh. Whoosh. One by one, the magical beings on the piazza marched calmly to the reflecting pool. Some waited on line to board the pirate ship. Others just dove in. All of them seemed ready, willing and able to go back to where they belonged.

Almost all of them, that is.

Titania stood reluctantly at the edge of the pool, whining, "But how can I *possibly* show my face in the faery realm again? All I know how to do is be queen! Without my career, who am I?"

Phinnbar hobbled over to her with his crooked old-man gait and threw his spindly arms around her waist. "You're still my mum! Perhaps we'll get to spend more time together now that you won't be so busy."

Titania unwrapped his arms with distaste. "Phinnbar,

darling. You are terribly sweet, but sooner or later a woman wants more in life than packing lunch boxes and wiping noses. Especially when the nose is so old and wrinkly."

Embarrassed, Phinnbar quickly morphed back into the cute teen boy I knew as Finnbar. He held out his arms for another hug, but Titania ignored him. "Oh, it's awful," she moaned. "How can I ever be happy as just another ordinary, gorgeous, brilliant, scintillating faery woman, when I'm used to being 'all that and a sparkly crown.' I wish I could forget I'd ever been queen!"

"Do you really mean that?" Epona asked, nostrils flaring.

"Maybe." Titania was petulant. "Why? What are you driving at, shiny pony person?"

"I think she's sayin' ye could have the veil of forgetfulness too," Colin suggested gently. "If Queen Morgan here so decrees."

"You mean, *really* forget I was queen?" She considered it for a second, then made a face. "But all of *you* would remember! You'd make fun of me behind my back. How perfectly humiliating that would be! Sorry, no can do."

"What if you defected and lived among the mortals?" I offered. "Like Glinda the Good Witch did when she wanted to be in *The Wizard of Oz*."

"Me? Mortal? That is *beyond* ridiculous!" She laughed wildly at the suggestion. "It's ludicrous! Absurd!" Then she stopped. "Tell me more."

"It's the perfect solution." I glanced at Epona to make sure this would work. The unicorn nodded, and I turned back to Titania. "I mean, isn't that why you lifted the veil to begin with? So you could share in all the really, really fun things mortals do?"

Titania took a fresh tissue and dabbed at her eyes. "You mean, I could take budget cruise vacations on the off-season and pay for them with my AmEx points? Use my cell phone to help choose a winner on *American Idol*? Shop at big-box stores and come home with a year's worth of toilet paper for only ten bucks?"

"And more." I didn't dare catch Colin's eye for fear I'd bust a gut laughing. "Being mortal's fun. You'll love it."

Now Titania was getting excited. "I must admit, it sounds relaxing. Especially after all these gazillions of years of being the gal in charge. 'Uneasy lies the updo that wears the crown,' as I once quipped to my old pal Bill Shakespeare. If anyone deserves a break, it's me."

She turned away from the reflecting pool and extended a hand in my direction, pirate-red press-on nails and all. "All right, Miss Queeny. It's a deal. I'm willing to be mortal—as long as I'm special."

"You will be, believe me." I shook her hand, still trying not to crack up.

"And what about you, Colin?" Epona asked gently. "Have you made up your mind yet?"

He looked at me, confused. I was confused too. "About what?" I asked.

Epona flicked her tail in concern. "The veil of forgetfulness is blanketing the human realm even as we speak. Colin will need to choose—is he one of them? Or one of us?"

The way Epona referred to Colin as "one of them" and

me as "one of us" made my stomach lurch. Colin seemed to miss the significance. He shrugged at Epona. "I'm a simple bloke. I can't imagine bein' anything or anyone other than who I've always been."

Epona looked at me. "You must understand: If Colin returns to the human realm as a mortal, he too will forget about all that has happened. As you yourself decreed, Your Majesty," she added, bowing her head.

"But—wait. I don't want to forget what I know about Morgan, now." Protectively, Colin put his arm around my shoulders. "It was bloody hard work findin' it out, ye know. I think I'm entitled to keep that information."

"Can't I also decree that everyone forgets except Colin?" I asked desperately.

"You could, of course. But be careful what you wish for," Epona warned. "A lifetime of keeping this secret from everyone you know—even the people you love—it will be difficult."

Colin stared at the ground. Right away I remembered what he'd said to me in the pub. *I'm a straight-shootin' bloke, Mor. I could never go through me whole life keepin' a secret from the whole world. . . .*

"I'll do what I have to do to stay with Morgan, then. That's all there is to it," he said quietly.

"No." I put my hand on his arm. "I can't ask you to do that. It's not right." He started to argue but I wouldn't let him. "And I don't want us to have to keep any secrets from each other, either. There's another solution."

I turned back to Epona. "I want to forget."

"Whaaaaaaat?" she whinnied, alarmed.

"I may be half-goddess, but I'm part of the human realm too. So let me forget along with them." I looked up at my royally excellent boyfriend. "There's no way Colin and I would be happy living a life based on lies. And there's no way I can be happy without Colin."

"Or me without Morgan," Colin said quickly. Then he turned to me, his eyes full of concern. "But, darlin'—ye want to forget all yer magic adventures? Are ye sure?"

Was I? The locket I wore around my neck felt like it was glowing. From somewhere I heard Granny's voice saying, *It'll remind ye what's important when all else fails. . . .*

"Colin, you and me living on opposite sides of the ocean is nothing compared to us living in opposite versions of reality. That's a kind of long-distance relationship nobody could make work." I reached out and let my fingers touch the side of his face. "Besides, I've had plenty of faery-world adventures. Now I'm ready for some human ones. With you."

He looked at me so tenderly I started to feel weepy again. "All right," he said softly. His fingers gently traced the chain of the locket around my neck, until they rested on the delicate silver heart. "But forgettin' feels kind of like a lie too, doesn't it?"

Epona shook her head vigorously until her silver mane flopped from one side to the other. "Remember: Even with the veil, humans never wholly forget the magic realm. The truth of our world will still be known to you, in the way it has always been known: in stories and dreams, in art and the imagination and in the wonder of childhood." She whinnied, full of feeling. "There are many kinds of magic, after all."

"Like photosynthesis," I said, turning to Colin.

"And them blasted Internets," Grandpap chimed in.

"Indeed." Epona stamped her front hooves in agreement. "And love is certainly one of them too."

Mr. McAlister had gotten Titania busy learning how to play Bejeweled on the oPhone, so he took the opportunity to sidle over to us and ask: "But if Morgan forgets she's queen, who will rule the faeries?"

"Don't worry," I said. "I'm not going to leave without appointing a successor. And I know the perfect person. He's one of the most reliable, trustworthy and bravest people I've ever met. And he's standing right here."

I turned to my mischievous, scatterbrained, but always clever and loyal faery friend.

"Finnbar. *You* will be king."

Finnbar was so surprised he almost fell backward into the pool. "*Moi?* Are you insane?"

I put my hands on his shoulders. "You're a natural born problem-solver. Think about it: You figured out how to get me to Wales, you found the Rules of Succession, you ran my campaign *and* you were brave enough to cast the deciding vote. You've been saving the world all along, really."

"Huh! You have a point about that," he said thoughtfully. Then he frowned. "But if I'm king, can I still be a part-time librarian? I do so enjoy the work. Mentally it's quite stimulating."

"Of course." I smiled. "Being well-informed is one of the requirements of being a good leader."

Colin slipped off his royal robe and draped it around Finnbar's shoulders. I spread mine at his feet like it was red carpet time at the Teen Choice Awards. Then I took the crown from my head and put it on his.

The moment my crown touched Finnbar's hair, the fireflies zoomed into the air to form a new image over our heads. It was like the front of a slot machine, with three windows scrolling rapidly through different pictures. Cherries, lemons, a crown, another crown, and finally—

"Three crowns?" Grandpap was baffled. "Does that mean we hit the jackpot?"

"Kind of," I said, suddenly understanding. "It means the prophecy has been fulfilled."

As one, the unicorns chanted and whinnied:

The Fey and the Folk are safe at last
When the Day of Three Crowns is safely paaaaaaast!

"Today's the day of three crowns," I explained. "Three rulers in one day: Titania, Morganne and Finnbar." *And boy,* I thought, *am I glad it wasn't clowns. That would have been really creepy.*

Finnbar smacked himself on the forehead. "So *that's* what it means! These prophecies are all alike. Completely inscrutable, and yet if by some accident you stumble upon the right course of action, the prophecy takes the credit!"

Then he adjusted his crown slightly to one side, until he

found the perfect, photo op–ready angle. "Given my new position of authority, do you think I should go back to my Mr. Phineas look?" He checked his appearance in the reflecting pool. "The citizens might find it more kingly."

I shrugged. "That's up to you. But you don't have to be an old guy with gray hair to be in charge."

"Really?" He smoothed his crimson robe. "I guess for now I'll stay as I am, then. Just your basic royal boy-band heartthrob! But I do like the notion of a long white beard. Perhaps for occasions of state . . ."

Epona turned to the rest of the unicorns, who were now doing stretching exercises and chugging bottles of what looked like Gatorade. "You heard your former queen: Let's give it up for King Finnbar!" She blew a trumpet blast through her horn.

The unicorns, though obviously tired and still on break, generously delivered another round of appropriate revelry. As a surprise finale the dragon swooped down from the sky and used its fiery breath to scorch an illustration into the boardwalk. Coughing from the smoke, the unicorns struggled to finish with a cheer:

Finnbar, Finnbar, he's our king,
For him we'd do most—cough! cough!—*anything!*
Goooooooooooo, Finnbar!

The unicorns gagged and wheezed and ran for their drinks. After a moment, the acrid smoke dissipated and I could see the image the dragon had scorched into the boardwalk. Three crowns, surrounding a massive book, arranged inside a circle . . .

"Fek—three crowns is the Oxford logo!" I blurted. "And I'm supposed to have my alumni interview now—or soon— or was it later? Oh my God, I hope I didn't blow it."

Mr. McAlister stepped forward. Despite looking like a drowned rat in an antique life jacket, he spoke with tremendous dignity.

"*I* am an Oxford alumni! And I can personally vouch for your character, leadership ability and civic-mindedness. With your permission, I will be proud to give my highest recommendation to the Special Admissions committee." He bowed humbly. "Unless you'd rather do your interview with the Archbishop of Canterbury? I shall take no offense if so. You might find it more interesting."

To be honest, the idea of meeting an archbishop didn't exactly rock my socks. For a minute I thought about requesting Hugh Grant. But that wasn't really necessary, either.

"You'll do fine, Mr. McAlister." I hugged him, which got my Natalie Portman's Shaved Head T-shirt all wet, but I didn't care. "Thanks for the recommendation."

King Finnbar inhaled deeply. "Can't the teary goodbyes wait until after dinner? The caterers are here! Mmm, I smell chicken with haricots verts and roasted new potatoes."

Epona's tail lashed from side to side, and she gave a loud, impatient snort. "All right, all right," Finnbar said reluctantly. "Let's finish what we've started; that's the kingly thing to do. I'll have a go at this forgetting business, but just to be on the safe side I'll rewind time a bit too. In my experience it's much easier to forget things that haven't happened yet. Mortals, front and center."

Grandpap and Mr. McAlister stepped forward, followed by a fluttery Titania. Hand in hand, Colin and I joined them.

Holding on to his crown so it wouldn't fly off, King Finnbar suddenly dashed forward and threw his free arm around me.

"Goodbye, dear Morgan! In one way I'll miss you remembering who I am, but in another way it'll be all the more amusing that you don't." He dabbed his eyes with the edge of his robe. "Of course, if you and Colin have children of your own, 'Bar-Bar' will be a frequent visitor."

"Promise?" I tried to smile, but I was kind of choked up myself. He nodded, and I kissed him on the cheek. "See you again someday, Your Majesty."

"Thanks for all the good times, mate." Colin gave Finnbar a fond buddy-punch in the arm. "It's been grand to see ye again. Congrats on the king gig. I know ye'll be brilliant."

"The unicorns will miss you too, Morgan-Morganne, who was queen for less than a day." Epona's horn started to shimmer, throwing off glittery sparks that gently rained down on me and Colin. "But we're happy that you and your royally excellent boyfriend will remain part of your world. We wish you only joy."

Then King Finnbar gave the order: "Now forget . . . forget . . . be kind . . . rewind . . ."

I squeezed Colin's hand. My vision started to blur and

my limbs felt heavy, like I was drifting off to sleep. "'Part of Your World'—that's a song from *The Little Mermaid*," I said dreamily. "It's my sister's favorite movie."

"Mine too," a strangely horsey voice replied. "I love all those Disney pictures . . ."

twenty-four

To: Special Admissions Candidate Rawlinson
<gddssgrrl@gmail.com>
From: Cornelius Phineas <urmajesty@phmail.com>
Subject: FWD: Campus Tour Itinerary

As promised, attached please find your printable
e-tickets, flight information, schedule of events and
other important information about your upcoming
campus tour.

In exchange for the free air travel and other amenities
provided by the university, we ask that all Special
Admissions Candidates provide ten hours of
community service while in residence at Oxford.

Service assignments have been made randomly. You have been assigned to:

> THE LIBRARY. As soon as convenient after arrival, please report to the Bodleian Library, Special Collections Department. The librarian will provide you with appropriate training.

Please note that air travel for Special Admissions Candidates has been generously paid for via the donation of AmEx points by individual Oxford alumni. If you would care to send a thank-you note, please write to:

> Mr. Devyn McAlister
> c/o Castell Cyfareddol,
> Tip of the Iceberg Cottage,
> Halftime-by-the-Sea,
> Wales, U.K. CF89

Note: In consideration of your participation in the campus tour, requirements for an application essay will be waived.

Congratulations on being selected for this prestigious opportunity, and thank you for your interest in Oxford University.

Sincerely,

The Admissions Office
Special Candidates Division
Oxford University

From: Colin O'Grady <Lovesdeathmetal@
dubcityu.ie>
To: Morgan Rawlinson <gddssgrrl@gmail.com>
SUBJECT: seems I'm "special"

Hey luv! How's my girl?

I'll be quick because Grandpap's waiting for me
to give him a lift, but I had to tell you right away—
there's gobsmacking news in today's mail. Seems
I've been invited to a "special campus tour" at the
last place you'd expect to find a simple Irish lad like
me: Oxford U (don't laugh!). The letter says something
about choosing promising students from colleges
around the U.K. to apply for a "special applicants"
transfer program, full scholarship, all expense paid, la
de da. And it's this week!!! And I'm going!!!!!

I'd never picture myself at a school so fancy, but
if Oxford offers me a free ride I'd have to seriously
consider saying so long to DCU. What do you make

of that? And how's your college hunt coming along? Be grand if we could end up at school together for a couple of years.

Patty at the bike tour company had a fit when I told her I'd be starting work late to do this Oxford shindig, but she'll get over it. If you want to help me make it up to her, why not work the bike tour with me? We're shorthanded this summer anyway, and it'd be a lovely wild adventure to have you aboard (he says, winkin' like a lovestruck madman).

Speaking of lovestruck, I've a wee gift to give you next time I see you. It belonged to my granny and it means a lot to me. I hope it'll mean a lot to you too. It's something for you to wear, and that's the only clue I'm giving—see how I'm trying to tempt you to come to Ireland for the summer?

Gotta run, Grandpap's howling to leave for his date. The man's found a lady friend, believe it or not. A tall bony lass who likes to bargain shop and watch telly, so they're a good fit in that respect. Tania (that's her name) is a silly bird IMHO, but Grandpap needs the company and he's happy, so I'm happy.

Love you, darlin',

C

From: Morgan Rawlinson <gddssgrrl@gmail.com>
To: Colin O'Grady <Lovesdeathmetal@dubcityu.ie>
Subject: RE: seems I'm "special"

[[[[[[[[hugging Colin!!!]]]]]]]]

WOW!!! Congrats about Oxford. Gobsmacking is
definitely my new favorite word.

I'll ask my parents about the bike tour. I'm in
their good graces at the moment because they
think I saved Tammy's life (she's fine, she
swallowed some water in the bathtub but you
know how the kid loves drama) so I fully expect a
yes. Wild adventure sounds like a plan [pumps
fists in air].

Want a good laugh? Somehow Sarah got it in her
head that I should run for senior class president
in September. Insane, right? But for some
reason everyone I ask says it's a brilliant idea.
My totally latent leadership ability must finally be
bubbling up to the surface. Anyway, if I win it'll look
good on my college apps, so I may give it a try.

My college search is also going gobsmackingly well!
In fact I just got some "special" news of my own.
As you will soon discover, heh heh. Sorry to be so
mysterious. But a girl's entitled to a few secrets, right?

Can't wait to wear my present (like you need to tempt me). Okay, time to pack my suitcase—oops! Almost let it slip!

Love you "mor" than I can say,

Morganne

p.s.—I know it's kind of lame but I just decided, I'm officially changing the spelling of my name to Morganne. Senior year, fresh start, blah blah blah. You know I always hated the boy's name thing. My mother will be totally insulted, but, duh, it's my name. She'll get over it.

p.p.s.—You still have to call me Mor, though. Nobody says my name like you do.

about the author

Maryrose Wood's previous books about the adventures of Morgan Rawlinson are *Why I Let My Hair Grow Out* and *How I Found the Perfect Dress*. She lives in New York with two kids, two kittens and a very patient pooch. Find out more at www.mary rosewood.com.